EBURY PRESS

# ONE AND A HALF WIFE

Meghna Pant is a multiple-award-winning and bestselling author, screenwriter, journalist and speaker. Recognized as one of India's best writers by national and international publications, Pant has published eight books to critical and commercial acclaim. These include *Boys Don't Cry*; *The Terrible, Horrible, Very Bad Good News*; *How to Get Published in India*; *Feminist Rani*; *The Trouble with Women*; *Happy Birthday! and Other Stories* and *One and a Half Wife*. Several of her works are under screen adaptation, including *Boys Don't Cry*, as well as a few screenplays that she has written.

Pant has been felicitated with various honours and shortlists for distinguished contribution to literature, gender issues and journalism, including the Bharat Nirman Award, Frank O'Connor International Award, Commonwealth Short Story Prize, Society Achievers Award, Laadli Media Award, FICCI Young Achievers Award, The Lifestyle Journalist Women Achievers' Award, FON South Asia Short Story Award, Muse India Young Writer Award and Amazon Breakthrough Novel Award. She lives in Mumbai with her husband and daughters.

*One and a Half Wife*, Meghna's debut novel, was first published in May 2012. The novel received critical and commercial acclaim. It went into multiple reprints and won the National Literary Muse India Young Writer Award. The novel was also nominated for the Cinnamon Press Novel Writing Award, Word Hustler's Literary Storm Novel Contest and the Amazon Breakthrough Novel Award.

# PRAISE FOR THE BOOK

'A delightful debut novel'—*Sakal Times*

'This is a refreshing take on the American Dream. Family, love, relationships and the pursuit of power emerge in this telling tale set in contemporary India'—*Mid-Day*

'An exceedingly readable novel'—*National*

'A well-crafted, warm story'—*Indian Express*

'Full marks for very lucid prose and some excellent characterization. The narrative keeps you turning the pages till the very end'—*Sunday Standard*

'Meghna's emotional wisdom as a writer, her sensitivity to the multidimensionality of the issues and her eye for the detail of social interactions result in an intelligent, satisfying read'—*Gulf News*

'An interesting read with powerful insights'—*Sahara Times*

'A worthy read'—*People*

'The book is a must-read'—*Deccan Chronicle*

# ONE
# AND
# A
# HALF
# WIFE

## MEGHNA PANT

EBURY
PRESS

An imprint of Penguin Random House

**EBURY PRESS**

USA | Canada | UK | Ireland | Australia
New Zealand | India | South Africa | China | Singapore

Ebury Press is part of the Penguin Random House group of companies
whose addresses can be found at global.penguinrandomhouse.com

Published by Penguin Random House India Pvt. Ltd
4th Floor, Capital Tower 1, MG Road,
Gurugram 122 002, Haryana, India

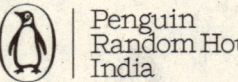

Penguin
Random House
India

First published in India by Westland Limited 2012
Published in Ebury Press by Penguin Random House India 2023

ISBN 9780143459859

Typeset in Bembo Roman by SŪRYA, New Delhi

Printed at Repro India Limited

www.penguin.co.in

# Acknowledgements

While there have been many influences in my life, some of which I'm not even aware of, I'd like to thank those who made this novel possible. I begin with my mother, to whom this book is dedicated, and whose strength of steel has been the ground I walk on. When I fall, I'm lifted by a sense of humour – the greatest gift my father has left me. And when I lose faith in myself, I'm lifted by my brother's single-minded passion, his belief in me that is more than my belief in myself. And none of this could have happened if my husband did not let me work behind closed doors for days on end, and still be there when I emerged, empty and happy.

# 1

The ringneck parrot hopped out of its rusted cage and cocked its green head, as if contemplating a serious decision.

Fourteen-year-old Amara Malhotra's right hand twitched. Her nails dug deep into her palm and she prayed silently, 'Mithu-miyan, please pick the right cards. I have a treat for you.' She was sure that the parrot, which knew everything, could see the plump red chilli inside her hand.

She watched as Hari Pundit, the parrot's master and Shimla's most famous astrologer, took a pack of cards out of a rectangular cardboard box and began laying them face down, one-by-one, on top of the steel trunk between them. Under his breath he chanted a Vedic verse. Although Amara couldn't see what the cards contained, she eagerly followed the astrologer's movements, not failing to notice his nails crusted with dirt and yellowing at the tip, or the hair on his knuckles, each as long as her little finger. When, amidst the humdrum of the marketplace, a song about gyrating pigeons reached their ears, Punditji raised his voice higher and higher, and swayed his pudgy body from left to right until all fifty-four cards – frayed and brown at the edges – stood back-to-back in five rows.

A smug smile skirted his lips when he looked up at Amara's mother, Biji, and said, 'Now, you may ask two questions.'

It was a cool autumn day, yet Biji dabbed at the sweat gathered above her upper lip. A sweet-sour smell of perspiration and talcum powder reeked through her blue Kanchi sari, the one she wore on every momentous occasion. She cleared her throat and stated her questions, both as banal as the henna caked on her orange fingernails:

Q1: When will the Malhotra family get their Green Cards for America?

Q2: When will Amara get married?

In anticipation of the parrot's answer, Biji clutched Amara's wrist, while Amara shifted uneasily on the straw mat, its ridges jabbing into her legs. But the bird remained motionless as though it hadn't heard Biji's questions.

'It is awake?' Biji asked, her voice husky and laced with concern. Regardless of people's grasp of English, or hers for that matter, Biji persisted in using it to establish that she was educated, a matric pass.

'Of course! He is smartest bird in India,' Punditji replied.

He gently prodded the parrot, which opened its red beak to nip his bony fingers, and seemed to remember, just in time, not to bite the hand that fed it. It staged a spasm as though shaking the boredom from its reedy plumage and hopped over to the first line of cards. It picked up the two cards nearest to it and after waiting for Punditji to take them, dipped its beak into its left wing and became completely still.

'What—,' Biji started to say, but Punditji raised his hand, motioning her to stop. He began studying the cards, while his free hand stroked the parrot gently.

After a few sombre seconds, he removed his Himachali cap, scratched his forehead and announced in a shrill emphatic voice, 'Green Card no problem. Marriage not good fortune. Babyji will be one-and-half wife.'

'One-and-half wife?' Biji shouted. The parrot startled and fluttered its wings. Biji glared at it as it squawked in self-defence: 'Karr.'

Amara was disappointed but she didn't disagree with Punditji. Biji had taught her that the best way to participate in a conversation was to say nothing at all. So her chestnut eyes slanted downwards as if in acceptance of everything, her lips remained firmly pursed as though to bar words from leaking out, and her ears perked upwards, a repository of people's opinions. She looked more closely at the parrot and noticed a yellow band tied around its right leg, as if the leg had broken and had been carelessly put back together. Could she trust the psychic powers of a maimed bird?

Biji apparently did, for she turned back to the astrologer and probed, 'What this one-and-half wife mean? Will Ammu become more than one person? Or grow extra leg? Extra ear?'

Punditji ran his hand through his grey beard and said, 'That is not for me to tell.'

Biji persisted, 'Is this bad luck from Ammu's father side? His family be full of half-halves and half-quarters. His niece have only four finger and his grandfather have no eyebrow, his mother no heart. Or this is because Ammu be dark, like her father? Or—'

'For that answer,' Punditji cut her off, 'extra twenty rupees.'

Biji had a cylindrical body with an enlarged head that lay in direct proportion to her torso, like a babushka doll. Her expansive nose sliced her face into two neat halves. She spoke from her stomach, as if the dewlaps below her chin had swallowed her throat. At that moment, Biji's throat lurched back to her neck and she bellowed, 'What extra? I give you money already. Read your sign. It say flat fee for reading and consultation.'

Her nostrils flared and collapsed like a giant heart beating.

Punditji didn't squawk, 'Karr'. He let out a long sigh that could contain a dissertation on martyrdom. 'This complicated case, Madam. Shani is in *tula rashi* and Rahu in eighth house.'

'I am fool? You say and I believe? This be cheating. I leave.'

Biji's knees creaked in protest as she got up and walked away. To show Punditji the seriousness of her offence she didn't wait for Amara. Biji maintained that if you had twenty rupees you had to pretend to have two, so Amara knew Biji wouldn't come back unless Punditji reduced his fee. Seconds passed – one, two, three, four, five – and Amara looked at Punditji holding out a half-eaten apple for the parrot to nibble on. He was not going to call Biji back. Relieved that her future was no longer going to be discussed, Amara dropped the chilli into the parrot's copper cage, got up and turned to go.

'Babyji,' she heard Punditji call out ominously. She turned around and saw him holding an emerald stone in the palm of his dirty hand. It sparkled in the sunlight, like a swan in a pigsty. 'Mithu-miyan pick this from bag. It means this for you and only you. You will see it true value when time is right. It will make your one wish come true. Only forty rupees for you.'

Amara touched the small round stone in wonder, feeling its smooth texture. She had fifty rupees on her; pocket money that she'd saved to buy a sweater for the approaching winter.

From somewhere Biji shouted her name: 'Ammu!'

'Thank you,' she said quickly, placing the stone in her purse. She pulled out the money and the parrot gently took the note in its beak.

~ ~

Amara couldn't find Biji in the crowd on Ridge Road, so she ambled along, enjoying a few moments alone in her favourite part of Shimla. The ridge overlooked hillsides dotted with slanted houses and teashops, grazing goats with bald expressions. The valley draped itself in forests of deodar, oak, pine and rhododendron, before modestly vanishing under the mist. Rising above it were snow-capped Himalayan peaks, so majestic that to lay prostrate before them, like the valley, seemed to Amara the natural thing to do.

For want of a clear destination, Amara followed the sweet-man, who was surrounded by rosy-cheeked children clamouring for the pink candy coming out of his jute pipe. She passed a group of forest monks in robes of heartwood dye and clunky wooden sandals, two old men on walking sticks drinking tamarind water from the golgappa stand. Voices rose and fell, among them the thin accents of tourists in the Tibetan market haggling over tiger miniatures. A whiff of oil and spices wafted in from the fritters stall behind her. She patted the silky dun-coloured skin of her favourite horse in all of Shimla — Shera — as his owner fed him whole gram.

Then Amara saw Langda Mr Lula — the boogeyman of Shimla — sitting by the burl of the Weeping Willow. The mendicant had once been the richest man in Shimla, simply known as Mr Lula. This was before The Big Fire (the cause of which was never determined) razed his restaurant to the ground. Children had run around the blaze singing:

> There's fire on the Lula's
> Run, run, run

The wind gathered stead. The Big Fire frolicked to his cinema hall next to his restaurant.

> There's fire on the Lula's
> About turn

And then The Big Fire leaped to his house next to his cinema hall. No rickety red fire engines gushed out water from their motion-sick pipes. Mr Lula rushed into his house to save — was it his wife and son or his lockers filled with cash and rubies and diamonds and gold? It didn't matter for The Big Fire licked his leg and made him Langda Mr Lula. The government declared his property unsafe, and modified the site into a guesthouse for its bureaucrats.

Langda Mr Lula prowled into the silence of every night, drifting in the smoky haze of a lit beedi he didn't smoke — for he liked to own fire at the end of his fingertips. When children's teeth, ladies' silver lockets and men's jobs went missing, everyone put it down to Langda Mr Lula. They never discovered his stolen stash or hidden ways, but when his metal stick went clickety-clock against the tar of the road, mothers silenced their children, 'Sleep before Langda Mr Lula comes to get you.'

As a one-and-a-half wife was Amara also going to be a reject like Langda Mr Lula? Alarmed, she turned her attention to an apple tree to count the number of fruits it bore. Like the fruit, each protected by a red covering, Amara's life was sheltered by the institution of marriage and expected to ripen within that calyx. Biji had predetermined this desire, along with Amara's other desires, before Amara was old enough to even understand what desire meant ('to wish or long for; to want'). This was her brief:

— Desires were pinned to sacrifice, acceptance and resignation.
— Desires were exiled from delight and from the self.
— Amara was to desire nothing except what she was told to desire.

And, she was told to desire three things.
The first thing to desire was whatever God desired for her.

Biji told her that the story, 'It Is God's Desire', began before Amara's birth. Biji had miscarried two babies when she found out that she was pregnant, possibly for the last time, with Amara. Amara's much-anticipated birth occurred on a torrential July evening in 1977 when there was blinding rain. Landslides buried buses rattling with people. Gushing water carried away bullfrogs, minnows and earthworms. Leeches dropped from trees and crawled from the earth to suck blood from people's arms, legs and places-that-could-not-be-mentioned. The death toll of flora, fauna and humans kept rising, making it seem as though murder was on everyone's mind. As this siege on the summer capital of British Raj's India continued, Amara slowly made her way into the world. When she came out of her mother's place-that-could-not-be-mentioned, she didn't utter a squeak.

Biji clutched the midwife, 'Is she alive?'

The mid-wife had another delivery to make across town in Chota Shimla. She didn't have time to play coquette with chota girls. So she grabbed a hot white coal from the pot of coals lying on Biji's stomach and brought it close to Amara's left foot. Amara wailed, declaring herself only under provocation.

Biji was so thankful to God for Amara's birth that she promptly took her daughter to the Baba Sheikh Omar Sahib Dargah in Musti village in Maharashtra. For five hundred years mothers had brought their newborn babies to this village so they could be thrown off the fifty-foot temple tower and come out healthy and strong and lucky. Amara too was dropped from this tower. As she fell through the abyss she didn't wail or howl like the other screaming babies, but landed quietly and precisely on a white bedsheet held by six men. A man picked her up in one bounce and handed her, amid much cheer and jubilation, to her proud mother. Back in Shimla, Biji boasted about this to everyone and the *Shimla Times* published a three paragraph article about Amara with the title 'Baby Buddha'. Biji carefully photocopied this article and sent it to her brother, Dua Mama, who lived in America. Six weeks later, in a fit of rare generosity, Dua Mama sent them a letter stating that since his niece's valour foretold a great destiny, he'd eased her path by filing for the Malhotra family's Green Cards to America. Amara was barely three months old then.

Biji was delirious with joy, for wasn't it every Indian family's dream to go to America? Wasn't life rumoured to be wonderful there, with its green parks, green dollars and green-eyed presidents, and did she mention, green dollars? There had to be at least one place in the world where life could be lived in accordance with the plans and dreams Biji had. She'd imagined that place to be Delhi, maybe Bombay, or in her bold moments, Singapore, but she'd never thought that America was achievable for her. She laminated Dua Mama's letter and placed it before Lord Krishna's statue, for, 'It Is God's Desire' would direct the Green Cards to their humble abode, even if it took – as Dua Mama had pointed out – more than a decade.

This led to the cachet of all desires: 'It Is Biji's Desire'. Biji took it upon herself, without any provocation whatsoever, to tame Amara, stating that America with its green dollars would spoil her only daughter. Growing up, Amara knew nothing but how to appease Biji, and this was difficult since Biji was pregnant, not of the body but the mind. She wanted two things but asked for three. Her needs charted the way of life for her – carrying her from the peak of perpetual wants to the trough of perpetual disappointments.

'It Is Biji's Desire' contoured Amara's identity and latched it on to 'It Is His Desire'. The 'His' was Amara's future husband, who existed as the epitome of Biji's unfulfilled dreams. Amara learnt 'It Is His Desire' during the amorphous beginnings of her childhood. Her doll Lily, with the pink satin frock and the ersatz blonde hair, became her training for His child. A gift of a tiny plastic tea set with tiny cups and tiny saucers was her fifth birthday present so she could learn to be a good hostess for His boss. Little tin pots and little tin ladles were placed before her to stir and roast His desires. His anticipated choices and needs filtered into the fibre of her childhood such that growing up she never felt like an only child. The spectre of another human being was so strong that Amara felt like she had an invisible twin, whose identity had been meshed into hers. She accepted that she was to have no 'I' in her life; before meeting Him she would be known as 'We', the Malhotra family; and after meeting Him she would be known as 'Us', the married couple.

~ ~

Amara saw Biji standing next to a long line of palmists, cowrie-shell-throwers and numerologists, conducting their business under the shade of the neo-Gothic Christ Church. It was going to be a long day.

Over the next three hours Biji and Amara walked from one astrologer to the next. One fakir studied the moles on Amara's face and declared her unlucky. Another poked her ears with a steel pin, and after comparing the wax inside her left ear to the one in her right, warned Biji of the presence of an evil eye. A holy man in orange robes determined the strength of the breath exhaled from Amara's nostrils and charted her husbandless future in accordance.

Biji threw her hands up in the air and declared, 'I am fed-dup.'

Fed-dup was not good. It meant Biji would try to find a solution.

Biji took Amara up the west slope of Mall Road (pronounced Maal Road) to the Kali Bari temple to pander to the omnipresent Goddess in her humble abode. Once they reached the temple, Biji covered her head with her dupatta, put on her temple-face (demure yet righteous), and bought grass from the holy-cow-man, the only man who could command his price without being questioned by her. She fed the grass to the holy-cow and whispered prayers into her ears. She always whispered in a temple as though her voice would – *and it could* – rouse God's anger. Then Biji walked up to a priest sitting on an old jute sack. The priest read a chant for Amara over mustard seeds in cheesecloth. Biji pocketed the seeds in her brown faux-leather bag, next to her prayer beads and areca nut silver box, to be put under Amara's pillow at night.

After appeasing Amara's fate they walked down one-hundred-and-eight stairs from Mall Road to their house in Lower Bazaar, assigned the name even though there was no Upper Bazaar. They reached a two-storied building in which they had a small apartment. On the ground floor of the building were two shops. The first was 'Snowflake', a woollens' shop claiming to sell authentic Pashmina shawls, which were in fact manufactured in the adjacent room. The second shop was 'Pinecone', that sold cigarettes – Gold Flake for adults and sweet Phantom ones for children – packets of *anardanagoli-churan-aampachan-lalimli-rasmola* and air pistols to scare away precocious monkeys. Boys, pretending to be men, roamed outside the shop with Phantom cigarettes in their mouth and air pistols in their hand. Girls, pretending to be women, smudged the red end of the Phantom cigarette on their lips and carried anardanagoli-churan-aampachan-lalimli-rasmola to feed the boys. Amara was not allowed to buy the 'un-lady-sweets', as Biji called them, but if Biji happened to be out of the house, Amara joined the children, holding a Phantom cigarette between her red-painted lips.

Like many houses in Shimla, Amara's home leaned on wooden stilts and tilted outwards, straight into the valley below. For optimists, the perched houses were a sign that magic lived – things could levitate between heaven and earth. For pessimists they were indicators of suicidal tendencies; their fears were realised every few years when homes tumbled into the depths of the valley. But nothing was done about it. After all, departed houses do not command the same respect as departed humans.

Amara's home was as simply laid out as the lives it was meant to shelter. Shaped as a long rectangle, the house was divided in half with cheap pinewood floorboards that creaked underfoot. On one side was the kitchen, the master bedroom and Amara's bedroom; while on the other side was a long verandah overlooking the valley, like a lover without a gift. As though to compensate for its loneliness, the verandah was filled with abundance. It had a brown sofa with teakwood armrests, matched with a red sofa chair whose cushion had been inverted, for it carried stains from a boy guest with an uncontrollable bladder. Beyond these stood a three-legged wicker chair, which had arrived on four legs, but was rendered lame a week earlier, at the same time that the Green Cards didn't show up. The culprit was better left uncaught. Next to the chair was a blue side table holding a foot-long Japanese doll encased in glass. The cracked side of the glass faced the white-painted walls as if glass were opaque and could hide a flaw.

The master bedroom belonged to Baba and Biji. It contained a wooden bed with a thin mattress and no headrest, a solid grey Godrej armoire with a full-size mirror (the only one in the house), and two large steel trunks put on top of each other. Mounted on the trunks was a tiny hand-carved marble temple, an undisputed indulgence. Amara's room had a floor mattress, a teak study table with a thin white lamp, and a small wooden cupboard.

Biji and Amara sat down to lunch and had finished a plate each of chickpeas and white rice when there was a knock on the front door.

'It is I,' a hectorly voice used to getting its way thundered. It was Bakshi Aunty, Biji's best friend and mortal enemy, as the situation demanded. Without further ado she entered in tow with her two constant companions: Arjun, her fifteen-year-old son, and the local gossip.

'Let me show you something,' she said. Bakshi Aunty had such flair for scandal that her eyes had become frog-like so they could see everything, and her skin had become porous so she could absorb tittle-tattle, like a frog's skin absorbs water. They followed her to the kitchen where she pointed to the road below and said, 'It's *her.*'

Amara looked down to see Shikha Arora – who lived in the adjoining building and whom she'd known as a sister all her life – at the *sabzi mandi*, where vegetables were laid out in multiple sizes, shapes and colours. Amara knew from hearsay that unlike the other customers, Shikha Didi would not get a free sprig of coriander or a fistful of green chillies from the vegetable vendor. She was divorced.

Bakshi Aunty gave a shudder and said urgently, 'Give me chilli to ward off her evil jinn.'

Amara watched as Bakshi Aunty spun the chilli thrice around each of their faces and threw it out of the kitchen window.

Amara looked at Didi again. It saddened her to notice that this black-eyed beauty, formerly known as Shimla Mirch, now looked ravaged and gaunt. Two years back she had got married and moved to Delhi. She returned to Shimla eight months ago and didn't leave. While she offered no explanation for her unexpected presence, her family said that Didi's husband had to go abroad on business and would soon take her back to Delhi. No one believed them.

Amara heard the word 'divorce' Shimla-whispered. It rolled out differently from different tongues, based on the educational background of the person uttering it: 'Die-force. Dee-boss. Die-wars. De-horse.'

The ignominy of a 'failed marriage' wheeled across narrow alleys reaching every house on stilts, climbing up the one-hundred-and-eight stairs to Mall Road, the hotbed of gossip, and sneaking into Gaiety Theatre to provide more entertainment than a pelvic-thrusting hero. Tongues of whispers stuck out, when people heard that a 'divorce refugee camp' had been set up within their town; the Aroras had allowed their divorced daughter to live with them. The denouncements gathered the destructive force of a tornado, loud enough to stir the jaded inhabitants of Scandal Point and the cosy inhabitants of Jakhoo Hills. Adults no longer shut children's ears when speaking of it. Children did not get punished for playing 'catch-de-horse-y.'

This was the first time that Amara heard of a marriage 'failing'. She couldn't understand what to make of it; was marriage a test to be graded on? She wondered who she should ask for the meaning of the word 'divorce'. Not her English teacher at Auckland House School, Mrs D'Mello, who was unmarried and hence had hair growing out of the three moles under her nose. Not her mother, who would make Amara wash her mouth with neem twigs. Not her friend, Charu, who had worms and could not keep anything in her stomach. So Amara looked up the word divorce in the English Collins dictionary:

1. The legal ending of a marriage
2. A separation, esp. one that is permanent

The word didn't fit into the brief Amara had been given. She'd learnt at a young age that marriage was eternity gazing at itself in the mirror. It was as irreversible as aging and as permanent as death. Its end was impossible.

Bakshi Aunty went to the sofa to do her cross-stitch embroidery, while Arjun sat next to her, holding the end of her sari. By virtue of being born to Bakshi Aunty, Arjun was a momma's boy. Amara and he used to play together as children, but after he turned ten, Biji and Bakshi Aunty drew an invisible iron curtain between them. Now wherever he was in Amara's presence, he sat close to his mother and didn't talk to anyone, as if there was shame in words too. Amara didn't mind. She had seen his short lanky frame being pushed and shoved by older boys, on those rare moments when he wasn't around his mother.

Amara watched as Biji made tea, pouring Amul Milk from a plastic pouch into the boiling tealeaves. This was not the milk Biji had stolen from the Aroras. For the last four weeks, Biji had sneaked to the Aroras' front door after the milkman's delivery, and emptied their milk pouches in the gutter for pye-dogs to feed on. Biji exacted what she thought was society's revenge on the Aroras and spoke proudly to Bakshi Aunty about the perils and thrills of every heist. Biji did not consider the milk suitable for her own consumption, contaminated as it was by Didi's jinn.

Amara didn't know how Didi or her parents felt about this, but she imagined they wouldn't be surprised. Already people had stopped buying grains and groceries from the Aroras' small storefront. They didn't invite them to weddings or parties, and avoided them during evening walks at Mall Road.

'Biji, we are out of apple biscuits,' Amara said, knowing Bakshi Aunty did not drink tea without apple-jam biscuits. 'Let me run down and get a packet.'

'Don't buy from you-know-who,' Biji said.

Biji had told Amara to stop talking to Shikha. Yet, whenever she passed Didi's store, Amara waved at her discreetly or dropped her a little present, like a toffee, or a letter with an update of her life. Sometimes she made a slight detour to General Talwar's bungalow – Kiara Mansion – famous for having the most beautiful garden in Shimla, and plucked purple roses from there to leave on the millets' sack outside Didi's store, hoping it would bring colour into her sister's life.

Amara grabbed some money from the tin box labelled 'Ghee' and sped out the front door to Didi's store. Since this was the time of day Amara came home from school, Didi was waiting for her. Seeing no one around, Amara walked up to her and said, 'Hi, Di. One Appi, please.'

Didi gave her the biscuits along with a packet of Phantom cigarettes, which she knew Amara loved, and said, 'You look pretty in this salwar kameez. No school today?'

'Biji wanted my horoscope read without Baba finding out. He doesn't like all this. So she made me skip school,' Amara said. Before she could say more, she saw an old man coming their way. She winked at Didi and left the store.

Back home, Amara laid the biscuits in a circle around a plate and carried it on a tray, along with the tea, to the verandah.

Bakshi Aunty took her cup of tea and turned to Biji, 'Did you hear the latest news? It seems that Shikha's husband threw her out of the house because he had a girlfriend. Arjun's father says, "Serves Shikha right." Remember how arrogant she was? "Look how beautiful I am. Look how intelligent I am, winning a scholarship to medical school." What's the point of all that now? She will spend the rest of her life alone.'

Amara listened carefully. Life was a book that had to be learnt; her elders imparted all the tried and tested formulae so she could adhere to them. Today's lesson was:

Women sided with men + Men sided with men = No one sided with women

'Let's talk about something else in front of children,' Biji said.

'Yes, tell me what the astrologers said about Amara?' Bakshi Aunty asked, helping herself to three biscuits, and putting one in Arjun's mouth.

Biji dipped a biscuit into her piping hot tea longer than required. It desiccated and fell to the bottom of the cup, something she never allowed to happen. 'They said Rajyog. She will live like princess.' Biji did not mention failures – the 'it that shall not be named'.

'Of course, why not? After all, daughters are reflections of their mothers. You want, we can start looking for boys now only,' Bakshi Aunty said.

'No need. My daughter will marry rich Indian boy in Amreeka. We will soon be there.'

A little less than five years ago, when Amara was nine years old, they had received a letter from the US Department of State National Visa Centre, stating that their immigration application was on hold, and they would be notified when further consideration could be given to its processing. Dua Mama, who had done all the necessary paperwork, including filing an Affidavit of Support, told them that his lawyer said this could mean a further wait of anywhere 'between two to five years'. Every Sunday, Biji argued with Baba about the meaning of the word 'between'– did it mean before five years or exactly in two years? Then, three months ago, they received the coveted Package 4 calling them for an interview with the US Consulate in Delhi and for their medical examination. Though Biji was the principal applicant, as she was Dua Mama's direct relative, it was Baba and Amara who were made to practice for the 'biggest test of their lives'. The interview went off smoothly, as an overprepared Baba deftly answered questions, even those related to their bank statements and their employment plans in the US. He was able to convince the consular officer that Dua Mama could financially support them once they reached America, if the need arose. Biji anguished for weeks thereafter about the consular officer's thin smile at the end of the interview, trying to ascertain whether it meant he'd approved them or not. Now they were waiting to see if their Green Cards would arrive.

'But what will you do there? At this age?' Bakshi Aunty asked with interest, as though she had not asked that question many times over in the past.

'What we have to do? We go for Ammu's sake. So she settle nicely. Anyways, artists like me can live anywhere.' For Biji, art meant dabbing water paint on their family's black and white photographs. She rescued the photos from what she thought was a sordid existence, and introduced them to the lively environs of fuchsia cheeks, violet saris and yellow daisies.

'And your brother? Is he excited?'

'He is too busy man for excited. But we are close like hand-to-feet,' Biji said. Dua Mama had moved to the United States twenty-one years ago to study accounting. He had worked with Arthur Andersen for nine years before starting his own successful accounting practice. He hadn't visited them in seven years.

'Will Ammu's Baba like it there?'

'He has to. For Ammu's sake. He not want to go. But what life is here? He works hard like a Chief Justice and earns like a peon. In Amreeka it will be different,' Biji replied.

Baba was a loving father who when faced with 'for Ammu's sake' could not reply in dissent. Though he was content with his middle-class existence and didn't share Biji's conviction that there was a huge world outside Shimla and it all belonged to America, he agreed to move.

Outside the entrance came the sound of shoes being taken off. Amara ran to open the door, even though it was, as always, open. She smiled widely, her biggest that day.

Baba was back from work.

He returned Amara's smile, his mouth disappearing under his moustache. His joy stopped short when he saw Bakshi Aunty and Arjun. Amara knew that in some odd way Arjun reminded Baba of Amara; and the injustice he felt and couldn't fight in his daughter's life, he tried to fight in Arjun's life.

'Stop sitting by your mother's *palu*, boy,' Baba said in his deep baritone voice. His tall body loomed in the hallway and his thin frame threw large shadows on the walls. Arjun clasped the end of Bakshi Aunty's sari more tightly and shifted closer to her.

Amara giggled.

'What is so funny?' Bakshi Aunty spluttered.

Biji chimed in, 'Where your manners, Ammu? Apologise to Bakshi Aunty.' Her strict tone was meant for Amara, but Amara saw Arjun straighten his back in attention.

'Sorry,' Amara mumbled. She had wanted to be a lawyer, like Baba, but Biji had dismissed the idea, convinced that the only thing Amara would learn from law school was to argue with her mother-in-law. 'It Is Biji's Desire' briefed Amara to study something intelligent but safe, like economics or accounting.

Bakshi Aunty gulped down the remnants of her tea. Without helping herself to more biscuits, she bid a hasty goodbye to Biji and left with her son and gossip in tow.

Biji turned to her husband. 'Why you always make her leave?'

Baba did not say anything. He often told Amara that he tried not to argue with his wife, knowing she was the judge, the jury, the witness and the verdict. He went into his bedroom.

Amara went to her room to do her homework while Biji sat next to her, painting an old photograph, where, all of six, Amara was sitting on a tin roof with Lily. Amara watched Biji dilute white paint and carefully dab it on Amara's forehead and neck. As Amara predicted, this reminded Biji of something. She went to the kitchen and came back with a steel bowl. With her bare hands, Biji applied ground lentil paste on Amara's face. Probably due to the one-and-a-half wife prophecy, Biji patted some paste on Amara's neck as well.

'This make you fair, like Amreekan *gori* memsahibs,' Biji said. Much to Biji's chagrin, years of this treatment along with generous dabs of Fair & Lovely cream did not lighten Amara's skin. 'Now don't talk. Or wrinkles you will get.'

Biji went back to her painting. She outlined the Himalayan background with black streaks so Amara would look whiter. She got engrossed humming her favourite tune:

*Eena, Meena, Deeka*
*We will go to Amreeka*
*Rum Pum Po, Rum Pum Po*

The doorbell rang. A blob of black paint landed in the middle of Amara's forehead. Biji cursed and went to the door, grumbling.

A second later, Amara heard her scream, 'The pink president have come.'

Amara ran out of her room, while Baba came out tying a white cotton lungi around his waist. At the door was a postman holding a white manila envelope.

'Take it to temple, Amara,' Biji said, in a voice like that of a dybbuk.

Amara took the envelope from the postman's hand and saw a pink stamp on it, with Abraham Lincoln's image. She walked towards the temple, with Baba and Biji following her silently.

'This be it,' Biji said with her temple-face. She lit a copper lamp and made clockwise circles around the envelope. Amara was nervous so she kept her head turned away till she heard Baba say, 'Open it before you burn the thing.'

With trembling hands Biji tore open the envelope along its marked lines. She pulled out three cards. 'They here,' she whispered in a raspy tone. The flimsy papers, which held within them such longing and agony, did not develop wings and fly, so she repeated more confidently, 'After waiting for fourteen year, I have got our Green Card!'

Tears rolled down her face.

Baba look stunned and Amara looked into his black eyes, which shone with flecks of brown when the sun was on them.

He said, 'Ammu, this does not mean that we have to go to America. We'll go only if you want to. Is this what you want?'

The only three desires Amara knew scrambled in front of her eyes. They crept up like vines from underneath the floorboards, jumped up from the third leg of the wicker chair and skipped atop the steel trunks. They danced in frenzy, whirring and whirring around her.

'It Is God's Desire.' 'It Is Biji's Desire.' 'It Is His Desire.'

Amara stared worriedly at Biji's earlobes. A few years ago, Biji had vowed that she would not remove her heavy gold earrings until the Malhotra family got their Green Cards. Every time Biji got excited – which was often – her ear lobes quivered, and over the years her ear piercings had grown larger and larger, like the fear in Amara's heart: what if her mother's earlobes succumbed to gravity and ripped?

'Why you are asking her? She too young to know what is good for her,' Biji said.

Amara saw Biji's earlobes trembling so hard that they could tear any moment.

She touched the smooth emerald stone that she had put in her kameez. The desires fell one by one and only one desire stood back up: 'It Is Biji's Desire'.

Amara knew that Baba's desire to let Amara retain a bit of her own life (for she had only one life) fell short before Biji's desire to suppress such moves. In front of his wife he too had no desires. He'd told Amara that after twenty-two years of marriage it was better that way.

As if his silence signified consent, Biji turned to Amara and said, 'Ammu, we are going to Amreeka. Don't fail us in journey.'

And so it was, on a sultry October evening, at the tail end of a day unwashed by rain, when the hills glowed orange from the setting sun and the yellow light from fireflies illuminated slumbering shadows, that Amara's fate was sealed.

# 2

Amara stared at the woman lying fast asleep across the aisle of the aircraft, snoring.

Biji noticed her too. 'Too shameful. What the Amreeka will think of Indians?'

An airhostess tapped the woman and woke her up saying, 'We have to serve snacks, Ma'am. Please clear the aisle.' The woman sat up on her seat, but once the airhostess turned away, she sprawled back on the aisle.

'She is delaying our food,' grumbled a man sitting next to Baba.

'I have packed aloo-puri. You want some?' Biji asked.

The man looked at Biji, moving only his eyes, 'Is this your first time flying?'

It was. 'Ofcoursenot,' Biji said, offended. She turned to Amara, 'Go tell Mrs Airhostessji please give to me glass of water.'

As a first-time flyer, Amara was uncomfortable dangling somewhere between heaven and earth. This suspended sensation was not entirely new to her however; over the last few months, ever since the arrival of the Green Cards, her life could neither be what it used to be, nor become what it could be, and Amara had been feeling like a flying trapeze artist frozen mid-air.

After receiving the Green Cards, Biji had placed a trunk call to Dua Mama to inform him that they were coming to America. On receiving a curt 'okay' from him she developed a great anxiety about Dua Mama and America, which became disproportionate as preparations to leave for America began.

First, she took a photo of the Dua family – Dua Mama, Sheila Mami, Riya and Tina – standing in front of a Christmas tree and scotch-taped it on their Godrej refrigerator. She instructed Baba and Amara to emulate the Dua family's lofty expressions and self-assured body language.

'But we don't celebrate Christmas,' Amara said.

'Now we will,' Biji replied.

Then, Biji declared, 'We need to train English.' Amara went to a convent school so her English 'train' was full. Baba had done his law graduation so his English 'train' was also full. The 'we' meant only Biji, though it was impolite to point that out. Under her tutelage, the Malhotra family had to say, 'Pass-the-potato-lentil,' instead of 'Pass-the-aloo-dal,' and 'Vegetable-Market' instead of '*Sabzi-Mandi*'. If Amara and Baba didn't speak in English they were fined; Amara had to study for an extra hour while Baba had to teach Biji English for an hour. Like a politician, Biji was exempt from punishment. Despite these efforts, Biji continued to speak English like one who dreamt in another language.

Fortunately for Biji, the year was 1992 and, as Baba told Amara, while America was caught in Operation Desert Storm, India was brewing in Operation Economic Reform. Prime Minister Narasimha Rao and Finance Minister Manmohan Singh were leading an era of economic and financial overhaul. Singh Bling. Rao Pow. India became globalised; global came to India and India went global, like one big happy borderless family. By the turn of the year, a bouquet was sent saluting this new relationship – StarTV-MTV – which people like Biji gratefully accepted.

So on an otherwise unmemorable day in January, two-and-a-half months after receiving the Green Cards, and amidst finalising Baba's job, Amara's school, their new home, and a million other things, Biji bought their first ever colour television set. With cable. Baba, Biji and Amara sat around the television as it flicked on. America burst into their room.

Biji clapped her hands in glee and said: 'My first Amreeka!'

'What about the tourists on Mall Road?' Baba asked.

'They not real Amreeka. Real Amreeka don't come to Shimla, they fly to Switzerland,' Biji replied. 'Real' Americans were rich, she assumed, and looking at the TV screen, Amara had no reason to contest this belief.

While Operation Economic Reform was able to fulfil Biji's desire to become familiar with American culture without leaving her living room, Amara was unsure of how it was supposed to make her feel. Precocious people in seraphic clothes and garish make-up were providing a new form of entertainment: guiltless and thoughtless. Heroes could be anti-heroes. Adults could be children. Blondes could be brunettes. Unlike Indian protagonists, these characters had no lessons to teach and no morals to emulate. They didn't saunter with bows and arrows to protect family honour or tear open their chests to show who lay inside their hearts.

From the comfort of a story she had grown up with, Amara was suddenly watching stories from the outside – alien stories that found no echo in her moral fibre, yet excited her. She understood then that children were taught things to unlearn them. Like Peter Pan. Easter Bunny. Santa Claus. Flying Monkeys. Indian Woman with Five Husbands. And adults were not immune to unlearning either, she determined, as she watched her family discard the old TV face – patronising and self-righteous – and develop a new TV face – vacuous and rapturous. Two weeks later, Biji bought Baba a pink terylene shirt and Amara a pair of purple pants.

Till the day they left, Biji made Amara watch TV everyday, sitting beside her to monitor the content and learn from the accent she couldn't quite follow. She 'tch–tch–ed' as Jasmine ran in slow motion in *Baywatch*. When Kevin and Winnie from *The Wonder Years* shared their first kiss, Biji stopped massaging castor oil on Amara's hair and placed her oily hand over Amara's eyes, 'This not meant for innocent Indian children.' And indeed it wasn't; Amara became a trailblazer in school for something apart from her studies: 'You are forced to watch *Baywatch*? I pretend to help with the TV antenna when the reception is not clear so I can catch a glimpse of the show. You are lucky!'

Seeing the people from behind the TV screen now come to life, Amara got so nervous that she threw up in the brown paper bag placed provocatively on her aircraft seat.

The woman on the aisle kept snoring.

At 1:47 pm EST on 6 February 1992 the Delhi–Dar-es-Salaam–London–Newark Air India flight landed at Newark Airport, New Jersey.

USA.

Biji puffed up like a dandelion. 'Smell the air. So pure. So clean. I love Amreeka.'

'We are still at the tarmac,' Baba said.

As the passengers got up to disembark, with Biji being first in line, Baba remained seated, playing with the earpiece in his hand. His expression was withdrawn, as if the cabin air had carved the edge of his mouth downwards.

'Baba, we have to go,' Amara said gently, as Baba got up slowly from his seat.

They didn't go far to catch up with Biji, who was on her knees at the airport vestibule, touching her forehead to the plush carpet. Amara blushed when the airport staff, in their clean, crisp uniforms and white-pink skin, watched Biji, much as hawk watch mice.

'Let us to pay respect for our new motherland,' Biji said on seeing them.

Baba walked straight past her. This time Amara and Biji played catch-up.

Within fifteen minutes Amara saw Biji reach the culmination of her Green Card dream. She glided past the long queues of Indians holding deep blue passports at the immigration line, to stand with the 'Amreeka', her bulbous nose high in the air. On reaching the immigration officer, however, Biji's sweat resurfaced on her upper lip. Amara sensed Biji's confidence floating away like a dandelion. Huff. Puff. While Baba fronted the officers' questions, Amara sang softly to her mother:

*Eena, Meena, Deeka*
*We have reached Amreeka*
*Rum Pum Po, Rum Pum Po*

At the luggage carousel, Baba went looking for trolleys because they had twelve steel trunks and six hands. He came back empty-handed.

'We have to pay for the trolleys. One trolley is for one dollar. Do you have change?' he asked Biji. Biji glared at Baba, as if he had asked her to sell the Godrej armoire (the one with the full-size mirror, the only one) that had come with her dowry.

'They think we fool?' she said and stared suspiciously at the white-gloved-not-empty-handed luggage porter. Her purse was strung diagonally across her crumpled cotton sari. She held it tightly, close to her bosom, as if someone would try to peel it off her. She wore thick white-soled sneakers as if to send a message to the peeler: I will – *but she couldn't* – chase you.

Amara observed the Real Americans; divorced from their seraphic clothes and garish make-up they still looked important and busy, making their way through the airport in long sure strides. The cafe, the money exchange joint, the information desk and the taxi service counter carried the same brisk and distinguished air as its customers. Standing still in the flurry of organised activity, amidst Americans passing by with 'excuse me' and 'sorry' at the tip of their tongues, Amara felt safe, for everything in America belonged exactly where it should.

Baba paid for the trolleys and the Malhotra family came out of the terminal, into the cold winter. They all lifted a hand simultaneously to tighten their jackets. Their winter clothes, which had protected them from severe winters in Shimla (with no central heating), seemed inadequate when confronted with this bitter wind howling in their ears. Amara stepped tentatively on the road, not knowing whether to look left or right before crossing, and was immensely pleased when a car, instead of speeding on seeing her, or honking, as would happen in India, stopped to let her pass.

'We be king here,' Biji said, before her teeth started chattering.

They reached the parking lot. Eight eyes (including the two on Baba's spectacles) searched for Biji's brother, Ashok Dua. Amara saw a stranger's hand go up in greeting. The man looked like a spick and span forty-two-year-old American, his clothes rich and creamy like the skin on gori memsahibs, his head covered with a blue Yankees cap embellished with a white NY logo, and his rimmed spectacles defining his face, instead of hiding it. He wore a black pea coat with a folded and looped black scarf. It was on coming closer to him that Amara recognised Dua Mama, for proximity helps dispel the illusion of perfection. The unadorned parts of him, his nose and mouth, gave him away, revealing a man who resembled an unkempt forty-two-year-old Indian. A mole at the bridge of his nose had a hair attempting to make a grim outward journey into the world. After he removed his cap, Amara saw that all his hair had leaped out of his head, leaving a mass grave of brown hair pits. Biji had told Amara that Dua Mama's success led to fawning relatives petitioning for money and favours, as if success were an incense stick whose fumes had to be distributed. Amara imagined that his lips must have grown brown-grey and curled from granting promises that she heard he sometimes kept and sometimes didn't. He had a metallic smell like one handling fistfuls of coins.

'We very much obliged, Bhai,' Biji said when she met him. She had on her temple-face as if her brother was God. She bent down to touch his feet, although he was the younger brother. Close as hand-to-feet, as Biji had told Bakshi Aunty.

Dua Mama shrugged his hands vaguely in the air, half a blessing, half a shoo-off-a-fly. He leaned self-consciously against his blue Cadillac (whose photo had driven across the Atlantic to parallel park on their Godrej refrigerator), as if it owned him and not the other way round. Unlike most Indian cars it was not scratched or bumped – a true beauty.

'I have coconut from India. Can I break it so we have auspicious start to Amreeka?' Biji asked him.

'Not here,' he replied quickly, with an accent that was American, yet not; Indian, yet not; Ind-erican, perhaps. In all likelihood, he realised that there was no need to shatter a coconut, for it symbolised dashing one's ego, and Biji's ego had already broken against his.

He shook hands with Baba, for they were as close as hand-to-hand. He turned to Amara and gave a little shake to the mound of flesh between her chin and lips, causing Amara to wonder if this defined their relationship – hand-to-mouth. To erase that possibility she bent down to touch his feet but he caught her halfway.

'There is no need for all this in America, Amara,' he said

grandiloquently, as if pronouncing a deep, long-pondered aphorism to a cult.

Not knowing how to respond, Amara helped Baba with the luggage and then sat inside Dua Mama's Cadillac, which quietly roared to life. The luggage forced her to press her face against the backseat window. She didn't mind, for this gave her an unobstructed view of USA. Images appeared and vanished, like photos on a slide projector. Grey highways. Naked trees. Stark buildings. The Real American, stepping out of the television's invincibility, battling the onslaught of winter, slipping and shivering on the hard teguments of sidewalk ice.

'People wearing clothes, thank God. Not like those Amreeka show,' Biji commented.

'It is the middle of winter, Didi,' Dua Mama said. His American-university and talking-to-real-Americans English sounded polished next to Biji's Hindi-medium-school English. He glanced fiercely at the red bindi on Biji's forehead, as if it had sucked all the blood out of her brains. And then, perhaps sensing the need for it, he pronounced a list of 'no need in America':

(1) No need to leave shoes outside the house.
(2) No need to make rangoli or have any religious talisman outside the house.
(3) No need to line-dry or hang clothes from windows or in the yard.
(4) No need to play loud Hindi songs or sing lyrics on the road or in the car.
(5) No need to be over-friendly (even dolphins sleep with one eye open).
(6) No need to wear bindis or dhotis or saris.
(7) No need to convert everything into Indian rupees.
(8) Absolutely no need to break coconuts outside their house or car.

During the car ride, Dua Mama explained that although what they did inside their home remained their business, their public conduct was of concern to society at large. The Statue of Liberty advertised America as open to immigrants, but some Americans deplored the success of such advertising and turned xenophobic. Just last week, Dua Mama explained (as if one incident defined the attitude of an entire country), young men prowled the roads for brown blood and yellow blood and black blood. They saw a Hindu lady in the parking lot (yes, she was also wearing a bindi) and descended upon her American dream. They called themselves Dot Busters.

It was consequently fitting for an immigrant to blend in with America like sugar with water, or better still – to avoid a fatal diabetic relationship – to blend in like air with water, Dua Mama finished, pointedly looking at Biji.

Amara realised that this counsel was directed towards Biji to help quell her enthusiasm for America. Dua Mama probably wanted her to wake up from the fantasy of the American Dream and realise the responsibility of such dreams.

Biji responded with a 'very nice', like an obstinate child impervious to reason.

Twenty minutes later Dua Mama drove past a green signpost that said: 'Welcome to Edison'. He took a turn at that exit and after a few minutes the Malhotras arrived at their new house. Amara got out of Dua Mama's car and stood with Biji and Baba, looking at the place they were going to call home.

'Very nice,' Biji said, again, as if her mind could process no word except what would please Dua Mama.

Though there was no 'Snowflake' and 'Pinecone' below it and it didn't lean on wooden stilts or tilt in any direction, the house was nice. Situated on New Street – although Amara could not see an Old Street – it stood alone, straight and solid,

rising out of the wood of elm trees to a shingle-style double
storey. Like the immigrant life it was meant to shelter, the
house blended in perfectly with rows of similarly landscaped
houses. Amara could hear the gurgle of a stream and imagined
that a small bank lay beyond the scanty wooded lot of poplars.
Beneath her feet were autumn leaves, a carpeted entrance to
her new home.

Amara believed that like second love, there could be no
second home, but she fell in love with this house immediately.

She was used to living in an apartment, and a bungalow like
this, small and compact as it was, seemed enormous to her. So
she turned to her father and asked, 'Have we become rich?'

Baba grazed her gently on the head. 'No, Ammu. We have
taken a loan from Dua Mama to buy this house.'

'Is it expensive?' she asked, worried about her family's
ability to pay back Dua Mama.

'For us it is, but not for the average American,' Baba
replied.

Amara looked more closely at the house and saw that there
was wild grass, weeds and brambles growing at the sides. She
noticed the cross-gabled skeleton of her new residence with
its irregular roofline, the splotched-on brown paint, dull and
listless, and the white colour peeling off the front door to
reveal a mouldy green. It looked like the kind of house that
would shine under neither sunlight nor moonlight, treating
both with a dignified indifference.

'I like it,' she said.

'Then I like it too,' Baba replied, and Amara looked up to
see him smiling, finally.

Biji lifted her hand in which she held the brown coconut
(whose hairy surface looked frazzled probably because of its
unfinished duties) and said, 'I will break inside house. Lucky
it will be.' She paused to see if Dua Mama would stop her

with a 'no need in America'. When he didn't, she ran towards the new house, before he changed his mind.

They walked into their residence, over shards of coconut, and entered a hallway. The living room was on the left and the kitchen to the right, absolutely bare. Wooden stairs with a wooden balustrade led to an unseen floor above, daring people to explore its hidden depths. Dua Mama told them that their house had two furnished bedrooms and Amara's was the smaller one upstairs.

Amara ran up. Outside her bedroom, she stopped beneath the wooden rafters and took a deep breath to pace her expectations. She opened the bedroom door slowly. A squeal of excitement escaped her lips. A bed lay by the corner of the room. She no longer had to sleep on a mattress! She ran up to the bed intending to sit on its plain beige bedcover but found herself sinking in its softness. A large window next to it overlooked a small garden with scraggly bushes and grass, beyond which was the high wooded border of their small yard. Since her room was on the underside of a sloping roof, a rectangular slanting skylight lay directly above her bed, looking up into an infinite sky, showing Amara the endless possibilities open to her in this new country.

If this was the not-rich life in America, Amara thought, then she was going to be all right. She was satiated, like a flying trapeze artist finally finishing a somersault. She went back downstairs, running her finger along the wall.

She asked Dua Mama, 'Is this wallpaper?'

When he replied in the affirmative, Amara turned to Baba and Biji, and said breathlessly, '*Wallpaper!*' She'd heard the word on TV and had never understood it, wondering if it was a wall made of paper. 'Now I know,' she thought happily.

Biji turned to Dua Mama, 'No light switch is here?'

Amara looked around. She could not see a light switch either. There were only plug points near the floor.

'Americans don't use tube lights like in India. They use lamps,' Dua Mama explained. Amara looked at her uncle, amazed at the confidence he expressed in the frailest of American concepts. How could a fringed lamp, the type she had seen clinging meekly to side tables, light up an entire room?

'Of course, Amreeka be smart,' Biji said, not wishing to ruffle the sentiments of either Dua Mama or Amreeka.

They declined offers of rest and, despite their jet lag, insisted that they wanted to meet the Duas. Dua Mama's house was five streets away, so they put on some extra woollens and strode towards it by foot. This way they could 'leg-stretch' and 'walk real Amreeka', as Biji put it.

While they were walking, Biji took Amara aside, 'Your cousin Riya go to same boy-girl school you will go to. She must know Indian boy. You meet her and put foot which is best forward.'

Amara was nervous, not because of Biji's dictum, but because she hadn't met or heard from Riya and Tina in seven years. They were dear to her, as cousins are to single children, and she hoped her move to America would rekindle their old friendship. She had so many memories of them, the loveliest being through a photograph taken on their last visit to Shimla, which captured the three girls posing as Gandhi's three monkeys: see no evil (Amara covered her eyes), hear no evil (Tina covered her ears), speak no evil (Riya covered her mouth).

Then there was hopscotch! The three monkeys' squealing voices ran through Amara's head as she remembered how they had played *stappoo* on squares marked with limestone.

And Ludo! A yellow square, a red square, a green square, a blue square and home.

And Statue! Freezing – staying frozen – in one position.

And Bingo! Each time someone else would declare a winning number to the game master, the three monkeys would sit together, chin-to-chin, knees-to-knees, and their jealous voices would sing:

*Fatty Fatty Tambola*
*Sitting on a bumbola*
*Bumbola broke*
*Fatty got a poke!*

And, the letter! Riya had written on a paper, which had a red ladybug on its bottom left, that Amara was her best friend and they would be best friends forever and ever and ever.

At this memory, Amara's reflections came to a halt. For it was another day, another season, seven years ago in Shimla. There was blinding rain. Amara and Riya played a game of Marco Polo in the torrent. A day later Riya got pneumonia. Death haunted the two families for twenty long nights and twenty long days. Riya survived, and the Dua family left Shimla to go back to their home in America. They never came back. Riya and Tina didn't reply to Amara's long letters, or call.

The spectre of death troubled Amara since.

She stopped playing Hopscotch, Ludo, Bingo or Marco Polo.

The red ladybug on the letter faded to pink, as Amara read and re-read Riya's words, longing to be Riya's best friend again.

Now, as they walked along a narrow road bordered by hedges, four pairs of feet with four sets of expectations, Amara tried to replace her nervousness with excitement. She convinced herself that Riya's letters were lost in the mail and Tina had the wrong phone number.

She walked over to Baba and said, 'Do you think Riya will remember me?'

Baba smiled and said, 'Of course she will. I am sure she's very excited to meet you.'

Amara could have hugged Baba in appreciation, but they were not the kind of family that did that. So, she used a voice as gentle and comforting as a hug, and said, 'Thanks, Baba.'

On reaching Dua Mama's house, Baba, Biji and Amara stopped short, as if they were at a road crossing. Rising above them was a three-storied Victorian mansion, with a winding driveway lined by pine trees, and an arched portico with marble pillars. The mansion resembled a palace and made Amara's new home look dilapidated and nondescript, like a slum at the foot of a high-rise. Amara remembered being told that no disparity existed in America. She realised that like children and adults, immigrants were also taught things to unlearn them.

'What a beauty house,' Biji said.

'Built by blood, sweat and tears,' Dua Mama said.

They entered the house and were greeted with a 'hello' by Dua Mama's wife, Sheila Mami. Behind her stood Riya and Tina. Biji and Baba waited in their place expecting Riya and Tina to bend down to touch their feet, till Biji whispered fiercely, 'No need in Amreeka.'

Amara was glad for the 'no need in America' because on seeing her cousins she had forgotten to touch Sheila Mami's feet. Like the house, Riya and Tina carried signs of both vanity and care. Amara had studied their Christmas photo and knew they'd grown, but in person they looked strikingly adult, even Tina who was younger than her. While Amara had remained at five feet two inches, Riya, who was a year older, was almost three inches taller and Tina, who was two years younger, had shot up to around five feet six inches. Their height lent an air of power to them. Amara remembered hot summer days, when the three of them had feared only one thing: 'the curse of shortness'. If anyone jumped over a recumbent person, they believed that person would not grow taller, and the only way to undo the curse was for the culprit to jump back over the supine body. Fighting for inches became a riotous game the girls played till the day Amara's jute cot, where the girls often played and slept, broke into two halves. Like a heart. Since then Amara had slept on a floor mattress. Now she felt that the jute cot had broken with a curse on its lip that left (only) Amara with 'the curse of shortness'.

Curses couldn't stand alone for that would be dull. Therefore, her cousins were also inflicted with 'the curse of beauty' (no one claimed that curses were fair). Riya's long hair, dark and dense, like raven wings, fell across the face. A yellow dress clung to her statuesque figure. Her skin seemed to take pleasure in the excessive pampering of make-up, something Biji always balked at ('you know that lipstick have fish scales!').

Tina, still in the body of a twelve-year-old girl, with the high cheekbones and almond eyes of her sister, had an impatient beauty waiting to burst forth, like a fairy backstage.

Amara imagined her cousins looking down at her from their silver platter of curses. She saw herself as she imagined they saw her. Her skin was besieged by pimples, denied the saving grace of make-up. She touched her uncombed hair self-consciously. As part of her convent school uniform, she'd always knotted her hair into two plaits with yellow and brown ribbons, but before coming to America Biji had unfastened Amara's plaits so she could look like a gori memsahib. Now her hair remained in the giddy hold of unruliness, indifferent to comb or conditioner. Amara looked at her hands, clumsy, for her fingers lacked the delicate finish of a manicure, and she looked at her feet, clunky in their rubber gumboots. Worse still, she was wearing her purple pants, purple.

Sheila Mami introduced Amara as if she'd never met Riya and Tina, 'Darlings, this is your cousin from India, Amara.'

Amara saw Riya and Tina size her up, and to distract them from dwelling on her flaws, she blurted out, 'Amara Malhotra.'

She looked from Riya's face to Tina's. They looked back at her vacantly. She felt sixteen eyes (including the two on Baba's spectacles and the two on Dua Mama's spectacles) bear down on her, particularly Biji's. The hair at the back of her neck rose.

'Pleased to meet you again,' she said quickly, almost taking a curtsey.

'Nice to see you too, Amara,' Tina said in a thick nasal drawl that Amara had trouble following. Tina pronounced her name as if saying it for the first time – Aa-maa-raaa.

Riya gave her a tight smile.

There was another long silence. This irked Amara more than her bashfulness.

'I bought you ink-pens, the best in Shimla.'

Amara had never used these expensive gold-plated pens for herself, happy with the ink-pens inside her He-Man pencil box that splotched her fingers or school pinafore with blue dots. She remembered Biji's surprise when she insisted on buying these pens and walked to over eleven stationary shops, till they got a five-rupee discount on each pen.

'How droll. I haven't seen one of these in like forever,' Tina said. Amara scratched the pimple on her chin as she realised she didn't know what 'droll' meant.

'And I made for you special painting from my own very hands,' Biji said. She handed a bundle wrapped in a Brijwasi Sweets plastic bag to Tina's outstretched hands. Tina opened the bag and pulled out a photo frame inside which was the three monkeys' photo. Biji had painted an extra spot of pink on the girls' cheeks, making all three of them look like monkeys. Amara saw Tina's eyes glaze over the frame with no recollection. She had a feeling that she'd never see the photo again; it would be lost among the hundreds of valuable things that rich girls possessed and didn't cherish. It was 'the curse of money'.

'Thanks, Bua,' Tina said, her smile a little less broad.

Riya looked from Biji to Dua Mama, rolled her eyes and said, 'Don't expect me to watch their backs.'

Amara looked at her favourite cousin ascend a magnolia wood staircase with gold-painted balustrades, and vanish from sight.

Amara tugged at her hair, as if punishing it for making Riya leave.

Baba put his hand on her shoulders. She couldn't meet his eyes.

Sheila Mami apologised on Riya's behalf. 'Don't mind what Riya said. She's tired from the Indian American classical dance competition she took part in yesterday.'

Amara knew that they were not in a position to take offence.

'Did she win?' Biji asked eagerly, for winning was everything.

Sheila Mami didn't reply, as though failure – the 'it that shall not be named' – was unmentionable even for Indians in America.

'Why don't you give her Hajmola? I have several bottle of it,' Biji said. Amara was surprised to hear this very generous offer because Biji never shared her Hajmola tablets. She believed that the digestive medical tablet could cure every ailment of the body – headaches, colds, migraines, cancers, ulcers and failure. Biji's generosity was probably to let the Duas know that the Malhotras were self-sufficient and helpful, not a burden as Riya thought.

Sheila Mami declined Biji's offer graciously, by making a counter-offer for tea.

Biji said to her brother, 'Too humble she is. Making own tea.'

'In America even the rich do their own work,' Dua Mama said, dismissing the compliment.

'Go, Ammu. Help Mami,' Biji said. 'Also, get water.'

Amara went to the kitchen and stood outside its door. She looked in at the glass cabinets, the limestone countertops and the dainty tea cups. Nothing looked like it could survive the boisterousness of cooking and cleaning and chopping and eating.

'Why are you standing there, dear? Do you need anything?' Mami asked.

Amara sought Mami's permission to use her fridge. 'No need to be so formal, Amara,' Mami said, beckoning her in with a gentle smile. 'Think of this as your house.'

If only, Amara thought, as she tiptoed to the fridge hoping she wouldn't break something. On opening the door, Amara stared in amazement because everything inside the fridge – the milk carton, juice boxes, tomatoes, eggs, apples – was double in size. Even the bread slices were bigger. And the water, the water had done a vanishing act!

'There is no water in the fridge, Mami,' Amara said, bringing the calm back into her voice, as if she watched magic shows everyday. 'Should I boil some?'

'We drink water from the tap here, Amara. No need to boil and refrigerate water,' Mami said. She grinned at Amara as if they'd just shared a secret.

After the customary service to tea, the Malhotras were taken on a grand tour of the Dua Mansion. Amara was struck by the fact that the ebony bed was American with an Indian batik spread, the granite floor was American with a Kashmiri carpet, the black walnut sofa was American with Jaipuri cushion covers, the stained glass windows were American with Indian silk shades and the walls were mounted with Indian Tanjore paintings. It was as if immigrants transported the soul of their culture to the skeleton of another culture, and then plastered the former so it couldn't come in contact with the host culture.

'And this is my most precious possession in America,' Dua Mama announced with a flourish. Amara followed the sweep of his hand that stopped at a wall-to-wall picture of a bearded man in orange robes. A plastic marigold garland covered the picture, leaving room only for the man's face, beaming mysteriously through sandalwood incense fumes. Dua Mama bowed down and Amara caught a glimpse of the temple-face, the first resemblance she saw between Biji and her brother. He added reverentially, 'This is my Swamiji. I have not made a single decision in my life without consulting him first.'

Amara was confused by all of this. While the Dua family appeared American with their car, mansion, clothes and 'no need in America', they were Indian with their Swamiji, decor, classical dance competition and 'it that shall not be named'. It was almost as if being Indian in America was to show Indianess only to other Indians. She realised that an immigrant's identity was a shifty-eyed monster, and that's what the phrase Indian American connoted: Indian on the inside and American on the outside.

Today's lesson was: Ind-erican = Indian for Indians + Indian American for Americans

After the tour the two families had nothing more to say to each other. An awkward silence followed before Biji said, 'We be leave. Must bath take before water go.'

Mami looked at the red bindi on Biji's forehead (though not as fiercely as her husband had) and informed her that America didn't have water cuts. Then she stated her own list of 'no need in America':

(1) No need to hand wash clothes.
(2) No need to buy fresh vegetables since frozen packets were available.
(3) No need to winnow rice or lentils.
(4) No need to expect home delivery of anything but pizza and Chinese food.
(5) No need to hire domestic help.
(6) No need to dust more than once a month or sweep more than once a week.
(7) No need to boil or refrigerate water.
(8) Absolutely no need to believe in any cuts (water or power) except budget cuts.

Like cue cards for a new life, 'no need in America' found use for Amara and her family almost immediately.

# 3

Amara came home from school at four o'clock. After fumbling with her keys, she entered through the front door behind which Biji had hung a thread of green lemons and chillies. The talisman, meant to keep away the evil eye, should have been on the front porch, but 'no need in America' compromised it of its due.

In the hallway rested the tiny hand-carved marble temple imported from their Shimla house – such indulgences could not be done away with. Inside the temple was a Hello Kitty penholder, now serving as an incense stick holder. Between the statuettes of a bronze Lord Ram and a wooden Lord Krishna were four photos: two black and white dog-eared photos of Amara's deceased grandparents – maternal and paternal, the Christmas photo of the Duas, and a sepia photo of Old Shimla.

Next to the temple, Baba had placed a plastic container still marked by the contents of its former resident: Kozy Rice Pudding. It served as a collection box. Since Baba could not afford to buy air tickets to visit India, he saved a little change everyday and put it in the box. Amara had started doing the same. Cents, nickels and quarters had accumulated and become thirty-three dollars and fifty-six cents. Amara dropped a quarter into the box, proud to have walked the five extra blocks to save on bus fare.

She went past the living room, now furnished with a brown IKEA sofa set, a wooden coffee table and a hand-knotted floral carpet purchased at an Indian shop. She opened the glass showcase (a feature in every Indian American house) and straightened the silver spoon that lay next to a porcelain thimble, china plate and clay figurines. 'No need in America' forbid Biji from wearing saris in public, so she'd hung them up as drapes across the house.

Their house looked as cheerfully reassuring as a matronly aunt in an old petticoat. It was almost like being in India. Amara cherished this, especially because in the last few months she'd been like a distracted parent whose undivided attention was on her newborn, America.

Suddenly Amara heard a door creak upstairs. She froze. A cold hand grabbed her heart. Her fingers dug into the clasps of her backpack. With growing dread she realised how alone she was. Accustomed to coming home to Biji, not to an empty house that made strange sounds in the absence of others, the first few weeks had been the toughest. Amara would forget the keys and wait outside the house, sometimes for hours, till Biji returned from work. Ravenous from school, she missed having a glass of warm milk and snacks ready for her.

She began reciting the *Hanuman Chalisa* that Baba had taught her to say when she was afraid:

*Jai Hanuman gyan gun sagar*
*Jai kapis tihu lok ujjagar.*

Fear can be allayed in no language except one's mother tongue, Baba had said, when Biji tried to find the English translation of the mantra. He was right. The cold hand on Amara's heart released, finger-by-finger, and the warm throb of blood flowed back to her limbs.

It wasn't so bad to be home alone, Amara thought. It made her grown-up and responsible. And, she didn't have to drink milk.

Amara shook the lingering dread out of her body and went to the kitchen to fix a snack. She glanced at the fridge door on which were tacked two foolscap sheets with instructions on the American English language. Amara had written these using a ballpoint pen, not an ink-pen that Tina had called 'droll' (which she found out meant 'comical in an odd manner'). On the first sheet were Indian English words corresponding with their American English counterparts:

| | |
|---|---|
| Lift | Elevator |
| Capsicum | Pepper |
| Torch | Flashlight |
| Cell phone | Mobile |
| Rubber | Eraser |

On the second sheet were commonly used words in America, with their corresponding pronunciation:

| | |
|---|---|
| Duane Reade | Do-ae-n Read |
| Jalapeno | Hal-a-penio |
| Manhattan | Maanhaatun |
| Schedule | S-ked-ool |
| Intestines | In-tes-tins |
| Route | R-ow-t |
| Data | Daa-taa |

The lists were for Biji's benefit, for she cared most about doing things correctly in America.

Amara took two boiled potatoes out of the fridge and mashed them to make potato-chutney sandwiches. Sheila Mami had mentioned that this was Riya's favourite meal.

A few minutes earlier, Amara had bumped into Sheila Mami.

'I'm going to the beauty salon and the girls are alone. Why don't you visit them?' Mami said, as usual trying for the girls to be friends.

Riya and Tina never came to visit Amara and during the few luncheons at the Dua Mansion, which were always initiated by Biji or Sheila Mami, they exchanged no more than perfunctory words with Amara. Tina was polite but distant, responding in monosyllables to Amara's questions, while Riya pointedly ignored Amara or stayed inside her room.

Seeing Amara sit alone on the couch or help the older women in the kitchen, Sheila Mami would remark, 'I wish my girls had spent more time in India so they could be like Amara. We try to raise them the Indian way but in the end they are born in America,' to which Dua Mama would say, 'They may wear American clothes and study at American schools, but in their heart they are Indian.' Dua Mama seemed to revel in his daughters' behaviour, as if approving of the distance between social classes, while Sheila Mami seemed apologetic, giving Amara something to take home every time – Riya's old clothes, Tina's old books or leftover food.

Amara rationalised that her cousins behaved awkwardly because they only met around adults. Once they were alone, she convinced herself, they would warm up to her.

Therefore, today's going to be different, she said to herself.

She opened the tin foil wrap in which she carried lunch to school and put three sandwiches inside it. Despite being famished, she waited to eat with her cousins.

She walked to the Dua Mansion and knocked on the front door.

No one answered.

She rang the bell. Once. Twice. And waited. She rang the bell again.

Finally, Riya opened the door. She stood before Amara with her mouth tight and her body frigid, as if playing Statue. Amara thought she was going to slam the door shut on her face.

When she didn't, Amara said, 'Hi! I heard you were alone so I came to say hello.'

Riya continued staring at her.

Amara held out the tin foil package. 'I made your favourite potato sandwich.'

Riya looked down at Amara's hand and said. 'I don't eat carbs.' She shut the door.

Amara waited. Riya was probably being funny in her usual caustic way. But no one opened the door. The house seemed as still as a monk in meditation. Amara turned around slowly. Riya must be in a bad mood over something else, she thought, and kicked a pebble on the road.

On reaching home, she found she couldn't eat despite her growling stomach. She threw the sandwiches in the garbage bin. Then she remembered that the Indian kitchen ran on the theory that 'every end is a new beginning'; nothing was beyond use. Nettle tea leaves were used for plants to grow, squeezed lemons were used to whiten nails, and fruit skin (especially orange) was used to scrub the skin. So she took the tin foil package out of the bin and put it in the fridge. She'd carry it for lunch tomorrow.

To distract herself from what had transpired with Riya, Amara sat down to do her homework. The same ninth-grade subject that took her an hour to study in Shimla now took three hours. Although her credits from India were transferred mid-year, she fumbled with learning several years of the American education system in a few months, and despite her accent training from StarTV–MTV, she couldn't follow a lot of what her teacher or classmates were saying. She dreaded showing Biji her semester report card.

Amara finished her homework by the time Biji came from work. Baba's salary couldn't sustain a household in America, so Biji had taken up a job for the first time in her life. She worked without a title at an Indian restaurant called Raj Mahal, owned by a Gujarati named Raj Patel. Biji had to manage the cash register from ten in the morning to three in the afternoon, and supervise the chefs for dinner from three-thirty in the afternoon to five-thirty in the evening. Her job also entailed pasting Raj Mahal's masthead on her car: 'Don't Worry. Don't Hurry. Eat Chicken with Curry.'

When Biji walked into the house, Amara started, as usual taking a second to recognise her mother; for Biji had taken Dua Mama's Dot Buster warning rather seriously and gone to great lengths to hide her Indian identity. She'd cut her long hair to shoulder-length (like a gori memsahib), wore only pants with shirts, and her forehead was empty, devoid of a bindi. Not surprisingly, Biji didn't change everything about herself; she still liked to carry niggling worries from outside to their house. She started a conversation with Amara as if they were in the middle of it, 'Patel not show up today so I stand at register whole day saying, "For here or to go?" Then customer say his ginger chai have no ginger. For one dollar what he expect?'

Amara knew that Biji's complaints had nothing to do with chai or Patel, but with 'little need' and 'big need' that had latched on to 'no need in America'. One such 'little need', which in Biji's irreconcilable eyes was a 'big need', was cleaning the bathroom at home. Biji scheduled it every Monday and called it 'untouchable day' because cleaning bathrooms was a job traditionally done by untouchables in old India. Since today was Monday, Biji was in a foul mood. She dropped her purse on the floor and walked towards the bathroom, wanting this 'little (big) need' to be over as soon as possible. Amara followed her, not daring to offer to do it by herself, for Biji believed that 'the curse of untouchability' afflicted those who did its work.

Biji was clutching the doorframe to the bathroom. Her knuckles were white.

'Let us to be strong, Ammu.'

She popped a Hajmola tablet, put on latex gloves and entered the bathroom. Amara followed her holding a Lysol bottle.

Later, while Biji took a bath, Amara made dinner. She put newspapers over the kitchen counter to avoid stains from turmeric powder, chopped gourd and potatoes on a cutlass, and put the potato peels inside utensils to help them shine, since 'every end is a new beginning'.

In fact, from this very theory, Biji had developed a new form of art. Since Baba had bought a colour camera, Biji's excuse for painting black and white photos had become invalid. So Biji saved discarded pistachio shells and eggshells, and made wall hangings out of them in the shape of elephants and tigers. They were hung all over the house — on Amara's bedroom door, below the kitchen cabinet, above the toilet seat.

There was a shuffle of heavy feet on the porch followed by the sound of a key rattling in the keyhole.

It was Baba. He was home.

Amara ran to the door, quickly looked through the peephole, as Baba insisted she do every time, and opened the entrance before Baba had a chance. Although Baba said he hated the idea of locked doors, he insisted upon this as a 'big need' in America.

The porch light threw Baba's shadow on the floor, small and shaky. His law degree had no relevance in America so he worked as an assistant manager in the home loans department of a local bank. He found the job 'brain-numbing' and returned home every evening looking like a wrung-out cloth on the clothesline.

He followed Amara to the kitchen quoting another new snippet about Shimla, 'Did you know that a new bird's been sighted in Shimla? I heard about it today from an Indian man who came to the bank for a mortgage. They're planning to name it after the chief minister's daughter.' The creases on Baba's forehead eased as he spoke about Shimla.

There was a knock at the front door. Maybe it's Riya, Amara thought, and almost dropped the pot of lentils in her hands. Maybe she's come to say sorry. Or hello. It didn't matter. She had come. Amara ran to the door and opened it without looking through the peephole.

It was Sheila Mami.

'I brought some lasagna for you. I thought you'd like to have it for dinner,' she said. Amara realised that this was Sheila Mami's way of apologising for Riya's behaviour; she must have somehow heard about the sandwich incident.

Biji came to the door, her skin pink and raw from the scrub she'd given it after cleaning the bathroom.

'Please to come in,' she said, and gave Amara a sidelong wink, their secret code to remove the tarpaulin on the sofa and chairs. Biji had put this to keep the furniture new and gleaming, hoping to impress the Duas when they visited. That moment never came.

It was not to come now either, for Sheila Mami said, 'Next time. I have to go back home for dinner.'

When the door shut, Biji said, 'Our house too poor for her? We so poor that she doing charity to show my brother?'

Baba said, 'She's just being considerate, unlike her hus—' when Biji threw him a 'karr' look.

Biji's leniencies were reserved only for her brother, while

Baba's leniencies were reserved for anyone but him. Amara knew that Baba had spoken the truth. By applying for their Green Card, Dua Mama behaved as though he had done a good turn to his less-favoured, less-educated, less-moneyed older sister, and was therefore rid of his duty. Performing a 'big need' gave him licence to ignore the 'little needs'. Biji justified her brother's detachment – 'he is too busy man and he have enough for us done.'

Before this turned into one of the many arguments Biji and Baba had started having, Amara turned on a local TV show that aired old Indian film songs at eight every night. Many of the songs were shot in Shimla, and Baba loved watching them so he could spot parts of his land. Even Biji got caught up in his excitement.

Since Baba and Biji worked so hard, Amara wanted the few moments they had together to be blissful. The three of them, home, together, back in the cocoon they had left, was the only time that Amara saw her parents escape from their drudgery, the life they were building. It was the happiest time in the Malhotra household, the happiest in their immigrant days.

As they set the table for dinner, Baba sang along with the songs he loved, and Amara took out a tape recorder to record her father's voice. It amused her to see Baba do household work, when in Shimla he had never lifted a finger.

'I am proud of you, Baba,' she said to him, half-joking, half-serious.

'Your pride may not last long. I'm not doing this when your mother and I go back to Shimla,' he replied, smiling. And in that jest the truth emerged. America was just a parenthesis for her parents. A slide that would transport their daughter to a life that they could only dream of. Baba and Biji's presence in this country was entirely incidental, even though they strove so hard to conquer it, Biji with her zealousness and Baba with his stoicism. This was all being done for Amara's sake and *His* sake.

Amara felt the onus of this responsibility. She looked at the grey hair multiplying on her father's head. She noticed that her mother sometimes walked with a slight limp because her legs hurt from standing long hours at the restaurant. Her parents were aging faster than they needed to so Amara could have a good life.

The house suddenly seemed stifling to Amara. She stepped outside under the pretext of taking the garbage bag and walked over to the empty patch of land behind the house. Bending down next to the yellow plastic swing, she dug her fingers through the mud and searched for the parrot stone. As soon as her hand touched its smooth surface, calmness descended upon her. She'd chosen this place to hide the stone from Biji, not knowing how to explain its presence or the sense of relief she got from having it.

'It will be different there,' Biji had always said, and Amara had believed that after coming to America, their lives would morph into an ideal picture, fall into the perfect slot. That faith was weakening under a thick weighty reality. Amara knew that her failures – her school reports, her cousin's rejections and her friendless existence – only accentuated Baba and Biji's disappointments. This could not be the way of life for Baby Buddha with a Green Card. Faith had to persist, out of sheer necessity.

Amara bowed down to the ground. As she did this, a plan formed in her head. She threw the mud back into the hole and patted it to level with the earth.

Tomorrow Amara would bring the Malhotra family's American Dream to life.

# 4

In order to achieve the American Dream, Amara needed to find *Him*. And for that she had to impress Riya, by putting — as Biji had said — 'foot which is best forward'. Since Riya was not warming up to Amara on the home turf, Amara decided to use the only other commonality she shared with her cousin: high school.

This was not going to be easy considering that Riya sauntered around campus as if she were encased in a plastic hamster ball and therefore untouchable. An apparition of beauty in her expensive jackets, fishnet stockings and mascara, Riya never acknowledged Amara, treating her as part of the riffraff, like the boys whom she swivelled past.

It also didn't help that everything about high school scared Amara.

This anxiety had started on the first day of school itself when she entered class a few minutes late and was asked by her teacher, Ms Sloss, to introduce herself. Amara stood before the whiteboard. The coloured eyes of thirty-six American students bore down on her. She forced open her mouth and self-consciousness strapped itself around her words as she became acutely aware of the heaviness of her Indian accent. The expression of the students confirmed her doubts.

Ms Sloss asked her to repeat her name five times and then pronounced it as if wrenching a meaning out of it — Aa-maa-raaa.

Amara hastened to agree with her, 'That is correct, Mrs Sloss.'

Ms Sloss looked taken aback, as if Amara had belittled her, before replying in a sweet dripping voice, 'You can call me Amy, like the other students do.'

That is wrong, Amara almost protested, for teachers should be addressed as (respectfully married) Mrs. She quietly walked to the row by the windows and – as Ms Sloss asked her to – sat at the front desk, where unfortunately the whole class could watch her. She fixed her eyes on Ms Sloss and didn't let go even when they became strained and wet. After class, when Ms Sloss began to collect her belongings, Amara stood up and said, 'Thank you, Mrs Amy.' There were snickers behind her back and Ms Sloss' kind expression did nothing to blunt the humiliation. Amara slouched as low as she could at her desk.

Once the bell rang for lunch, she could no longer hide under the organised chatter of a classroom. Lacking the courage to approach someone in class, she picked up her bag and went to the hallway in the hope of finding a friendly face. But all she saw were smokers walking past her with a brash languor, fighters with booming voices, danglers sitting on trashcans and windowsills, and kissers with tight curls and spiked hair. With her eyes peeled to the ground, she walked fast, avoiding the boys and girls.

She went into the cafeteria and saw students sitting together on benches. Everyone seemed to know one another. Although she knew Riya would be of no help she looked around for her. On not seeing her, she wondered whether she should grab a tray and wait in line like the other students, but the smell of greasy food – French fries, chilli on buns, macaroni and cheese – made the bile in her stomach rise. In need of fresh air, she came out of the cafeteria and walked around campus until she stumbled upon a small and empty cathedral with a sign that said:

*Ad Moira Nati Samus.*
*We are born for greater things.*

She went inside and sat on the wooden pews, praying for time to fast forward. The bell rang for her next class. From that day on, knowing that lunch would be school's most dreaded time, Amara carried food from home and sat in the cathedral, eating on the pews, hoping she was not desecrating something.

Over the next few weeks, Amara made no friends. In Shimla, her shyness had been offset by several commonalities with other students, like games or festivals or tuitions, none of which she had with American students. Even the occasional Indian American student she was hopeful about seemed turned off by her; she wondered if it was her accent or clothes. At those moments, she wished she had been born in America like them or had stayed in Shimla, instead of being an outsider to both places.

With boys around, she was even more self-conscious. Having spent her entire life in a convent school, she was awed by the sight of boys and girls together, nonchalantly teasing, laughing and hugging, even in front of the Mrs teachers.

*American students are so adult, so sophisticated,* Amara thought.

Biji had strictly forbidden Amara from befriending boys or teaming up with them for school projects. She would have put Amara in an all-girl's high school were it not for the high private school fees. To save her daughter from the wiles that inflicted gori memsahibs, Biji developed her own form of sex education. She forced Amara to watch Hindi movies that followed the same storyline: a hero and heroine would stand in front of a roaring fire, two birds would peck, flowers would sway in the breeze, the heroine would become pregnant, doomed, the world would call her – gasp! – unmarriageable. 'This happen if you think of boy in *that* way,' Biji warned, her hand crossing over Amara's wrist, leaving her fingers' impression. Due to StarTV-MTV, Amara knew this couldn't happen, but she still lived under the shadow of the warning.

This was before Amara saw Bob. Bob, with long brown hair that fell below his forehead, and made Amara want to pull them aside like drapes, so she could see the colour of his eyes. Bob, with legs like drinking straws on which he walked with a slouch. Bob, with creases on his unironed T-shirts, as if he'd just woken up. Amara wondered if Bob, cuter than Kevin Arnold in *The Wonder Years*, would notice someone like her. She daydreamed about meeting him and what he would say to her, what she would say back. She wrote his name at the back of her notebooks, and crossed out Malhotra from her name to write Bob on it: Amara Bob.

But two weeks prior, Riya had shown up at Bob's side, or telling by the lovelorn look on his face, he had shown up at Riya's side. In the mornings, Bob would tag behind Riya as she headed towards class. During lunch, they'd be eating off each other's faces instead of their plates. After school, they'd be inside his Firebird, driving out of the parking lot together.

Amara almost convinced herself: I am in America to study, not to make friends.

Now, in order to achieve the American Dream, Amara had to make friends, at least with Riya. For that she would have to look and behave like her cousin, become one of Riya's posse, the clique with whom Riya stopped to chat, even laugh. These girls typically wore short skirts, even in the winter; their eyes peeked from under the smoky haze of black eyeshadow; and their lips puckered beneath hues of red lipstick.

Amara would have to wear a short skirt and make-up to get Riya to talk to her.

The problem was that Amara did not own clothes that were above her knees or elbows. Sheila Mami had donated Riya's old clothes to her, but Biji – the clothes police – had scoured through them and picked out what she thought was inappropriate. She was scandalised to find a short denim skirt in the pile – *she trying to show us we too poor to buy own underwear!* – and now used it as a dishrag.

Amara had to get hold of that skirt.

That night, after Biji and Baba went to bed, Amara hand-washed the dishrag and put it to dry over the heater in her room. When her parents left for work early next morning, she ironed the skirt and slipped it on. Amara had never worn a short skirt before. Her embarrassment was so acute that she could spot the goosebumps on her legs. She couldn't carry off the skirt, she realised, so she put on beige thermal underpants from Shimla Knits and Knots underneath the skirt, thinking they were thin enough to pass off as stockings. She paired the skirt with a hand-me-down pilled black sweater from Betsey Johnson, bought before Riya's size-two days.

Satisfied with the clothes, Amara dwelled on the next problem: make-up. Biji did not use any, saying the chemicals and fish scales would injure her skin and religion, so there was no make-up in their house. Amara got creative. She took talcum body powder, used to stem Biji's incessant rivulets of sweat, and patted it onto her face as she had seen other girls do. For rouge, she rubbed a pinch of *kumkum* – which Biji used for her bindi – onto her cheeks. She mixed Nivea cold cream with the kumkum, and lined her lips with it like lip-gloss. Then she took a glass kohl stick, that Biji used to keep away the evil eye, and dragged it under her fluttering eyelashes. As a final step for 'the day to impress Riya', Amara took off her glasses, a hand-me-down from Baba that covered half her face, and put them inside her bag.

A feeling of guilt roused Amara. She was going against 'It Is His Desire', for he would not approve of her dressing up like this. But she firmly pushed the thought aside. After all, this was for *Him*; Biji had said that Riya could help Amara find *Him*, and for that Riya had to first like Amara.

Amara stepped out of the house as an icy draft inched up her legs. She was tempted to go back home and change into something warm, but she couldn't let the weather determine the course of her life. Instead, she put on her red and white reindeer snow cap, which Biji had picked for her at a post-Christmas sale at Walmart (the biggest store Amara had ever seen) and took a bus to school. By the time she reached the school gates, Amara still didn't feel like herself and took a deep breath to calm her nerves. That's when she saw that people were turning to look at her, some even twice. This is how Riya feels everyday, Amara thought with glee as she quickly entered the campus grounds. She walked confidently to the North Wing where the tenth graders had their classes. Riya's first-period class on the fifth floor would be over at nine, after which she would take the elevator to her next class on the first floor. Amara went to the fifth floor and waited by the elevator.

It was a quarter to nine. She was early. Sophomores came out of the elevator and got in, giving Amara strange looks when she kept standing. So she walked to the nearest water cooler for a drink of water and took long sips with her mouth. She couldn't see very clearly but she kept her ears perked for Riya.

Soon Amara heard a gritty voice coming down the hallway: 'I didn't open my mouth during class because the new guy passed me a note saying that I looked exotic. If I'd said something he would've totally realised that I've grown up in America. You jealous?'

Amara began to panic. Riya was with someone, probably Bob. She couldn't face both of them together. She wouldn't be able to carry this through. She turned in the opposite direction and began to walk away. Then she saw a boy pass her by and turn around to stare at her. Maybe it was a good idea to let Bob see her this way. She swung around and walked back towards the elevator. When Riya was close enough, Amara saw that she was with Bob. Her knees became fluid, as if the water had gone straight to her limbs, but she managed to walk up to them.

'Hello,' she said to Riya.

Riya looked at her from top to bottom with her mouth ajar.

The elevator door opened and the three of them stepped in. Riya and she had not stood this close to each other since childhood.

Bob, cute as ever, probably embarrassed by the long silence, leaned over and introduced himself, 'I'm Bob. You are?'

Amara didn't reply. She was seeing Bob's eyes for the first time. They were minty blue-green and wider than any other pair of eyes she had seen.

Riya replied to Bob, as if apologising, 'This is my cousin. She just got here from India.'

'Yeah? You know my friend Sara, she went to some beach in India and all the women were inside the water with their freakin' clothes on. Now Sara was wearing a bikini, so everyone stared at her and these kids started taking her photos. Crazy right?' Amara didn't know how to respond. Americans had a story for everything, but she did not.

'You want a smoke?' Bob said, as if fumbling for something more to say. Amara saw that his shirt was ironed and he was wearing converse low-tops, the rage on campus. Riya had changed him.

'Hey, she's a good Indian girl, not a bad American boy like you,' Riya said, playfully hitting Bob's arm.

They reached the first floor.

'Does that mean I can't ask her out on a date?' Bob said, letting out a loud snort. Amara was stunned. What would she say if he did ask her on a date?

Riya laughed as they both got out of the elevator. 'Are you crazy? She'll think you want to marry her.'

Why did Riya think of her this way? Then Amara remembered: Biji.

'Are you jealous 'cos you can't behave like a good Indian girl?' Bob asked.

'And look like her? Did you see her clothes? And make-up? What was she thinking?' Riya's voice trailed behind her.

Amara thought she had been slapped.

She was sure the whole school had heard Riya.

With quivering hands, she took her glasses out of the bag and put them on. She wanted to make sure that it was Riya she'd seen. Riya's figure was receding in the distance, swinging in a peplum ruffle top and a grey mini skirt. That's when Amara realised that people were still turning to look at her, not with the awed expression they held for Riya, but with contemptuous smirks. They had not been admiring Amara's new look but laughing at it.

Amara had to escape. She ran out of the building into cold drops of rain. Her teeth chattered like dice being shaken. Her glasses became foggy but she kept them on because they made her feel invisible. She ran till she reached the ladies room in the old brownstone building where no one ever went. She looked at herself in the mirror and realised with swelling dread that she looked like a circus clown. Her face was sheet white with patches of powder, the kohl had smudged around her eyes like a raccoon's tail and her cheeks were red like a monkey's ass.

Embarrassed, she ran into the big toilet stall for people in wheelchairs. She wanted to wipe away the stains plastered on her face. Her hand dug inside her bag for some tissue paper. She yanked it out and in the process her history term paper fell to the ground. Amara looked at the first page, marked by big red circles, bright and jarring like her flushed cheeks.

The roaring haze in her mind reached a point of calm. She began to see things clearly.

The first thing that struck her was the foolishness of her ambitions. She could never be Riya. And she could never impress boys like Bob, who dated girls like Riya. She realised that maybe Riya and Bob didn't even matter because in trying to impress them she was going against 'It Is His Desire'. He would be ashamed to see her like this, trying to be someone she wasn't, failing tests, having crushes on boys who said 'freakin', wearing make-up and short skirts, such an aberration from the good Indian girl he was seeking.

Amara wanted to skip school and go home. She could tell her parents and teachers that she wasn't feeling well. Instead, she wiped the make-up from her face, adjusted her glasses to nose level and went to class.

The day passed in a blur, but when Amara reached home that afternoon she knew exactly what to do. She walked straight into her room and took out The Letter kept in the shoe-box below her bed. She looked at the pink ladybug, tired and 'fed-dup', and ripped the letter, forever and ever and ever.

# 5

The icy stillness of the sealed winter lake was replaced by the sunny waves of a freewheeling spring ocean.

Amara came home at the end of the term clutching something in her hand. She didn't let it go till Baba and Biji were home, and then she held it out to them like an offering. It was her report card. She had got straight As and an A+ in math (she'd taken the exam without even using a calculator).

Biji and Baba were sedately euphoric, the proletariats' reaction to success. Baba offered Amara a Coca-Cola, an American product he was inherently suspicious of, and while she was sipping her reward, he walked up to the refrigerator, removed the yellowing foolscap sheets, and tacked on her report card.

Biji said, 'Good, I be fed-dup of American words.'

Biji was happy. Amara's intelligence had given credence to her immigrant cause. After a few minutes of admiring the curve of the 'A' on Amara's report card, as compared to the straight lines of the B and D on her previous test papers, Biji grew impatient.

She yanked the report card from the fridge and declared, 'We be going to Duas.'

Baba said, 'Now? They may not be home. We may disturb them.'

'Stop your Amreeka way. My brother not mind me. His house be my house.'

This was one of the few times Amara agreed with Biji; she wanted to see Riya's reaction to her first success since coming to America.

They reached the Dua Mansion. Biji knocked on the door. Once. Twice. Thrice. 'They're not home, let's go,' Baba said. Biji ignored him and knocked again. Once. Twice. Thrice. No one came to open the door. They waited for a few minutes like devotees at the gate of heaven. Finally, as they turned to leave, the door opened. Dua Mama stood there but didn't invite them in. Heedlessly, Biji barged in, while Baba remained rooted to his spot till Amara walked in as well.

The Dua family was watching *Roman Holiday* on their VCR. Their TV faces were neither vacuous nor rapturous, but steady and bored, for the dreams shown on TV are accessible to the rich. Riya was filing her nails on the sofa. Tina was flipping through a magazine. Sheila Mami was peeling cucumbers.

Biji interrupted them without a thought and showed off Amara's academic performance.

'I wish my girls would study as hard,' Sheila Mami said, not succumbing to the bait of jealousy.

'We are not freshmen nerds, Mom,' Riya chimed in, without missing a beat.

'Riya is right,' Dua Mama said, for he always agreed with his eldest daughter, the way his sycophants agreed with him. 'But Riya, we have distracted you from your academic work by putting you in extracurricular classes, like dance and music and Hindi. We need to stop one of them. I'll pull you out of the violin class. It is useless to learn something that no one in our community appreciates.'

Riya stopped filing her nails. 'But I love the violin, Dad.' Amara was surprised to see a shade of vulnerability pass across her cousin's face.

'Not till your grades improve,' Dua Mama said definitely. He turned to Amara, as if he wasn't quite done with her, and said something she would recount for many years, 'It is good that you are studying, Amara. But remember that in America it is not only intelligence that matters but opportunity. You will soon learn that.'

~ ~

True to Dua Mama's words, 'the curse of opportunity' was something Amara learnt over the next three years. Despite her academic success, Amara could not afford a private college. The scholarships that she was offered by some universities did not cover the high costs of living or meet Biji's condition that Amara continue living at home. So she went to study accounting (as per 'It Is Biji's Desire') at Edison State Community College.

Riya, at that time, was starting the second year of law at Columbia University.

Despite not studying in a field or college of her choice, Amara enjoyed college life. She took the bus to school, spent the day with accounting students typically as diffident as her, and studied hard. She was able to step out of Riya's shadow for the first time since coming to America.

Sometime after the first month of college, Amara was sitting in the Internal Audit class. Next to her was a girl with a curly red mop of hair that she kept twirling with her fingers. Midway through the lecture she turned to Amara to ask what page they were on. After a few minutes, when the professor told them to take notes, the girl began fumbling through her large bag. She pulled out a pack of gums, a lone cigarette, a hairbrush embossed with Bill Clinton's photo and a few crumpled dollar bills. Amara took an extra ballpoint pen from her bag and gave it to the girl, who in turn looked up. Amara noticed her angular face and startled grey eyes as she took the pen with a quick 'thanks'. As class was coming to a close, the girl put her paraphernalia back into her bag, and before the bell finished ringing, she had left the classroom.

The next day Amara was in the cafeteria, having lunch in a corner and reading one of her accounting books, when the red-haired girl came and sat next to her.

'Hey! I've been looking for you all over the place. Wanted to return this,' she said, and held out Amara's pen as if brandishing an honour. 'You are one lucky girl. I never remember who I take pens from, but you I've noticed since school began.'

Amara was surprised that someone as gregarious as this girl could show interest in her.

'Why?' she asked.

'You know, you don't look from around here. And, I've heard you talk to the prof during class and you have like this different accent.'

Amara couldn't be shy around this girl, so she smiled in response and said, 'It was our karma to notice each other. You stood out too, because—' she looked at the girl's hair as bright as a fiery sunset '—you don't look like you're from here, and your accent sounds foreign to me too.'

The girl gave out a loud laugh and her whole body shook, like a jelly dancing.

'Karma, nice word,' she said. 'Yes, I guess it was karma.'

Amara asked her if she'd like to sit with her for lunch.

'I can't eat this cafeteria crap. Let's go to McDonald's and try the new ShamRock shake.'

Although Amara was halfway through lunch she didn't get many opportunities to eat outside home, especially not fast food. So she agreed, though she'd have to cut back on her Kozy Rice Pudding donations for a few days.

'I don't do lunch with strangers. What's your name?' the girl asked.

'Amara.'

The girl repeated her name, and Amara was impressed with her exact inflexion and tone.

'And your name is?'

'I'm Stacy and I've never shopped at Macy's.'

Amara burst into laughter at Stacy's sheer silliness.

They went to the nearest McDonald's where Stacy ordered a cheeseburger and ShamRock shake, while Amara ordered French fries since there was nothing vegetarian on the menu. Once they sat down, Stacy asked Amara where she was from.

'Edison,' Amara replied.

'But you're so, you know, exotic-looking. Where are your parents from?'

Once Amara said India, Stacy couldn't stop asking her questions about India, her move to America and her migrant life.

'You know, I'm so impressed that you and your parents were brave enough to give up everything to move here and start from scratch. It must be tough,' Stacy said.

'Not always,' Amara replied, meaning it.

'Is there anyone here to help you?'

Amara thought of Riya and Dua Mama. 'Not really.'

'There should be something to make it easier for immigrants like you.'

'Well, many immigrants are worse-off, they don't know anyone or anything when they come here,' Amara said.

'Then, let's help them. Let's bring some good karma in our lives.'

Amara looked around her, 'Karma in the land of McDonald's?'

'Yes, McKarma,' Stacy said and laughed.

Stacy made Amara feel like she could say anything and be understood, so she said, 'I hope you don't mind me saying this but you don't behave like an accounting student.'

'You guessed it, sister. I hate it. The problem was that I didn't know what I wanted to do with my life, and since everyone in my family is an accountant, they told me to become one too. So here I am trying very unsuccessfully to survive accounting.'

'I didn't know that American families functioned like that too,' Amara said, immediately realising how little she knew about the people whose land she lived in.

'Not all Americans are the same,' Stacy said.

They went back to class together and over the next few weeks became fast friends. Before Stacy, all of Amara's relationships had conformed to a strictly marked social and economic hierarchy, so she liked that with Stacy she felt suspended, borderless, not knowing her exact place. She began to stay back after school to hang out with Stacy. Most days they remained on campus but sometimes Stacy invited Amara to her dorm room in a building off-campus. The building was buff-coloured brick with a sandstone trim, and encrusted with dirt. Nonetheless, Amara loved going to the dorm and seeing students living without their parents, learning the responsibilities that came with this freedom.

One day Stacy asked Amara to come on a double date with her boyfriend and his best friend. Amara declined. They were in class, so when Stacy asked why, Amara whispered, 'I am not allowed to go out with American boys.'

'Ah-ha,' Stacy said, as if Amara had divulged her biggest secret.

A boy on the bench in front of them turned around and said, 'Shhhh.'

Stacy ignored him and continued, 'You know, I thought

your disinterest in boys was due to religious reasons or something. So if you're not allowed to date Americans, are you allowed to be friends with them?'

Amara thought about it. Had 'It Is Biji's Desire' covered that realm? She tore a small sheet of paper from her notebook, wrote 'I don't know', and passed it to Stacy.

'Does that mean you're not supposed to be friends with me?' Stacy said, in no mood to stop disturbing the class. The boy in front turned around again and narrowed his eyes at Stacy.

'No,' Amara wrote back.

'Then why do you never call me to your house?' Stacy asked.

This time three students turned around and glared at Stacy and Amara. Amara ignored them and furiously scribbled on the note: 'You can come home anytime.'

Before Stacy could open her mouth, Amara covered it with her hand, and gave Stacy a pen and sheet of paper. Stacy scribbled: 'WHEN??????'

'Tomorrow?'

'Awesome,' Stacy said loudly, and raised her hand in a high-five to Amara.

Just then the professor turned towards Stacy and said, 'Miss Stacy, I couldn't help but notice that you've been talking since class began. Why don't you leave if you're not interested?'

'I'm not some crazy who talks to herself, Prof,' Stacy said. 'I was talking to her.' She pointed to Amara who had hidden her face behind a thick book. The class guffawed. They were both thrown out and spent their time of punishment doubled over laughing.

~ ~

Three nights later, Biji was removing the tarpaulin from the sofa and chairs, when the doorbell rang. Biji had agreed to have Amara's 'Amreekan' over for dinner. She had invited the Duas as well, so they could see that Amara had met a gori memsahib, but Dua Mama, as always, declined the offer. Amara saw Biji put on her temple face and open the door. She had warned Stacy: 'My mother is a traditional woman,' but Stacy was confident, 'Don't worry, I'm reading a book about Indian culture. I'll charm her over. Besides, all my friends' parents love me.'

Stacy entered the house, with her hands folded in a Namaste, the way Amara guessed the book must have instructed her, and said, 'Good evening. I got some wine for you.'

Amara couldn't see Biji's face, but she knew it was disapproving. Biji was holding the wine bottle as if it were a leper.

Amara wished Baba was home and not stuck late at work.

Amara sat Stacy in the living room and went into the kitchen to help Biji. Biji was holding up the denim dishrag, which had survived 'the day to impress Riya', and said in Hindi, 'She be wearing clothes we clean sink with.'

Amara almost snapped back that Biji's niece Riya did the same, but an odd sort of loyalty stopped her. Despite Biji's curiosity, Amara never told on Riya's conduct or boyfriends.

They went into the living room with a plate of vegetarian cutlets.

'You have a lovely house, Radha,' Stacy said. Stacy must have picked up Biji's name from the nameplate outside their house.

Biji's jaw dropped. No one younger had ever addressed her by her first name.

'Call me "Aunty,"' Biji said, her voice as sharp as a stapler. Then she directed a barrage of inquiries at Stacy that covered

Stacy's family, religion, siblings, career goals, parents' job and house. Stacy, who usually enjoyed a long talk, looked exhausted by the end.

'I hope you learning to cook for husband,' Biji said.

'Me? No way. I can't even boil water.'

Biji pinched her face as if expressing frustration on behalf of Stacy's future husband. 'But learn you must. Take water in vessel, turn gas on, and it boil.'

'I don't have pots and pans in my dorm room, which is cool 'cos my boyfriend cooks at his place.'

'No pans? Boyfriend?' Biji asked. She glared at Amara as if she had confessed to having a boyfriend and no utensils. Before Biji's heart stopped, Amara showed Stacy Biji's pistachio painting collection. Only on Stacy's generous praise of her 'artwork' did Biji somewhat warm up to her and allow Amara to serve her dinner.

～ ～

The next morning, Stacy walked up to Amara as they were making their way to class.

'You know, Am, I don't think Radha liked me,' Stacy said.

Amara couldn't help but smile. 'I like you all the more for that, Stace.'

'You should've seen her face when I mentioned my boyfriend.'

'That is definitely something she didn't expect.'

'So you can never have a boyfriend, not even an Indian one?'

'I don't want to,' Amara said, her words clipped and sure; not having a boyfriend was as much a consequence of 'It Is Biji's Desire', as it was 'It Is His Desire'.

Stacy leaned over, 'You know there are a lot of guys here who would love to be your boyfriend. But they call you the

Cold Mountain because they think you're impossible to know.'

Amara was flattered to be noticed. She had been taking care of her appearance. Her glasses fitted her face and her clothes fit her size. Unknown to Biji, she had purchased a kohl pencil and a pink lipstick that she enjoyed wearing on campus. Then she looked around. There were three Indian boys walking into the building together. Any one of them could be her future husband. She didn't want them to think that she was the type of girl who would date boys. She would rather live with the moniker of Cold Mountain.

So she dismissed Stacy's comment. 'I'm glad that's my reputation.'

'Suit yourself,' Stacy said, shrugging her shoulders.

Amara watched as Stacy ran up to her boyfriend of the month: Derek. He scooted Stacy off her feet and held her above him, planting a long, hungry kiss on her lips. The sun bounced off them, their young love, off Derek's honey-coloured hair, the sparkling gloss on Stacy's lips, her soothing laugh that turned sharp and loud when she was really happy.

The sun threw a glare into Amara's spectacles and made her eyes water.

She hurried on alone to class.

~ ~

After graduation Amara wanted to apply to the Big Five accounting firms in Manhattan but Biji insisted she find a job in Edison and continue living with them. She was convinced that seeing more of America would make Amara independent and spoil her marriage prospects.

Dua Mama, who had heard about Amara's academic prowess for five years, told Biji that he'd hire her as a junior accountant in his accounting firm, Sheila Accounting. Biji accepted the offer on Amara's behalf, and since Amara didn't have any other options, she went to work for Dua Mama. During the year, Amara grew bored with her stuffy colleagues, whose minds concentrated on their ledger sheets as if those contained the meaning of life.

One day, she got a call from Stacy who'd been fired from her job because her boss did not like her attitude towards work. To Amara this was no surprise, for Stacy repeatedly said that she was meant to do more than tally up Excel sheets all day, even though she didn't know what the 'more' was. Fortunately, there was an open position at Sheila Accounting. Amara told Stacy to apply for the job and recommended her highly to Dua Mama, exaggerating her skills and passion as an accountant. 'Stacy is the reason I did well in college,' Amara lied. Dua Mama hired Stacy.

And so it came to be that Stacy and Amara worked together in the same company. Even though Amara had to watch Stacy's back through this tenure and cover up her mistakes, it was worth it, especially as Amara would learn in time how priceless her decision to work with Stacy was.

# 6

The hand of time moved like a cop directing the flow of traffic and stopped on a day in 2000.

Amara closed her Hyperion file and logged off from her desktop computer.

'I'll be off then,' she said to Stacy.

'Adios, you slave of nepotism,' Stacy replied, as Amara pulled out her employee card to clock herself out. Stacy held up a customised bumper sticker that said: Sheila Accounting – We Promote Family Values More Than Family Members. She had gifted this to Amara on her previous birthday, and when Amara returned her gift saying she couldn't use it, Stacy kept threatening to paste it on her car.

Amara laughed at Stacy's theatrics even though there was a ring of truth to her mockery. Amara worked harder and longer than most of Dua Mama's employees. Yet she was the only employee who had been overlooked for a promotion or a raise in two years.

Today Amara was leaving early from work for the first time and it was – of course – on the boss's command. It was Tina's twenty-first birthday for which Dua Mama had planned a big party in the evening. But indulgences had to be preceded by prayer; the soul cleansed before being corrupted again, so Dua Mama wanted his family to visit the local Hindu temple. Though he did not believe in all familial duties, he believed that a family must pray together for his daughters. So Biji and Amara took half-day from work, Tina came from Illinois University where she studied public health policy, while Riya came from New York City where she worked as a corporate lawyer. Biji and Amara met the Dua family at the local Indian temple, located on the first floor of a nondescript brownstone building with a Chinese dry cleaner and a UPS store at the ground level.

Amara hadn't met Riya and Tina in months, but she wasn't hurt when they gave her a lukewarm response. She expected nothing else. She handed them extra dupattas to cover their heads within the temple. She had correctly anticipated that they would forget to bring these or perhaps they had correctly anticipated that she would get them.

They went inside the temple and, like sincere devotees, lay prostrate before the statues. Unfortunately, some devotees – overwhelmed by God's munificence – were unable to express their piety. Sheila Mami, who had plastered her face with an expression similar to Biji's temple face, got up with a sudden yowl. Her salwar kameez was embroidered up to her neckline with Swarovski diamonds. Like a porcupine turned over, she could not lie down.

Biji, who had a double temple-face in front of God and Dua Mama, looked at Sheila Mami with absolutely no expression on her face, as if superior beings did not take kindly to emotions. Without a word, she began to roll clockwise around the statue of Lord Ram. This was her way of compensating for her sister-in-law's inability to lie down before God.

Amara ignored Riya as she (surprise) rolled her eyes.

'That's enough, Didi. I'm sure God has got the message,' Dua Mama said.

'I be praying for Riya and Tina hard,' Biji whispered, as if her voice would – *and it could* – rouse God's anger. 'May they soon find good boy.'

'As long as they don't bring home a BMW, I'm fine,' Dua Mama added.

'BMW?' Biji asked.

'Black, Mexican or White.'

Amara had learnt that in Indian society, everything – prayer, education, family, beauty, chastity and career – was a rung of the ladder of life, which had to be climbed to reach the top rung: marriage. So Tina's birthday party was a ploy to find a suitable boy for Riya, while also laying the groundwork for Tina. Amara's shot at the top rung was neglected due to 'the curse of money' that did not allow her marriage to be mentioned in the same breath as Riya's or Tina's.

Amara didn't mind; she was used to being her cousins' backdrop. Even Biji, with her ambition for Amara, bit her tongue. Instead she told her daughter, 'On Tina birthday we must prove we be grateful. We must show that we also give. This be our test.'

She saw Biji get up from the floor, open her purse, take out a twenty dollar bill, fumble for her glasses, pretend she had forgotten them at home, and then loudly ask Amara if she was indeed holding a twenty dollar bill. Once its value had been established to everyone, Biji put the bill with slightly quivering hands into the donation box. Biji usually donated a quarter; this extravagance was to show her brother how devoted she was to his family. Since she could not perform her familial duty with one 'big need', she had to do it with a hundred 'little needs'.

Dua Mama was not to be outdone by his less-favoured, less-educated, less-moneyed older sister. He slowly unrolled a hundred dollar bill and nonchalantly put it in the donation box.

After God was (hopefully) appeased by the drama humans enacted for him, they all went to the Dua Mansion. Biji, Amara and Sheila Mami cooked *puris*, *halwa* and *chana* – 'sacred food for the poor'. In India, Amara had celebrated every birthday serving this food to girls from less privileged families. For two hours, tall and short girls would line up outside her door, playing their role as God's humble and hungry children. They'd sit on the floor, shy and wide-eyed as Amara served them food on banana leaves, eat only a little and fold the rest for their family. This happiness found no place outside Indian shores. For real Americans were rich. They didn't send their daughters to Indian homes to be fed 'sacred food for the poor'. Therefore, the Dua family, Biji and Amara played the role of God's children and ate the holy food. Then they began work for the party.

Dua Mama's status ensured that the best and worst of the Indian community would attend his party. Dua Mama needed the worst, as much as he needed the best, for he waded through his cesspool of power like a hippopotamus, with parasitic birds, in the shape of sycophants, pecking at his discarded offerings.

For the sake of the hippopotamus and ladder, preparations for the party were made weeks in advance. Riya and Tina had to look their best. Dua Mama had to call important people. Sheila Mami had to put the house in order. Biji and Amara had to prepare 'sacred food for the rich'.

Biji, whose culinary skills had grown as formidable as her weight, volunteered to cook for Dua Mama's sixty-odd guests and designated Amara as the informal *sous chef*. Amara made her way around the Dua kitchen on tiptoes, still scared that the kitchen wouldn't survive the boisterousness of cooking and cleaning and chopping and eating. Biji started kneading the dough and Amara noticed that her sari – which she'd worn to the temple despite the Dot Buster warning – edged inches above her ankles, its length compromised by the breadth it had to cover.

Amara let out a long yawn. The last few nights and dawns were a blur of mincing mutton for curry, freezing chicken for kebabs, buying the right size green mangoes for chutney, peeling onions for fritters and skinning potatoes for samosas. Their task was tougher because they didn't eat meat and Biji didn't let Amara touch it, saying that working at a place with the masthead, 'Don't Worry. Don't Hurry. Eat Chicken with Curry' had already corrupted her soul.

They continued working and before they knew it the guests began pouring in.

First came 'the earlys'. In the index of human value they were the minus x-axis. They were the parasitic birds on whom the hippopotamus had bestowed favours, and they repaid this by grovelling, seeing themselves as either family (mistakenly) or lucky (correctly). They were told to set the napkins and light the porch.

Then ambled in 'the equals'. In the index of human value they were the x-axis. Like Dua Mama, they had achieved the American Dream and were reaping its benefits. Their children went to medical school and held cushy jobs with which they paid off enormous student loans. They were offered samosas and limewater.

Late to the party were 'the beyonds'. In the index of human value they were the y-axis, having achieved more than just a dream. Their sons went to Ivy League colleges with no student loans, such were the deep pockets of their ambitious parents, and their pretty daughters snagged another 'the beyond'. Scotch and kebab was placed before them.

As if doctored by slot machines the guests fell into sections – 'the beyonds' stood at the centre, surrounded by 'the equals', while 'the earlys' flitted nervously around both.

In the index of human value Amara knew she was the minus y-axis. So she remained in the kitchen and listened to people cackle like roasting rice grains.

'The earlys' tried to prove themselves by listing out the failures of India in belligerent voices: 'When is India going to catch up with America? When do we have to stop sending dollars to sustain the economy?'

'The equals' spoke in studied shrill tones: 'My Varun is going to medical school in Columbia.' 'Well, my Kaishav is on a full scholarship at Harvard Med.'

Then came the voices of 'the beyonds', languid and persistent, least eager to please, for success had made them impervious to social faux pas: 'Where is the Blue Label bottle?'

Sheila Mami strolled into the kitchen and told Amara, 'Riya and Tina are still in their rooms. I can't leave the guests. Can you please go and call them?'

Amara walked up the magnolia wood staircase and knocked on Riya's bedroom door. 'Come in,' Riya said. Amara went in. Riya and Tina were sprawled on the bed, surrounded by hundreds of photographs of boys, like pixels on a computer screen.

'Look at this guy,' Tina said to Amara, handing over a photo. 'Isn't he adorable? He's going to be here tonight.'

'Why are you so obsessed with looks, Tina? They're all going to be fat and bald by thirty. Think practical. Look at candidates like this one.' Riya held up a photo. Fat and bald stared back at Amara. He was not someone she saw with her glamorous beautiful cousin.

'He's the one I'm going to snag. His name is Prashant Roy. He's studied at Harvard, works as a partner at a hedge-fund, is the only child of rich parents and he was voted Ivy League Matrimonies' bachelor of the month.' The words rolled off Riya's tongue as if she were clinching a deal.

'Didn't you say his mother wants a traditional girl for him?' Tina said, sounding unconvinced by her sister's bravado.

'That's just a silly mind game. We have to overplay the whole *sati-savitri* thing and the guys have to overplay their success.'

'So all you have to do is fake it till you make it,' Tina said, laughing. Amara looked at her giggling cousins, wishing she could feel like she were a part of their world.

'*Ammu!*'

Amara was shocked to hear Biji's voice through the party noise.

'Mami is asking both of you to come down,' Amara said quickly.

Riya replied in a mock-sweet voice, 'Can't you see I'm still in my hair curlers?'

Amara retreated and went to the kitchen where Biji's space was in a state of disarray.

'I forgot to take chicken kebab out of skewer. It outside on table. I go make it okay,' she said. 'You make samosas. Hurry!'

Amara bent over the dough and potato stuffing, her lips pursed in concentration, and spent the next thirty minutes rolling and frying the samosas.

The party was on in full swing. Men engaged in a battle of wits. Peals of laughter rose and fell like beads. Someone started the karaoke machine and people took turns to sing Hindi movie songs. Above that din, Amara heard a round of hoots and claps. She realised that it must be for her cousins inflicted with 'the curse of beauty' and 'the curse of money'.

Biji came into the kitchen, thrilled. 'Peoples love the food. Even Bhai say he know I love his children like mine own.' She looked at Amara and said kindly, 'Our job be over. You go change and then talk to the peoples.'

But Amara did not know what to say to these people. Like the outside of a tornado staring at the eye of a storm, she was invisible to something that she had a 360 degree view of.

Nonetheless, she changed into a salwar-kameez that Sheila Mami had left for her in the guest room, put on the little make-up she was carrying with her and went outside. The first people she noticed were Riya and Tina. Gone were their western garbs; they were draped in saris and pulled off the yards of cloth with the astonishing grace of those with 'the curse of beauty'.

She noticed Riya talking to the fat bald guy whose photo she had shown. Prashant Roy. He was dressed in a suit as though at a job interview. She thought how heavy-set his face was, like a claw hammer, as though to deliver a blow and drive home a point. His nose protruded out, seeking more excitement than the mere drudgery of breathing. His head was balding at the centre; possibly his hair had missed that vast airstrip. Yet his body was erect and there was something commanding in the manner he stood, as if he owned the room and everything in it. And indeed he did. She saw a line of aunties with their trailing daughters, hovering around Riya and him, waiting for a break in their conversation that never came.

Riya and he were standing head-to-head. He was leaning over and saying something while Riya bent her head slightly, coyly, seemingly receiving an award she didn't deserve. It was only when Riya lifted her head to take a sip of water (for tonight she was a teetotaller), that Amara realised that the man was an inch or two shorter than Riya. Such was the regal air of a powerful man, and the diminution of a woman pretending not to be.

Amara grabbed a tray of appetisers and started serving the guests. She moved like a phantom through the crowd. When people came face-to-face with her, their eyes searched for a defining feature. They found nothing. An old man, standing alone, asked her for a quiche. She handed him one. 'This is like putting a cumin seed in a camel's mouth,' he joked. Amara put three more quiches on his napkin. He smiled and thanked her by placing his large gnarled hands on her head, like a blessing. 'I wish there were more traditional girls like you nowadays.'

At that moment, Amara saw a lady nearby pirouette on her heels and turn around to look at her. She must have overheard the old man's comment. The woman was wearing an expensive Kanjivaram sari and an enormous silver pendant with a tiny marble elephant engraved inside it. Amara found her eyes locked with a woman she didn't know. She pulled away and walked to the other side of the room, expecting the woman to lose interest in her, as did most people. But the woman trailed Amara as she served the guests.

Amara was not used to being observed.

She went back to the kitchen and stayed there, busying herself with trivialities. Fifteen minutes later, after she'd shaken off the woman's presence, Amara came out. She set the dining table with the entrees – rice pulao, mutton biryani, tandoori chicken and *shahi* aloo-palak. This time the woman came out of nowhere and startled Amara, causing her to drop some napkins on the floor. Before Amara could recover, the woman lifted a samosa in her hand and asked in a deep voice that was used to getting its way, 'You made these samosas?'

Amara picked up the napkins from the floor and looked around the busy room. She was on her own. 'Yes.'

'Your name is Amara?'

'Yes.'

'Amara Malhotra? Daughter of Radha and Madhur Malhotra?'

Amara didn't know why the woman was asking questions to which she knew the answers, but since she hadn't adopted the 'mind your own business' style of the Americans, she replied in the affirmative.

'You've never been married?'

'That's correct.'

'How much have you studied?'

'I have a bachelor's degree.'

'No master's?' the lady asked, frowns lining her forehead.

Amara looked away for a second to relieve the weight of that question, for she hadn't been able to afford to study further. 'No. But I have studied accounting.'

'Accounting?' the lady repeated, forming an opinion around that word. Amara looked at her eagerly. She was willing to spell out her grades if the lady was not impressed, but the lady smiled at her, as if approving of her choice in study.

'Tell me, do you follow the stock market?' the lady asked.

Amara concluded, even though the thought was far-stretched, that the lady may have mistaken her for some sort of financial advisor or stockbroker. 'I'm no expert.'

'That's all right. Which mutual fund would you recommend to buy?'

Amara saw that Riya was looking at her for the first time that night. She was surprised to see her pause in the conversation with the Harvard guy, and though she couldn't read Riya's expression from the distance, she didn't want her to think that Amara was antagonising her guests. She took a moment to think, remembered a snippet from a business newspaper, and said, 'Any fund with technology shares is a good bet.'

'Good,' the lady said, taking a long sip from her glass of red wine. Maybe she's had too much to drink, Amara thought, and was wondering if she should go find the lady's husband, when the lady asked, 'Do you have white friends?'

Amara would definitely have to find her husband. 'Um. What?'

'Go on. Do you?' The woman's dark eyes were sanctimonious under a cocked eyebrow.

Amara realised that this was no drunken conversation. She was being judged. This made her eager to please. 'Two or three,' she replied tentatively, immediately thinking that she should have said less.

'Are they close friends?'

Instinct told Amara to say what this lady wanted to hear. 'No, not at all.'

'Good. Do your parents own property?'

This was getting too much. Amara didn't want her parents to be brought into this bizarre conversation. She didn't reply.

The lady understood her silence and asked, 'If you were married, is this the kind of food you would make for your husband every night?' She pointed to the spread on the table that had taken Biji and Amara five days to prepare.

Amara was a little 'fed-dup' of this lady's questioning. 'Only if there's no KFC nearby,' she said and laughed, hoping a light jab would end the conversation.

The lady opened her mouth to say something when Sheila Mami came up to them and grabbed the lady by the elbows, 'Why, Daminiji—' Amara was surprised to hear Sheila Mami address someone with a respectful 'ji'. 'I've been looking for you. Please come with me, I want you to meet my daughters.'

Daminiji gave Amara a last look-over as Sheila Mami led her away. The conversation had rattled Amara and she needed to find a safe spot. She looked for Baba but couldn't locate him in the crowd. Then she went to the back garden where Baba was standing alone, smoking.

'Baba, cigarettes are not good for your body,' she said, walking up beside him.

'No matter how you treat the body, Ammu, it punishes you with disease or decay. It's not the body I'm worried about but the soul. It's poor and neglected, yet it stays eternal.' Saying this Baba stubbed out his cigarette, for he was a loving father who when faced with 'for Ammu's sake' could not continue smoking. 'Why are you out here? Aren't you having fun inside?'

Amara looked at her father's buttery eyes melting on sacs of kindness and said, 'You know I don't fit in there.'

'You shouldn't expect to. Everything fits together in America except the immigrant's identity.' Amara knew that Dua Mama had tried to shape the Malhotra family's identity, but since he acknowledged only two types of identities − those above him and those beneath him − and since he wouldn't think of Baba as superior to him and Baba refused to be viewed as inferior, the family had no definite identity; it didn't fit in anywhere.

'Are you happy here, Baba?'

'What is happiness in a foreign land? It's like waving a picture of water to a burning man. My happiness will be to see you settled.'

This path did not seem to promise happiness at all, Amara thought.

'You hate being here as much as Biji loves it,' she said.

'In America I have learned to love and hate with a straight face. Now go back in and try to have fun.'

Amara went back to the house. She thought of the Kozy Rice Pudding containers at home, occupying half their storage room; they got the highest contribution from Baba.

When she entered the Dua Mansion, an old lady sitting on the corner chair asked her to bring her hot water in a plastic tub. She wanted to soak her aching feet. Amara got it for her and spent the next hour sitting with the lady. She listened to her as she spoke softly, uncomfortable in her chair and trying to stay awake for the sake of her fifty-five-year-old son who was somewhere in the crowd, among 'the beyonds'.

Suddenly Amara noticed Daminiji standing next to an M.F. Husain painting and staring at Amara again. This time Amara didn't look away.

Daminiji walked up to her and said, 'Do you know this is my mother-in-law?'

'No,' Amara replied. 'But if I were her son, I wouldn't leave her alone like this.'

'Some habits are hard to fix,' Daminiji said. Before Amara could ask her what she meant, she spun around and walked straight towards the kitchen, where Biji was adding sugar syrup to bowls filled with sweetmeats. Amara watched as they spoke, or rather as Daminiji spoke. Biji had put on her temple-face and her expression was indiscernible. Amara wondered what they were talking about. Was Daminiji complaining about Amara to Biji?

Just then Daminiji's husband came over to take his mother home. Amara helped the old lady to her feet and by the time she looked back, Daminiji had left the kitchen, and Biji was leaning her head against the refrigerator. Amara went over, concerned on seeing a look on her mother's face that she'd not seen before and couldn't place.

As soon as Biji saw Amara, she grabbed her and gave her a long hug. When Amara recovered from her first recallable hug from Biji, she asked, 'Are you all right?'

'Bless you, Ammu,' Biji said, tears rolling down her cheeks. 'Today I knows I raised you well.'

'What are you talking about?'

'That lady be Damini Roy, mother of Prashant Roy.' The same guy that Riya was trying to hitch. 'Rich Indian family. She look for bride for Prashant. She say she like you. She watch you full night and see you be good traditional girl.

Homely, she say. Just what her son needs. She ask us to come to their home.' Biji sat down on the kitchen stool as if the burden of this information was too much to bear.

Amara watched Biji's expression change as she realised that her American dream had started taking shape. She watched her mother's smile stretch from one end of her mouth to the other before it reached her eyes. Biji had not smiled like that in years.

There was a distant throbbing in Amara's heart: 'It Is Biji's Desire.'

'Biji, Riya is after this guy. We can't just take him from her,' Amara said, knowing her cousin wouldn't be pleased.

'Daminiji talk to me about same thing. She laugh and say that she see Riya want her son. But she have hear about Riya from other Indian families, and she not want such rich, spoilt girl with too many boyfriend to marry her son.'

Amara guessed that the same 'Indian families' must have briefed Daminiji about the Malhotras as well.

'And what about Dua Mama?'

'Dua Mama?' Biji repeated, as if the thought had not crossed her mind. She looked down at the apron wrapped around her, stained with oil, turmeric, ketchup and some unidentifiable brown sauce. Suddenly her voice was angry, as if the throat in her stomach had lurched back to her neck, 'We not worry. We not need him anymore. No more this.' Biji threw down her apron. She looked at Dua Mama and Riya standing together in the warm afterglow of another success, receiving the gratitude of enchanted guests. 'You not be able to beat these girl in money, looks. But now better than them you will be.'

Her words fell out, as if blown by the force of long-held breath.

Amara looked over at the man she could possibly marry.

Her invisible twin. The one whose expectant desires she had stirred all her life. He was still standing head-to-head with Riya, as if the pain of being parted from her was unbearable.

Amara felt like a gold miner who'd discovered gold to find it belonged to someone else. Was she doing the right thing by agreeing to this? She thought of Riya and her relationship, the inheritance of sisterhood that had turned into the inheritance of rejected sandwiches, cold shoulders, snide comments and elevator rebuffs. Suddenly, she didn't feel sorry for what she was about to do.

She saw Daminiji pull Prashant away from Riya and bid the Dua family a curt goodbye. She watched Riya stare at Prashant's back as he stepped out of the front door. She saw her face turn ashen.

Suddenly, Prashant glanced in her direction. Amara hid behind the fridge. She didn't want her future husband to see her for the first time in tired clothes, especially after he had spent an evening looking at Riya.

After they left, Amara turned her attention to Biji who was still talking. She listened, not happy, not unhappy, as her mother said, 'You have make our coming to Amreeka worth it. You have make us proud.'

# 7

Amara dipped her fingers, covered with intricate henna designs, into the tray of water, vermilion and milk. Her fingers touched the bottom of the tray and grazed against Prashant's fingers. This was their first touch and a quiver ran up Amara's body, like seltzer rising in a tumbler. She gave what she hoped was a delicate shudder.

They were playing Aeki Beki, a wedding game, in which – according to marriage folklore – the person who found the ring the most number of times in six turns, ruled the household. Amara had found the ring in the last three turns, so now she stopped moving her fingers to let Prashant win. There was stillness inside the clouded water. Was it her imagination that Prashant's fingers hadn't moved at all?

A guest shouted, 'All okay? It doesn't take this long to find the ring.' Amara looked up at the expectant faces around her. Though she couldn't look directly at Prashant in front of so many people, she gathered that perhaps he wanted her to win. So she rummaged for the ring and held it up as people cheered.

Their marriage had been fixed six days after Tina's birthday party when the Malhotras met at the Roys' Long Island house. The elders decided to hold the wedding after three weeks, giving the couple no time to get to know each other. To add to that, Prashant sat quietly between his parents through the seven-hour meeting, neither contributing his thoughts nor displaying any eagerness. On Amara this behaviour was becoming, but on Prashant it was baffling. Even when, at the end of the meeting, Daminiji asked Prashant if he'd like to ask Amara something, Prashant said, 'Nothing.' His voice was gruff and heavy, as though forced awake from sleep. That singular word took on so many nuances that it was difficult to peg it to a mood or emotion. Was he being dismissive, submissive, pensive or buoyant? Yet none of this flustered Amara, for having spent her entire life learning how to be a good wife, she was positive that she would please Prashant. Plus, Biji claimed to have run a check on Prashant: 'He don't drink cigarette. He don't get pitch drunk. Too good, he is.'

Biji was too awe-struck to complain when the Roys told them to pay for the entire wedding. Even Baba desisted from his usual sarcasm when the Roys picked a five-star hotel — that Baba would normally never enter — as the wedding venue and invited four hundred guests. 'That's what we've been saving for,' he said. What hadn't been spent on Amara's education or clothes was spent on her wedding. They emptied their savings and investment account. The Kozy Rice Pudding containers (forty-one and counting) were cleared of their metallic content, rendering a potential visit to India unfeasible. This wasn't enough. Biji and Baba took a personal loan from Baba's bank. To repay this, it was decided that Biji would work an extra shift at the restaurant, every Saturday for a year, while Baba would start law consultations for Indian immigrants.

'None of that matters now,' Amara thought, as she dressed for the *pheras* set to start in a few hours. She pictured the ceremony scene-by-scene: the glint of a diamond ring on her nose, the filigree of henna on her hands and a deep red sari swathing her. She saw herself heading coyly to the melody of the *shehnai* towards the heavily decorated canopy, her senses tantalised by the smell of jasmine and marigold. She heard the crackle of puffed rice, ghee and flowers tossed into the ceremonial fire, as Prashant and she walked around the fire seven times, taking their marital vows of loyalty and compassion. She saw the seven Gods perched on top of the canopy's flagpole, raising their hands to bless their union. She imagined Prashant slipping his hand into hers, though that was not part of the ritual.

But by evening a heavy downpour started, a freak shower in an otherwise hot June. The venue was shifted from the open lawn to a hall suitable for a hundred people.

'The beyonds', 'the equals' and 'the earlys' stood elbow-to-elbow.

A guest remarked loudly, 'This is worse than travelling in the subway.'

Another guest retorted, 'This is worse than a Mumbai local train at peak hour.'

Despite the daunting task of greeting and appeasing the guests, Biji and Baba looked happy surrounded by people, reminding Amara of them in their Shimla days, when they were wrapped in the laughter and love of friends.

Dua Mama and Sheila Mami were standing in a corner. Unlike the other guests, they didn't have a drink or plate in their hands, and weren't talking to anyone. Their behaviour underscored their disapproval of Amara marrying a man reserved for Riya, marrying before Riya, and jumping several rungs of the ladder to become one of 'the beyonds'. By virtue of being struck by one curse – 'the curse of opportunity' – Amara had broken all other curses: 'the curse of shortness', 'the curse of beauty' and 'the curse of money'. After all, no one claimed that curses were fair.

Biji was thrilled with her brother's discomfort. She no longer put on a temple face in front of him and when he didn't offer to help with the wedding preparations, she became giddy from gloating, 'Too much jealous they are.' Riya did not attend the wedding. Amara tried to push the creeping guilt out of her head. Someone came up to her and said that she was the epitome of a 'glowing bride'. Perhaps Biji's insistence on Amara wearing lenses and getting her first facial was the reason for this glow. Amara flushed. The flattery distracted her from the groom's absence for only a short time. It was silly to stand alone under the canopy, awaiting Prashant, when the auspicious time for their wedding was half-an-hour away. The bright lights around the hall were beginning to hurt her eyes. There was a whiff of something burning.

There came a churlish scream. Amara looked around. Had her worse fear been confirmed? Was the groom not coming?

She dived into the crowd towards the source of the scream. A guest told her that a boy of six had put his hand into the water fountain, intending to play with the colourful string of lights behind it, and got mildly electrocuted. Someone was asking for plastic buckets to throw at the boy. A woman was wailing loudly. The hotel staff called 911 and began to clear the guests from the hall so the paramedics could do their job. By the time the boy was taken to the hospital and people trickled back in, Amara thought the hall looked bigger, as if many guests had chosen to leave without eating, an insult in Hindu tradition.

Amara tried to remain unfazed. She spotted Stacy among the crowd, flirting with a young Indian guy. Stacy met Amara's eyes and gave her a thumbs-up sign. Amara had told her not to act friendly with her during the wedding because her mother-in-law would not approve. Stacy was too familiar with Indian customs to protest.

Amara's heart burst with joy at seeing the most beloved people in her life – Baba, Biji and Stacy – as a part of her happiest day. How could things get better?

The auspicious time for Prashant and Amara's wedding was over. Baba and Biji consulted the priest. Baba, who never lost his composure, was dabbing his forehead with Biji's handkerchief. Did he share the same fear as Amara? She saw him slip the priest a crisp hundred-dollar bill so he could set a new auspicious time to an hour away.

/ By this time the groom's wedding procession arrived, wet and cranky, blaming the rain for their delay. The girl's side ignored their excuses and set straight to task. Baba washed Prashant's feet with honey and milk. Biji lit the wicks soaking in purified butter inside the clay lamp and rotated it around Prashant's head as a welcome blessing. Since the second auspicious hour was ticking away and Amara was already near the ceremonial fire, Prashant was led to Amara by his parents instead of the other way round. The wedding ceremony was done in fast-forward. Amara wished she could see Prashant's face in order to memorise his expression when they exchanged garlands and walked around the pyre, but his face was hidden behind a drape of flowers. They didn't exchange a single word throughout the ceremony.

When asked later, Amara would always smile and say, 'It was the perfect wedding.'

# 8

On Amara's wedding night, Biji gifted Amara her most precious possession: a year's supply of Hajmola. 'You will be woman from today. This will help.' But by the time they reached the Roy Mansion, 'It Is His Desire' was in no mood to make Amara a woman.

A flock of giggling relatives took Amara to a room lavishly beset with chrysanthemums, tulips and orchids. She was made to sit in the middle of a four-poster bed strewn with rose petals, bleeding deep magenta on the white bed sheet. Once the relatives left, Amara sat alone, her discomfort amplifying with every moment. What was she supposed to do on her wedding night? The heaviness of her nine-pound sari, which she'd carried with élan through the night, weighed down on her. Its embroidery chafed her ankles, elbows, arms and neck. Her diamond nose ring seemed to obstruct her heavy breathing. Where was Prashant?

There was a knock on the door. Startled, Amara crushed the rose petals. She looked at her hands covered in deep red. How would Prashant find his initials in the henna now? Without this wedding night game, they had no icebreaker.

When Prashant entered, Amara sat still, not sure how he expected her to behave. Of the many lessons taught to her, why had Biji skipped this one? A silence swallowed the air in the room. Amara looked up gingerly to see Prashant opening his mouth. What was the first thing her husband would say to her?

'Why don't you get into something comfortable?' he said, each word as distinct as a hammer driving in a nail.

Amara almost ran to the bathroom, happy to have something to do. She removed her jewellery and yards of cloth, and slipped into a fuchsia cotton tunic laced with crotchet and extra-long slim pants. She popped a Hajmola tablet to calm her nerves and came out of the bathroom.

Prashant's snoring had filled the room.

She walked up to him and seeing that nothing was going to happen, heaved a sigh of relief. Although she wanted to sleep, having never lain next to a man before, she could only stare at him, expecting him to do something out of the ordinary. But the only thing that caught her interest was the flesh between Prashant's chin and neck, giving him the appearance of a cherubic baby, not a twenty-eight-year-old man. There's nothing to be scared of, she realised with consolation, and put her head on the pillow next to his. A surge of warmth ran through her body.

Sleep searched for her but Prashant's increasingly loud snores echoing past the expansive walls chased it away. She waited for an hour. Two hours. Three. She was tired, very tired. She rolled off the bed and practically crawled to the nearest unoccupied room. Before her head touched the tiled floor, she was fast asleep.

The next morning she woke to the sound of laughter. Amara was filled with horror when she realised that she was in the kitchen, surrounded by Prashant's relatives. Her horror didn't abate when Prashant's relatives teased her good-naturedly, calling her the 'kitchen bride'; Prashant didn't join the banter.

That afternoon Prashant took her to his Manhattan apartment on Fifty-fifth Street and Sixth Avenue. Amara stepped out of the cab, awed by the ambition and power of his building. The wonder continued when she entered his apartment and looked at the sweeping view of Central Park, the décor borrowed straight from *Millionaire* magazine.

Prashant told her that they were going for dinner to 'one of New York's finest', 'Nobu 57', 'with the boss and his Mrs'. He gave her a five-hundred dollar bill and told her to buy a nice dress and make-up. Amara almost said, 'No'; she didn't wear dresses or make-up. Then she remembered Prashant's preference in women. After he left for work, saying there was an important meeting that he couldn't miss, Amara looked to the street below to see what the well-dressed women, of the many New York had, were wearing. She went to Zara, Mac and Nine West, which she had been scared of entering before, and bought two dresses, a lipstick, rouge and eye-pencil, as well as a pair of silver sandals that went with both dresses.

She spent four hours getting dressed. To avoid repeating the mistake of 'the day to impress Riya', she carefully followed an online step-by-step guide on how to apply make-up. She wore a purple velvet dress with a bow tie in front. Right before they were to leave for dinner, she emerged from the guest bedroom where she'd been trying to transform herself, and stood before Prashant, proud and shy, wondering what he would think of her new look.

He was reading *Barron's* magazine but looked up immediately. Amara smiled at him widely, glad to have so easily caught his attention. He sucked in the air between his teeth and turned his face back to the magazine. After a moment of silence, she asked him, 'Am I looking okay?'

He replied without skipping a beat, 'You should look like the wife of a hedge-fund partner, not a 7-Eleven cashier.'

The humiliation of 'the day to impress Riya' resurfaced, for all it took to strip away someone's worth was a scathing remark, a pointed finger, a derisive look. But she held back her tears; she was not a fourteen-year-old girl anymore.

'Was this the dress you bought for five hundred?' he asked. 'No,' she replied slowly. Maybe what she said next would impress him, 'I spent three hundred on make-up, shoes and two dresses, and saved the rest.'

Prashant sucked in his breath loudly, as if wind was knocked out of him, and said, 'When I give you money it's meant to be spent. You're not a middle-class girl anymore.'

Amara didn't say anything. She realised that he was right. She didn't know how to dress like a rich woman because she'd never been one. She apologised to him and changed into the other dress, which she had been saving for a special occasion. Prashant still didn't look impressed but he didn't say anything.

At the restaurant, Amara introduced herself carefully to Prashant's boss, Adrian Jones, and his wife, Betty. Prashant held out a chair for her and she was relieved that she hadn't bungled up so far. She wanted desperately to impress Prashant and his boss. During the day she'd run a Google search on Adrian and Betty, and learnt that Adrian had studied at Columbia University. So she researched more about the university and its history. Betty was on the board of an Indian charity for the visually impaired, Sankara Eye Foundation; she made a donation to it so she had a talking point with Betty. She rehearsed in front of the mirror, about what she would say and what questions she would ask them. She looked online at the Nobu menu and learned the correct pronunciation for the vegetarian dishes she decided to order, so it looked like she ate at fancy restaurants often.

She needn't have bothered. Prashant ordered dinner without asking her what she wanted, and he didn't order any vegetarian dish save seaweed salad, which she wasn't sure was even vegetarian. He took care of the conversation as well, and she was surprised to note how glib and witty he was. She hoped that in due course he would become that way with her too.

Prashant worked with a 'hedge-fund on the short side' and she memorised that line without really understanding what he did. On the way to Nobu, he had tried, rather impatiently, to explain his job to her and his deliberate tone had suggested that it was a role of some significance. Now, as she watched figures roll out of his mouth in millions and billions, she realised just how important his job was. She watched him, amazed and a little mesmerised.

A waiter put a small plate of dumplings in front of her. Her stomach growled. She hadn't eaten the whole day, saving her appetite for the fantastic meal she thought she'd be having. Without knowing what was inside the dumpling, she took a bite. Her mouth exploded as something warm and slimy, like a foetus, made its way in. She almost gagged. Noticing that the other three were engrossed in conversation, she lifted a cloth napkin to her mouth and spat out the food.

Suddenly, without warning, the spotlight turned to her. Adrian looked at her and said, 'We are being very rude talking shop and boring this young lady. Are you enjoying the *foie gras* dumplings? They're my favourite.'

'Delicious,' Amara said, glad that he couldn't see the contents of her napkin.

She felt something at the right side of her lip but dismissed it as he asked, 'Can I get you something to drink?'

Amara wasn't prepared for this question, so she mumbled, 'No, thank you. I don't drink.'

'Really?' he laughed, not unkindly. 'What a refreshing thing to hear. Have you recently moved from India?'

Amara was prepared for this question. She was often asked this because her accent was not Ind-erican. 'No, I've been in the US for almost nine years now,' she replied and went on to explain her Green Card story. Betty and Adrian listened intently, but she saw Prashant shift in his chair. He interrupted her mid-sentence and asked Adrian if he would like a refill of his drink. After that, he didn't look at her.

On the taxi ride back to the house, Prashant didn't say a word. Heaviness lingered between them but once they reached the house, Amara mustered the courage to ask, 'Are you angry with me?'

Again, Prashant didn't hesitate for a moment before turning on her. 'Why were you behaving like a girl from the village?' His words came out sharp and categorical like bullet points:

- Why did you talk with a piece of food stuck to your lips?
- Why did you refuse to drink?
- Why did you spell out your whole life story?

Each bullet point left a bullet-sized scar on her body. He continued his barrage. 'Haven't you been here long enough to know that Americans want a slice of someone's life, a short riveting story, not a novel? You made me look like a damn fool through dinner.'

He decided that she had purposely humiliated him, first in front of his family by being the kitchen bride and then in front of his boss by being the village belle. Amara apologised and cajoled him, but he went to sleep in the guest bedroom saying he didn't want his snoring to bother Amara's 'beauty sleep'.

Amara tried not to let this minor spat dampen her enthusiasm. So excited was she to be married that she was beside herself, and wanted to express and emote like a harmonium. Since she hadn't known Prashant before marriage her expectations from him were not formed by compatibility or differences. She wanted to know him fully, as much as it is possible to know someone, so as a new bride she probed like an archaeologist. Every small discovery thrilled her. She skimmed through books he read and was thrilled to find that he underlined sentences he liked, just like she did. When she found out that he liked cold showers while she enjoyed hot water baths, she turned the shower knob to blue and on feeling the biting water pierce her body, tried to feel what she imagined *he* felt.

She wanted them to be woven together, like clematis in a basket, looking up in the same direction at the sunlight and growing together in harmony, tendril to tendril, shoot to shoot and leaf to leaf; each life protecting the other.

But Prashant reciprocated her enthusiasm by keeping his emotions at bay. His words were measured and deliberate, as was his manner. Amara was surprised that she had married someone quieter and shyer than her.

'I love you,' she said after three months. He didn't reply. Her voice slid thickly across the heavy air as she said more slowly and loudly, 'I love you.' She waited for a few seconds – one, two, three, four, five – and on not hearing his response, she ran in the other direction, as the defeated are wont to do.

She tried to suppress her affection for him so she could ease him into their marriage, but over time, Amara realised that whenever she tried to stir and roast *His* expectant desires and anticipate *His* needs, things got worse. He had made up his mind about her and she could do nothing to change it. Instead, anything she did reinforced his belief that she was a village belle. If she asked him to dab sugar on his tongue before leaving the house, in order to ward off evil spirits, he refused. When she said she didn't enter the kitchen or look at herself in the mirror during her periods, he invited his friends for dinner, so she would have to go inside the kitchen and use the mirror to dress up. He did not go out with her unless they were meeting Indian American families. Worse still, he didn't allow her to demonstrate the skills she'd learnt on her tiny plastic tea-set; she could never be a good hostess for *His* boss.

In no time, so many bullet-size scars filled her body that she didn't feel whole anymore; she wasn't what she thought she was; she didn't know what she was anymore. She became empty. Her emotional struggles became an emotional violence against herself and him.

Chaffed by his disapproval, Amara could not stay oblivious to his faults; for once the floodgate to human flaws opens it's difficult to stop a tsunami. Living with him made it easy to stumble upon his defects. She realised one afternoon, while reading George Orwell's *Nineteen Eighty-Four* (his favourite book), that he was a 'totalitarian'. He lived with a restraint that was entirely his own, and his words were uber-structured, like his days. Most people mistook his reserve for maturity, just like they mistook laughter for immaturity. Amara knew it was not maturity he possessed, but self-absorption, a detachment from anything that didn't involve him.

He expected visiting friends to stay in hotels. He would not pick up or drop anyone, even if they were on his way. He was paranoid about his own safety, never Amara's, and before entering a cab would take down its plate number and save it as a draft on his cell phone so he could send it to his mother in case of an emergency.

Amara didn't like the way his left toe curled in, like a shrivelled prune.

Around others, he'd say things that were the opposite of who he was. He said he enjoyed exercising four times a week at the New York Racquet Club, where Amara knew he never went. He'd say Amara and he went to the movies once a week, for the wife had to be pleased, but they had gone to the movies only once in the first three months of their marriage, and that too with Mummyji (previously known as Daminiji), for he did things in two ways: his or Mummyji's. Despite her best efforts, Amara could not be the wife Prashant wanted.

She needed to talk to someone about Prashant. She couldn't talk to Baba, for his happiness was in seeing her settled, which gave her no happiness whatsoever. So she went to Biji, woman-to-woman, mother-to-daughter. Biji dismissed her concerns, saying, as if the crime had been pardoned before trial, 'Marriage like that only. Don't be asking more than you deserve. And don't be talking bad about new family in front of me or other.'

It troubled Amara that Biji had not said this before Amara's marriage. It was like throwing a child into the deep end of a pool before teaching her how to stay afloat.

Since Biji made Amara feel guilty for going against 'It Is His Desire', Prashant's faults festered inside her like a large bullet-size scar. Husband and wife started growing apart, downward, instead of growing together like clematis.

The attention and respect that Amara didn't get from her husband came to her from the Indian American community. 'You are such a "lucky" girl, Mrs Roy,' they would say. The problem was that the lucky girl's marriage sounded good on paper – beautiful apartment in Manhattan, a husband earning a six figure salary, vacations in Hawaii (with Mummyji) and movies every week. In the index of human value she was the y-axis. But, she hadn't earned this respect – which really was no respect at all.

Scotch and kebab were placed before her. But she didn't drink or eat meat.

People flattered her. But she knew she meant nothing to them.

In a room full of these people, someone would come up

and ask, 'Why *such* a sad face on *such* a lucky woman?' Amara would be surprised to hear that she was looking sad. She'd slap the smile back on her face and wonder what would happen if she suddenly screamed. After all, she was one of 'the beyonds'. She could do anything. What was holding her back? Where did the words that formed so spontaneously in her head go by the time they reached her tongue?

In the fifth month of their marriage, Prashant came to the house only twice for dinner. One day he texted saying that he was staying at work the whole night. By that time Amara had spent eight days inside the house without seeing him, for he left for work before she woke up and came back when she was asleep. The walls in the house bore down on her. She had to leave. She had to be around people. She stepped out of her apartment building to take a walk around the block.

She pulled her jacket tighter around her. The weather had jumped a season ahead and brought cold winds in its wake. A blast snaked its way between the buildings on Broadway and sliced across the Hudson plane. Amara inhaled deeply as an icy draft ran up her nose and chilled her bones. She saw chestnuts being roasted by street vendors, chimney smoke rising from a Fifth Avenue penthouse and steam dashing from a pizza box being opened by a Manhattanite. Walking among the mass of people going home from work, she savoured these cheerful touches before a gust hit her full in the face; there were tight lines on her cheeks where tears had dried.

Amara had thought that her marriage would give her no time to herself. Yet the invisible twin, whose spectre she'd grown up with, left her alone, and for the first time in her life, Amara felt like an only child.

In a short time, she walked so long and so hard that she wondered if she was lost and could ever remember the way home.

# 9

Amara set the long-stemmed basmati rice to soak for twenty minutes. In the last five years of marriage she had learnt that was the way Prashant liked his rice cooked. Two years back, when he had stayed at work for three straight days, she had burnt his rice on purpose, and in protest he had not eaten at home for six months. After that, she made food to perfection for him.

She stirred lamb curry in the pot. Like Biji, it irked her to cook meat, but Prashant liked food with eyes. Still she made a mistake whenever she cooked meat — like today when she had added bay leaves in the curry when he didn't like its flavour. She fished them out, one by one, counting eight in total before throwing them in the bin.

The only sounds in the house were the little ones, the simmer of curry on the gas, the bite of the knife wedging onions on the cutting board. The silence sliced through Amara. She started the mixer though there was nothing inside it.

Her head didn't stop throbbing.

She stepped out of the kitchen and onto the hallway. Her naked feet didn't make a sound against the marble flooring. She straightened the picture of Gandhi ('my mother thinks a lot of him,' Prashant had said) and turned right to look at the dining table where she had already set the glassine lace doilies, a teapot with matching china cups and a bright hand-knitted cosy. She would fill the teapot with freshly brewed tea exactly five minutes after Prashant came to the house. She looked over the living room, where a pale light from the dipping sun streamed in through the French windows, highlighting the details in the house, the lived-in order of the minimalist furniture that Prashant had bought before she moved into his Manhattan apartment. She straightened the Persian rug, which perfectly matched the vintage cream chenille sofa set, and arranged the Moroccan throw on the cream chaise lounge so it hid the dinky tea spill she had once made on it. She remembered with fondness the comfortable brown sofa at her parents' home, on which she could eat a mango if she so desired. She looked at the reflection of the room on the flat-screen TV ('with surround-sound') to see if it was tidy.

Satisfied, she went towards the master bedroom. Before entering through its door, she knocked on the wall to her right. A hollow sound reverberated. Like a heart. She smiled. She loved producing a sound from what she imagined to be an empty expanse.

She entered the room feeling, as always, like an intruder. Maybe this was because she couldn't find the I in theIr room. After all, scarcely a few hints indicated that she lived there, like her clothes that lay inside the pull-out white cupboard and her thin white cotton towel that she left on the bed when Prashant wasn't there, only because he hated that habit. She removed the other few signs that she cohabited this room: her alligator-skin spectacle case, a half-open Dostoevsky she was pretending to read on his recommendation, and a Mills & Boon whose pages she knew by heart. She put them inside the drawer of the side table. She pulled out her hair from the silver hairbrush, rolled it into a ball, and put it inside the step-bin below the magnolia dressing table. After her afternoon nap, she hadn't made the bed, so she straightened the Egyptian sheets and the silk mosaic duvet, and leaned the patchwork pillow shams against the platinum bedstead.

Prashant had agreed to sleep in their bedroom, but only after Amara told Mummyji that Prashant hadn't snored since their wedding night. A lie was not a lie if it saved a marriage, she rationalised. When his snores filled their bedroom at night, Amara tried to pace his contractions with her breath to trick her brain into thinking that his snores were a soothing melody. It never worked. She started taking afternoon naps.

Amara opened her cupboard and took soap-nut out from a shoebox. She hid this stash from Prashant because it fit her village belle image. She went into the bathroom and ran the bath. She took a bath before Prashant came so she could look her freshest, even though he never really looked at her. She turned to the sink to wash her face. Prashant had harsh lights installed over the mirror. He liked to see himself at his worst so he could put his best foot forward in front of others. And now, under these harsh-lights, Amara watched herself critically.

For most women, looks ceased to matter after marriage, as personality took centre stage. For Amara, it was the opposite. She couldn't impress Prashant with her village belle personality, so she desperately tried to make herself physically attractive to him. As in the case of all his possessions, Prashant demanded perfection from her. She was to be his − his definition, his vision and his parody.

'Your nail polish is chipped. Look at American women. Their hands are always perfectly manicured.' Amara set up a weekly manicure and pedicure session at the local beauty salon.

'Why do you wear scuffed box heel sandals?' Amara switched from her comfortable cherry red Doc Martens to Jimmy Choo slip-on dress shoes.

'Do you have to wear this cheap shirt?' Amara began to buy branded clothes with two-hundred-dollar plus price tags.

'Isn't this dress a size six?' Amara cut down her meals to twice a day and went four times a week to Equinox gym. Even though people looked alarmed on seeing her − 'so thin you have become' − their concern didn't matter, for she became a size two like Riya.

This wasn't enough, for sex remained a hurried process between them, without affection or foreplay. Amara still did it because it was the only way she could keep her hopes of a baby alive. She had wanted a baby as soon as they were married, but didn't talk about it, afraid that she'd sound as if she'd entered this relationship just to start a family. Fortunately, Mummyji asked them about it once, and while Amara's ears perked up to listen, Prashant dismissed the idea. 'What's the rush? We'll have a baby when she's thirty.' Amara was disappointed but pushed her expectations back into the pit of her stomach where they had resided for so long. 'I shouldn't be selfish,' she told herself. 'I shouldn't want a baby because I'm lonely. A family should be started when the time is right,' she told herself firmly. Maybe he was saving his sexual appetite for when she turned thirty.

Every time someone asked, 'Is there good news?' she would say to herself, 'I am still young, I have time.' And looking at her one would think so. At twenty-eight years of age, under Prashant's regimen, Amara's beauty blossomed. When she stepped out to buy fruits from the stalls run by Bangladeshis and Pakistanis, she would get four peaches if she asked for three, or a free Brazilian mango when she bought a packet of blueberries. American men, who'd never been interested in her, propositioned her on the road and held open doors for her. She enjoyed the little attention she was getting for the first time in her life.

Yet her young soul felt like that of a forty-year-old's. Some of her scars were physical, like the lump that throbbed in the small of her back after a workout, or the scar on her left little finger from when a can opener slipped and peeled her skin off. Most, however, were emotional, a result of Prashant's constant scrutiny. She was never at ease with her looks, for he would not allow her a moment to be herself. So she worried that her eyes didn't carry a spark anymore and that her hair looked listless. There were aches and pains in places she hadn't sensed problems in earlier. The marriage that she had got into fearlessly, she now lived in fear of.

After the bath she pulled the plug out of the bathtub. Her body became heavier as the water drained and pressed against the bottom of the bathtub. Sometimes, after waking up from her afternoon slumber, she felt like this, when she'd pull the sheet over her face and search for something inside her that would compel her to rise and go back to living.

The phone rang. Amara let it ring. She felt too weak to climb out of the bathtub without help. Then she remembered that it was six o'clock and Stacy was calling.

During college, Stacy and she had deliberated starting their own business – McKarma – to help Indian immigrants come to terms with American society, but college loans (for Stacy), and family pressure (for Amara), led them to join Sheila Accounting. Three years back, however, Stacy decided to pursue her vision instead of someone else's. She asked Amara to join her. Though Prashant didn't want her to work, Amara agreed instantly. She became the silent partner of the firm, doing business over the phone while Prashant was at work. She told no one about this. To assuage her guilt she worked pro-bono and her foregone salary was re-invested into the business. The company grew slowly and now had enough capital to rent a small office in downtown Manhattan.

Amara put on her bathrobe and answered the call. Stacy wanted to know if an Indian driving licence was a valid document to apply for a new driving licence in New York State. Amara gave her the necessary advice.

'You should swing by the office. We need you,' Stacy said.

'You know I can't.'

'It would be great having you around. Anyway, when are we meeting?'

'I'm a little busy.'

Stacy was quiet at the other end of the phone line. Amara knew she was being unfair to her, for she barely met her anymore and had never invited her to her marital house. Prashant did not want Amara to have white friends. 'Remember, we need this land, not its people,' he said by way of explanation. He didn't mind working or networking with them, but when it came to friendship, he wanted only Indians.

'Marriage is a compromise, Am, not a sacrifice,' Stacy said and hung up.

Amara knew what compromise and sacrifice meant, but somewhere in the last five years the line between them had become blurry. She looked up the meaning of the word compromise: 'a settlement of differences by mutual concession.' She looked up the meaning of the word sacrifice: 'the offering of animal, plant, or human life or of some material possession to a deity, as in propitiation or homage.' Stacy hadn't been briefed on 'It Is His Desire'; she wouldn't understand that in marriage there was no line between compromise and sacrifice.

Yet, she hoped Stacy wouldn't stop calling her. McKarma gave a counterpoint to her days; it was the reason why she was able to get up from bed and pull herself out of the bathtub.

Darkness crept in. Amara's mood changed with the colours of the sky.

She put on her clothes, finished her cooking, and switched on the TV. She stopped at a channel where a child was gently holding a cerulean butterfly in his palm. 'How beautiful it is,' Amara thought. Suddenly, the child plucked out the butterfly's wings. The butterfly fell to the ground, quietly and precisely. It remained there without moving. Amara shut her eyes but already the image was a part of her memory; it would come back to her when this moment was long gone, in a dream, in a stimulating conversation, at a time and place where it would matter most.

She switched off the TV. She couldn't watch it anymore.

Another day had wrapped itself in a shell of emptiness, and brought another night of new promises that would be broken once morning set in.

The quiet got on her nerves as it usually did by this time of the day. She put on a CD in which she had recorded Baba singing Kishore Kumar songs. His voice, deep and thick, like warm honey, was the link running through her past, present and future. It amazed her that his was the only voice she could find solace in.

Amara walked over to the living room window and peered out. Like an old woman she spent a lot of time at the window, but unlike an old woman the outside didn't interest her as much as the eighteenth floor of the apartment building opposite her. For the last four months, everyday at around seven-thirty, she noticed a man come home to a woman and their baby. After placing a kiss on the woman's lips, the man held the baby in his arms and smiled; his smile held all the love, longing and beauty with which this baby had been born into the world. The woman then set something to heat in the pot while the man swayed around the living room with the baby in his arms. Amara imagined soft music playing in the background. The woman lifted a spoon from the pot and held it to the man's lips. He said something. The woman threw her head back and laughed. That's how simple love was, to create a life within life.

For the first time Amara was jealous of something: this harmony, this understanding, this completeness. But what had she expected? That her husband would kiss her hello after returning from work? That they'd talk deep into the night, sharing their secrets? That she'd have his baby as soon as she wanted? Foolish girl, she chided herself. She chanted the marriage mantras that Biji had taught her: 'Don't expect anything. Don't say anything. Your husband is always right.' She realised that like everything that was important to her, Prashant didn't even know that this couple existed.

She heard a key turning in the lock on the front door. Quickly she switched the CD in the Black & Decker music system to Bach's *A Minor Violin Concerto*. Prashant opened the door in the same precise fashion as he did everything else. It swung out obediently. He entered. Short, fat and bald. Stacy had laughed when Amara first described her soon-to-be-husband. But it was true, despite Biji's vehement denial that Prashant was either short or fat or bald. Since he was a man, a rich and successful one, people took it for granted that he was tall and grand. Details, Stacy had wanted more details, and Amara had given them. He had the darkest shade of black eyes, a neck that didn't quite begin or end, and angry carmine pimples that always clumped in two or three across his forehead and chin.

Prashant removed his shoes and socks, tucked the socks into the shoes, and placed them in the shoe rack. He went straight into the bedroom, after muttering a soft 'Hi' that could fall anywhere. That was of no concern to him. Amara knew he would change into his nightclothes – a white kurta-pyjama – after folding his trousers by the seam and hanging his shirt in the 'dry-cleaning' section of his cupboard. He usually wore beige pants, always from Charles Tyrwhitt, along with a striped shirt, usually in light blue or dark blue. On weekends he liked to wear horizontally striped T-shirts, bright as he deemed suitable, in orange and green. He liked to wear branded clothes to work because others could see it, but inside the house he wore clothes and underwear from discount stores. Amara didn't tell Stacy that.

He came into the living room where Amara had heated and laid out his food and tea. He turned on the TV and sat at the dining table. Amara admired the confident way with which he sat on the white cushioned chairs, something she never dared to do for fear of spilling something as she had on the chaise lounge. Prashant neatly pushed the bite-sized lamb pieces to one end of his plate, the mounds of rice to the other side, and left the centre of the plate free, so he could mix each side in a ratio of two to one. He brought the food to his lips. He ate with a fork and knife even in the house. Not a drop spilled on his white kurta or the white cushion.

Amara stood between the dining table and kitchen, waiting for the moment he would address her, a comment, an order, anything. 'The cumin seeds are a little strong,' he said, when he was finished. 'Sorry,' she replied.

This could become another long silent night, which she couldn't bear. He would be interested in a conversation about her appearance in front of others, so she added, 'I bought two saris today from the tailor shop that Mummyji had recommended. I thought I'd wear one of them for her party next week.'

There was a long silence from his end. The conversation, if one dared call it that, had stalled. These very silences around Prashant made Amara feel like she was doing or saying something wrong. To rebut the silence's rebuke, Amara ran into the bedroom to fetch the two items of clothing.

She'd read several magazines and internet articles on how to manage her marriage. They told her that married life was like a second birth. A woman began her marriage by behaving like a newborn baby who was utterly helpless and whose life depended on her caretaker, that is, her husband. Slowly, like a growing child, she had to pretend to gain ability as per his rules. Once she won over his loyalty and love, she could turn hostile, like a surly teenager, and live under a show of deep offence, mythical and hurtful to those who loved her most. And then, only then, could she come to a level playing field, come into her own, become her own person and lay her own rules. Marriage was — after all — a battle of wits and constraint, exercised in order to win the war for a peaceful life.

Amara sat quietly at parties when women discussed the mind games they played with their husbands, and more importantly, for their husbands, wondering why such an opportunity had not presented itself before her. Was she incapable of manipulation or was her marriage not strong enough to play games?

This is all hogwash, she told herself. All marriages were a consequence of security, tradition, money and beauty. Love was a chance, a lucky coincidence. Its existence was an afterthought, for more serious matters cemented marriage.

Prashant looked at the saris she was holding. Maybe he would notice the new earrings she was wearing, bought from Tiffany to impress him. He pointed to one of the saris, which blended in with the wall. 'Wear this,' he said and went back to watching television.

Amara walked slowly back to their room, weighed down as though lifting Prashant's dusty dumbbells (lying below the guest cupboard).

She realised that all things considered, Prashant and she were like any ordinary couple, married, sometimes happily, sometimes unhappily. At least unlike other couples, she consoled herself, they didn't live in the fear that something, or worse, someone, would snap.

# 10

'Mother will be moving in with us,' Prashant announced over the phone line.

It was a Thursday morning in February. 'It's temporary. Dad is travelling on business and I don't want Mom to stay alone,' he added with finality, as if Amara's opinion on that subject was of no importance.

After all, a man was allowed to decide who could enter the circle of marriage, and for how long. Prashant's diktat was that his family and friends be allowed while Amara's kept out. Biji and Baba justified this ordinance with their own; 'a daughter's husband's house is no place for us,' they said; 'we're not supposed to even drink water in her husband's house.' In accordance, they treated Amara with reverent love, as if she was the diamond on someone else's tiara.

Between these two diktats, it had taken Amara years to broach the topic of inviting her parents to visit them. Prashant agreed dismissively, as if Biji and Baba's presence or absence was of no importance to him.

'But my parents are coming tomorrow,' Amara said. She'd made plans to show Baba and Biji the Statue of Liberty, the Empire State building and a Broadway musical, none of which they'd seen despite living in America for fourteen years.

'Well, they can't now, can they?'

Amara had never raised her voice in front of Prashant before, but his cavalier tone was getting on her nerves. 'What am I supposed to tell them?' With much effort, Baba and Biji had got leave from work at the same time. How were they going to postpone their leave at the last minute?

'Tell them what you think is best. But don't tell them or anyone else that Mom is going to live with us.'

Amara couldn't retract the anger from her tone. 'You're not leaving me with many options, are you? If I don't come up with a proper excuse, don't you think I'll end up hurting my parents?'

'I have to go. Mom will be there in two hours,' he replied curtly and hung up.

Amara put down the receiver and leaned her head against the white wall. This had been their first argument and they hadn't been able to see it to its final conclusion. She sensed that they would find excuses to never discuss it again. She knew that couples argued, some less, some a lot, and many of these arguments were interrupted or forgotten by sleep or work. But somewhere, somehow, these arguments were resolved, for the couple was smitten by love. The contents of her arguments with Prashant never escaped Amara's mouth, for they didn't have the luxury of landing on a field of understanding. She stored them for later use, and they accumulated like rocks in a river, steering her life off-course.

First, Amara called her parents and told them that Prashant had to go on urgent work out-of-town and she had to go with him, so their trip would have to be postponed. It broke her heart when they innocently believed her flimsy excuse and made plans for a future visit. Even the mention of Prashant, leave alone his presence, made her parents behave like bowling pins before the ball, ready to roll over.

'Where we will go? We be here only,' Biji said.

Baba and Biji had become like many other immigrants, who knew that they were free to leave America at any time, and this made them want to stay. So they found excuses to still their torn minds; they'd leave after their children were born into American citizenship, after their son finished college, after they paid off their mortgage, after they married their daughter, after they saved another hundred-thousand dollars for retirement, after they played with their first grandchild. America had become an addictive habit even for Baba; he no longer spoke about going back to India and didn't fill another Kozy Rice Pudding container.

Her parents' complicity made Amara angrier with Prashant. But where could she go with her anger? She dug her hand below her bed and fished out a packet of 'Cheetos', food Prashant had forbidden her to eat. She hopped on to Prashant's side of the bed. Without holding a plate, she bit into a fistful of crunchy cheese curls and watched the crumbs fall on the sheets he was so possessive about. She smiled. She ate another fistful, closed the rest of the bag with a chip clip and got up, feeling calmer.

As she put fresh sheets on the bed in the guest room, she thought about Prashant's parents. Amara did not see much of Daddyji. When he was there, he gave the impression of lurking around, as if he was scared to join in and scared to appear detached. He'd stand near Prashant or Mummyji as if not fully present, yet he wouldn't stay away and be completely absent. Prashant often said that his father was a busy man because of his thriving diamond business. Amara and Daddyji had a polite, formal relationship.

Mummyji made up for her husband's remoteness. Every alternate weekend, she came to visit them, usually showing up unannounced. Every other weekend, when Prashant wasn't playing golf with his clients at the Forest Park Golf Course, they went to visit her. In that brief interlude Amara had no time alone with her, for her Long Island house was filled with guests who came for lunch and stayed for dinner. Even when Mummyji came to Manhattan, she invited several of her friends and it would be the same affair in a different house.

Mummyji was demanding with Amara, like an artist who expects his masterpiece to carry through. Since she had selected Amara to be part of the Roy family, she expected Amara to perform her duties as the perfect daughter-in-law and wife. Amara didn't have a problem with that since she'd been raised to orchestrate such demands. This made Mummyji happy and Amara was relieved that she wasn't critical of her like Prashant was. In fact, Mummyji never mentioned Amara's errors of judgement, like during their first meeting, when Amara had suggested she buy a technology mutual fund, just before the dot com bubble burst. Moreover, between Prashant's aloofness and Daddyji's absence, Amara preferred Mummyji, for on a cold night even a spark is appealing.

With these thoughts Amara walked into the kitchen. A turmeric stain had yellowed the white linoleum since Prashant did not like Amara spreading newspapers across the countertop while cooking ('village belle,' he said). Amara placed a toaster on the stain to hide it. These small giveaways would undo her efforts to be known as a good wife.

Amara then called up Stacy to let her know that their daily calls would have to be aborted till further notice.

'I need you, Am,' Stacy said, her voice stretched.

'I'm sorry, Stace. Send me everything on e-mail. I'll try to reply everyday. I'll make up for this, I promise,' Amara said before hanging up.

The doorbell rang. Amara walked to the front door slowly, still angry about her parents' visit being abruptly cancelled. On opening the door, she bent down to touch her mother-in-law's feet. Only when she came to eye level with Mummyji, did she notice that her mother-in-law looked like a boxer who'd just lost a big fight. Her eyes were unfocussed, sitting on dark sacs beneath; her skin had lost its glossy sheen; and her shoulders, which she held erect like a pole, were slouched. Amara's anger vanished, replaced by a concern, for when strong people break, their vulnerability seems doubly accentuated.

'Are you okay?' Amara asked, bringing Mummyji's two duffel bags into the house.

'Leave the bags in the hallway for now. I need to rest. Don't disturb me,' the lady replied, her voice barely audible. She headed straight into the guest room and didn't come out of her nook the whole afternoon.

When Prashant came to the house that evening, much earlier than usual, he headed straight into the guest room. Amara heard fierce whispers. She hovered around the living room, not daring to go into the guest room for fear of breaking orders, and not daring to go into her bedroom for fear of appearing disinterested.

Prashant's behaviour around his mother was something that Amara found overwhelming. He was so eager to impress and please his mother that he obeyed everything she said. Amara had not expected a man to stand up to his mother – after all, she had married an Indian man – but she had not anticipated such absolute compliance.

Prashant was caught in the perpetual feud that exists in human beings, between adulthood and childhood, but it grew pronounced when he was around Mummyji. He tried to send a message that he was ready to take care of his mother, but he used the language of his childhood, making the memo garbled, and putting the onus of this responsibility's execution on Amara. If he wanted his mother to have a comfortable night's rest, he expected Amara to fluff the pillows, bring out the most darling comforter and warm the milk. At those times, Amara thought the word 'wife' was too small to accommodate its responsibility. Of all the roles Amara had played – daughter, student, employee, sister and wife – wife was the only syllable and disproportionately the most difficult.

When Prashant came out of the room two hours later to bring Mummyji tea and dinner, which Amara had kept on the dining table, Amara asked, 'Is she okay?'

'Let her rest. She's not well,' he said.

'She doesn't seem unwell, just upset,' Amara said. 'Is something wrong?'

'Why must you question what I'm telling you? Have you seen her ill before? Then how do you know how she'll behave?' Saying this, he went back into the room. He did not eat that night and went to bed early.

Despite his warning, Amara knocked at the guest room door. She entered carrying a drink of *kadu* in her hand – a concoction of bitter aniseed, ginger, black pepper and honey.

'Sorry to disturb you, Mummyji,' she said. In the beginning, the word 'Mummyji' had rolled out with difficulty from Amara's mouth, as if unwilling to accept another mother, but now she was accustomed to it. 'I made kadu to help you feel better.'

Mummyji sat up on her bed. Amara could tell she'd been crying but didn't want to ask any questions after Prashant's outburst. Mummyji took the glass from Amara's hand and whispered hoarsely, 'My mother used to make this for me when I was little.' She took a sip and pinched her face, for the taste of kadu is bitter. 'It's perfect.'

Without being asked, Amara sat down on the bed and began to press Mummyji's legs.

'You don't have to,' Mummyji said as she pulled her legs up.

'Let me know what you need to feel better,' Amara said. She took the empty glass from Mummyji's hand and wished her goodnight.

The next day, while Mummyji stayed in bed, Amara made her more kadu and cooked light meals to help her recuperate. Prashant had skipped work, much to Amara's surprise, for she knew he didn't miss a day's work even when he was sick. He stayed in his mother's room and came out only to bring her meals. That weekend he didn't play golf. For two weeks things remained the same. Mummyji stayed in her room while Prashant and Amara took care of her in shifts, Amara during the day and Prashant after work.

One day after Prashant had left for work, Mummyji came into the kitchen. She looked much better. Her eyes were almost back to their sharp selves, her skin had lost some of its dullness, and she was not slouching anymore.

She asked Amara, 'When will Prashant be back?' Amara confessed that she didn't know. They went to the living room and watched TV together.

'No Zee TV?' Mummyji asked. Operation Economic Reform had enabled Indian TV to be brought to the TV screens of Indian Americans. They happily boycotted the American shows they'd had no choice but to watch and embraced the Indian shows, which they believed kept them in touch with the motherland.

Mummyji started working on a blue sweater for Prashant. Her tongue rolled as fast as her knitting needles, purling through most of Amara's favourite afternoon shows. Amara reminded herself to have Indian stations installed; for that was the only time she'd seen her mother-in-law's face become rapturous.

A scene from *Ugly Betty* came on, where a young man and woman were shopping for a cashmere gift for their boss.

Mummyji stopped knitting and said, 'You know, I've always wanted cashmere. So soft it is. Prashant's father kept telling me he'd gift it to me and because of that I've never worn one.'

A few hours later when Prashant came from work, early again, Mrs Roy got up to give him a long embrace. He looked happy to be in the house, a first. He sat next to his mother and listened to her speak about what she was knitting for him. Amara was startled to hear him laugh loudly as his mother made a silly joke about one arm being longer than the other. The laugh seemed like such an indulgence within these walls that had seen only his tight smiles and frigid stares.

When they were around each other they didn't need Amara, or miss her, as if she was the guest sitting in between a happy couple. Her point was proven when Mummyji asked him questions that Amara never could, like the pin number for his ATM card, in case she needed to withdraw money, or the key to his secret drawer where he apparently kept his passport and some important papers.

This was despite the fact that Mummyji did things regardless of Prashant's approval. While cooking, she placed newspapers along the linoleum. She did not allow meat to be cooked in the house since she was a vegetarian. She loved sweetmeats and fried snacks, and though Prashant said that it was bad for her cholesterol, she continued eating them.

That night Mummyji called Amara into the kitchen. She opened a small silver box inside which lay bright-red saffron threads. 'I want you to have this with milk every night before sleeping. It'll give you fair babies.' Amara smiled at her mother-in-law and drank the milk. She would do anything to have babies, leave alone fair babies.

The next day Amara forgot to take her birth-control pill. The day after, she did not take it on purpose.

It didn't matter, for Prashant didn't touch her while his mother was under the same roof.

~ ~

The weave of time pushed their lives into a pattern.

During spring, Mrs Roy spent every free moment with Amara. 'I feel alone here,' she said. 'Whom will I talk to?'

Amara didn't mind that Mummyji's 'short visit' had turned into a 'long stay'. She enjoyed being with her. They started their morning by praying for an hour. Mummyji chanted devotional songs while Amara read from the Bhagvad Gita. Amara grew accustomed to starting the days with calmness. They spent the rest of the time cooking, going for long walks, shopping or watching TV. They began trading secrets. Amara showed her the yellow turmeric stain shyly. Mummyji rubbed lime over it instead of Lysol, and it was gone. Mummyji made a joke about their first meeting. 'I'd heard that you were a sweet, well-behaved girl but I wanted to see how you reacted when pushed in a corner. You didn't lose your temper or become rude, nor did you break under pressure. You showed me that you are a good person who can be tough.'

Prashant seemed oblivious to the growing relationship between his mother and wife. The only difference in his attitude was that he smiled more at Amara but the smile never reached his eyes.

One day Amara found Mummyji crying in the kitchen.

'What's wrong? Are you missing Daddyji?'

Mummyji looked at Amara with her dark eyes, wounded, 'How can you ask me that?'

'Well, I thought you'd miss him since he's been away on business for so long.'

'Business? Is that why you think I'm here?'

Amara looked at her surprised.

'Didn't Prashant tell you about his father?'

Amara shook her head.

Mummyji stopped cooking the lemon-grass tofu she was making for Prashant, and said, 'I don't know why Prashant didn't tell you. I'm trusting you with what I'm about to say, so don't repeat it to anyone.' She took a deep breath. 'Prashant's father has a second family.' At this, her words choked on themselves and she stopped talking. Amara gave her a glass of water. After taking a sip, Mummyji continued, 'Ten years ago he had an affair with one of his employees and they have a daughter together. His other family lives in Austin and he goes to meet them for a week every month. During that time, we tell everyone that he's away on business. Recently, this other woman was diagnosed with cancer and he decided that he wanted to go live with her. I couldn't stand being alone in that big house. That's why I'm here.'

'I'm so sorry to hear that. But isn't Daddyji scared that someone in our community will find out?'

'She's not from our community. She's a gori memsahib.'

On hearing this, so many things began to make sense to Amara:

— Mummyji asking her if she had any close white friends.
— Prashant's attitude towards white people.
— Prashant's protectiveness towards his mother.
— Prashant and Mummyji's closeness.
— Daddyji's aloofness and absence.

She realised that this information would have helped her understand Prashant and his family better, but he hadn't wanted her to. As Mrs Roy spoke, Amara's own pain circumnutated like a tendril around the older woman's words.

Mummyji looked at her. 'I'm surprised Prashant didn't tell you. I had told him that he could.'

Amara didn't reply but rubbed some lemon on a new turmeric stain that had gathered on the linoleum. Mummyji didn't pursue the matter, but said, 'I have learnt that a good marriage is healing for the soul, something to relish. But a bad marriage is a long sentence, suffering, a thing to be endured. I guess the only good thing about a bad marriage is that it's perishable like human life.'

Amara wasn't sure whose marriage Mummyji was referring to, but she realised that the big hurt growing inside her now had a witness.

'Promise me you'll never talk about this to anyone,' Mummyji said.

Again, Amara wasn't sure what Mummyji was alluding to. She simply replied, 'I will not speak of this pain to anyone.'

~ ~

One Monday afternoon Amara took Mrs Roy to the Central Park Zoo.

After seeing the penguins, they stood behind a glass pane watching the graceful swim of a bulky white polar bear. Amara said to Mummyji, 'Did you know that penguins live in Antarctica and polar bears in the Arctic? Because they live on opposite sides of the world they can never meet.'

'We live on the same side of the world and we never meet,' a thin voice chimed in, interrupting them. They turned around to see who it was.

Riya.

Amara had not seen her or anyone from the Dua family since her marriage. And although the scales between Riya and Amara had tipped — not only were they both 'the beyonds', but Amara was now also inflicted with 'the curse of money' and 'the curse of beauty' — Amara still tugged at her hair self-consciously, wishing she had blow-dried it this morning.

Riya greeted Mummyji warmly, as though she bore her no ill-feelings for selecting one cousin over the other. Riya had no trouble finding a 'the beyond' groom shortly after Amara's wedding, and now she stood with her two daughters, telling them, 'Say Namaste to Aunty.'

The girls put their hands together clumsily and said, 'Namaste', in synchronisation. Amara couldn't help but give them both her biggest smile. Riya didn't introduce her toddlers to Amara, as if she didn't exist even now.

But her older girl, around four, tugged at the end of Riya's leather jacket, pointed to Amara and asked, 'Who this?'

Faced with no choice Riya said, 'Shezan and Mallika, this is—,' apparently Masi was too personal, '—Mrs Roy.'

Amara bend down on her knees and hugged both the girls.

'Why don't we go and grab a bite?' Riya suggested.

They went close to Alice's Tea Cup and Amara listened as her cousin spoke of her apartment in Fifth Avenue, her husband's investment banking job, her plans to go back to work and her children who even at this young age wanted to wear only Gap.

'Speaking of clothes, I notice you're wearing very nice clothes, Amara,' Riya said, addressing her for the first time.

'Yes, Prashant likes to spoil me,' Amara replied, as her mother-in-law looked at her.

'So, did you buy this from Barneys' or Valentino?'

'I bought this at Bloomingdale's,' Amara replied.

Riya snorted. 'If he was really spoiling you, he'd take you to Bergdorf.'

Amara couldn't fall from the y-axis. She changed the subject, 'I recently bought an impressionist painting of the Tuscan countryside.' She realised how much like Prashant she was sounding. 'You must come and see it.'

'Why do people buy art when pictures are so much more distinct?' Riya turned to Mummyji and asked.

Amara shifted uncomfortably in her chair. 'I think I'll order the blueberry ginger scone to take home for Prashant. It's his favourite,' she added, to change the topic again.

'You've been trained to be a good wife I see, Mrs Roy,' Riya said.

~ ~

Later that evening as Amara was cutting the blueberry ginger scone for Prashant, she reflected on the chance meeting with Riya. Her finger nicked under the knife. She put it to her mouth and picked up the blood's sharp copper taste. Mummyji came up behind her, held her cut finger and sprinkled turmeric powder over it. She looked into Amara's eyes and said, 'From the moment I laid eyes on you, you reminded me of who I was thirty years ago. The world will do what it wants with you and you'll have to learn to stand up for yourself.'

~ ~

Spring was coming to an end. Prashant's blue sweater was ready to wear for the next winter. Mummyji started knitting another sweater, a tiny one, meant for a baby. She told Prashant and Amara over dinner one day, 'My old ears are aching to hear the pitter-patter of tiny feet. I don't know if I can wait for Amara to turn thirty for that.'

That night Prashant made love to Amara and held her in his arms after. Amara didn't dare breathe, in case whatever spell Prashant was under, broke. He surprised her further by saying, 'Thanks for making such a great effort with my mother.'

Amara looked at him to confirm that it was really Prashant talking. He'd never thanked her for anything before. Tears streamed down her face. Her marriage could turn around; it could be what she had always strived for. Biji was right – she just had to be patient.

The next morning was a Saturday and Mummyji commented at the breakfast table, 'Amara, you're glowing. Good news already?'

Amara smiled and didn't say anything. By virtue of the fact that they'd made love, she wasn't on the pill and she'd been regularly drinking the saffron milk, there was a good chance that a baby was being made now. Amara gently patted her stomach.

The doorbell rang. Prashant got up to open it. It was Daddyji. Tension curled its fist around the apartment.

Prashant hustled his father into the guest room but Mummyji didn't move from the dining area. 'Whatever has to be said must be said in front of Amara.'

Amara looked at her mother-in-law gratefully. Despite the overall mood, this was the happiest she'd been since her wedding day. She was finally a part of Prashant's family. She could barely pay attention to what her father-in-law was saying, but gathered that he was apologising to his wife and asking her to move back with him.

'People are beginning to talk, Damini. You can't keep living with your son,' he said.

They went back and forth, till Daddyji said, 'At least think about Prashant and Amara. Imagine what they must be feeling having you around all the time.'

Amara was about to say, 'Wonderful!' when Mummyji said in a voice without hope, 'Yes. We must do what people say. Our life is their desire.'

She was a loving mother who when faced with 'for Prashant's sake' could not reply in dissent.

'Mummyji, please don't go. This is your house. Stay as long as you want,' Amara said, speaking for the first time in the family discussion.

Prashant gave Amara a bruised look, as if she had stolen his line in a play.

'I have to follow my destiny and it doesn't involve me being here forever. I'll leave tomorrow,' Mummyji replied with a heavy voice.

The next day after Daddyji and Prashant went down to load Mummyji's bags, Amara handed her mother-in-law a gift. It was an Ann Taylor cashmere sweater.

Mummyji had tears in her eyes as she said, 'You are the best thing to happen to me in a long time, Amara.'

She leaned over and gave Amara a hug. This was the first time Mummyji was hugging her.

'I feel like I've found a life partner, not for my son, but for myself,' Mummyji added.

Amara looked down, unable to meet the eyes of someone who was this kind to her.

Mummyji pulled her chin up and said, 'I'm sorry you're not getting what you deserve in your marriage. But I don't regret bringing you into this family. I'd do it all over again. Prashant is a lucky man and I'll talk to him next weekend when you both come home.'

'I'll miss you till then,' Amara said.

Mummyji's absence left a giant-size hole in their house.

The silence returned. Prashant went back to his hectic hours of work, as if his mother was the only inducement to loving Amara. Amara again started the mixer when there was nothing inside it and knocked on the hollow outside their bedroom. Every evening at seven-thirty, she watched the couple opposite her building whose baby had grown big enough to walk.

Five days later, tragedy struck as it always does – without prelude. It was only foreshadowed by the bitter wind that blew in through their big picture window. Amara went to shut the window when she heard Prashant taking a call.

It was about Mummyji. She had died.

# 11

Amara snapped awake from a black dream. Water was dripping from a tap in the bathroom sink. Beyond that came the sound of keys jingling.

It must be Prashant.

He hadn't come to the house for two days this time.

Amara got up, slowly she thought. But her feet landed so unexpectedly on the floor that she must have jumped out of bed. A chill coursed through her body. Yet she was sweating. 'It must be a hundred degrees inside the house,' she thought, 'and possibly outside.' 'No, it's winter,' she reminded herself, for it had been six months since Mummyji's death. Another chill ran through her body and she drew a woollen stole across her chest.

Her right eye twitched. 'Not today, don't cry today,' she told herself firmly, for her eyes were gouged out, numb. She placed her hand over her heart feeling its strong beat. Ever since Mummyji's heart failure, Amara's own heart had started beating more rapidly, as if her mother-in-law's heart had come into hers.

It was not only her heart that felt different, but also the house, for it had become a place where death resided. Its dust settled on every corner, clinging to every picture frame and every table edge. Its heavy breath rotted everything from the inside out, not even sparing the inhabitants.

Amara patted her hair down and went towards the front door just as Prashant was entering. He walked in with his shoes on, straight past her and went into the kitchen. He fumbled inside the fridge before taking out leftover lentils and rice from two days ago – the untouched dinner she had made for him.

'Shall I heat it up for you?' Amara asked softly, for this house had become a still place where every sound echoed.

'No,' he replied and heaped the food on a plate. Without heating it, he took the food to the living room and sat on the chaise lounge. Amara followed him and watched as he ate with his fingers, something she had never seen him do before. She saw a little food fall on the white chaise lounge. He didn't notice.

When Prashant was in the house these days, Amara spent hours studying and analysing his habits and moods, to gain some insight into his mind. She tried to listen to him even when he said nothing. This consumed her entirely. In spite of these efforts at familiarity, Prashant grew distant, and they lived as strangers, now more than ever.

Amara stood next to the dining table, her fingers playing with its edges, and said, 'Daddyji called. He said he's been calling you but you don't answer. He wants to talk to you.'

Amara didn't tell him that Daddyji had said that he was worried about his son, not having heard from him since Mummyji's funeral. He wanted to come and visit, but never did, knowing his presence would exacerbate his dwindling relationship with his son. He hadn't waited long after Mummyji's death to marry his lover, who'd fully recovered from cancer; and now he lived in Austin with his new family. His timing and marriage had created a scandal in the Indian American community, but it was short-lived because he was a man and one of 'the beyonds', which invalidated social failures, and most importantly it seemed that everyone, save for Biji and Baba, already knew of the family secret, for such is the fate of all family secrets.

With no father or mother to ask after, people questioned Amara: 'Is Prashant okay?'

Amara didn't know whether or not he was okay. Since the telephone call that fateful night, he acted as if he too had ceased to exist. He vanished for days on end without informing anyone of his whereabouts. He never answered his phone. He didn't reply when spoken to. He did not ask questions. Amara didn't know if he was going to work, for he always wore a white shirt and black pants, as if that was the official uniform for mourning. He came to the apartment at any odd hour, and went to sleep on the couch, in the guest room, once on the bathroom floor, and rarely in their bedroom.

Amara understood his pain, for she was grieving too. She tried to be there for him, but he didn't grieve in front of her and did not ask for her support. Silence grew between them, hardening into tiny rocks and then huge boulders, throwing the river of their lives off-stream, drifting them far apart. They moved forward because that's all they knew to do, having been told there was a sea ahead that they had to enter as one.

Amara needed to find that sea. She was fed up of the rocks and boulders. So when Prashant didn't look up from his food, Amara did something she had never done before; she went and sat beside him. He didn't respond, but didn't move from his seat either.

'Prashant, please talk to me. You haven't spoken to me for so long,' she said.

Prashant mashed together his rice and lentils in response.

Amara could have retreated, as she always did, but today she couldn't. She was like an egg that had been put in the microwave and turned, under heat, into something fuming and hard, ready to burst with a gentle poke.

'You have to say something, Prashant. Please.'

He looked up from his plate. Their eyes met after so many months, so many.

'What do we have to talk about?'

'Something. Anything.' She found that she couldn't actually think of a topic.

'What I mean is—' and here he articulated each word slowly '—that we have nothing to say to each other.'

'What is that supposed to mean?' she asked in surprise.

'It means, Amara, that you and I have nothing in common. Therefore, we can't talk about "something" or "anything".'

'Don't say that. We have a lot to talk about. There is really so much to discuss. We – I am worried – about you. I don't know where you are all day long. I don't know how you're feeling. I'm concerned.'

Prashant stretched his hands out and rested them on his lap. Amara could see the rice and lentils still stuck on his fingertips.

'Then don't be concerned.'

Amara reached out her hand and put it on his, 'How can I not be concerned about you?'

He looked straight ahead and said, 'Why would you be?'

'Why? I'm your wife, Prashant.'

'Wife,' he repeated in a sad low voice. He raised his eyebrows in question and then gave a loud unhappy snort. 'Yes, yes, you are my wife.' He laughed; his laughter bounced off the sides of the empty walls, and echoed with mock horror inside Amara's ears.

'Prashant?' Amara asked. She pulled her hand away, thought better of it, and put it back again. He started, as if she had jolted him, stood up all of a sudden, and flung his plate on the marble floor.

'Don't touch me,' he said.

'Prashant!'

Amara looked at the pieces splayed on the floor. Broken and dangerous. She hoped he wouldn't step on them.

'Wife? Concern? What are you talking about? If you must know why I'm gone all the time, let me tell you. I stay out of this house because I can't walk through that door knowing I'm coming home to you.' He stood in the light, flailing his arms, pacing.

'What are you saying, Prashant?'

'What I'm saying, goddamn it, is that we are living a lie. Everyday before entering home from work I pause at the front door. I can hear your Hindi music playing all the way in the corridor. I pause for a second before I enter so you can switch the music off. I do this so I don't embarrass you, so I don't catch you red-handed. Because I know that in this marriage you're living a lie too.'

'I don't understand what you're saying,' Amara said, very softly, as if afraid to give shape to the feelings in the room.

'You understand, Amara. You know exactly what I'm talking about. This marriage is a sham. We are not like a normal husband and wife. I don't love you. I never will.'

His voice was like a knife slicing the house into two.

Amara looked at him. His words should have shattered her into a million pieces, like a jug hit with stone. But she didn't break. She didn't shatter. She wasn't surprised by his words or the emotions behind them. She just hadn't expected them to be said out loud.

He ran his fingers over his head as if lining his muddled thoughts into order. A tear rolled down his eyes. The anguish and helplessness in his voice tore her apart.

She realised that he wasn't angry. This was a cry of help to her, and her alone.

'Why don't you love me?' she asked slowly. She was surprised that her eyes remained dry.

He said without hesitation, 'We have nothing in common. I have no field of reference with you. You are more Indian than anyone I've known. Mom assumed that being Indian was enough for both of us. It wasn't.'

Things that Amara had buried deep inside her sub-conscious came back to her. For that night when Daminiji had proposed Prashant's marriage to Amara was not a victorious night; it was a night of failure. Prashant had not even noticed Amara; he had eyes only for someone he connected with, someone he could be happily married to: Riya. He knew that. Daminiji knew that. Amara knew that. Riya knew that. Biji knew that too.

He continued, 'Mom wanted me to be with someone like you. Her love convinced her that's what I needed. How could I say no to my own mother?'

He had married her out of duty to his mother. A familial duty executed out of love could not translate into marital happiness. They finally had something in common, they shared an understanding now.

'I understand,' she said.

'No, you don't understand. I tried to love you, I really did. But I couldn't bring myself to, because I was so angry with myself for agreeing to this marriage without thinking what I was getting into.'

He made her realise what she didn't want to.

'And you didn't hate me for not loving you. You didn't demand it, as you should have. You didn't need me to love you because it wasn't important to you whom you married as long as you were married. I could have been anyone and it wouldn't have made a difference.'

She had made him realise what he didn't want to.

'I'm glad we spoke about this, Prashant. We can take it from here and make this marriage work,' she said.

'No, we can't. I can't be bothered with this anymore.'

'What do you mean?' Amara heard herself say.

He gave a mirthless laugh. 'See. This is what I mean. I have to explain everything to you. Every reference, every allusion and every context.'

Amara got up from the chaise lounge and started walking towards the bedroom.

'You can't walk away from the truth, Amara. It has to be said. It has to come out. If you hadn't brought it up today, I would have tomorrow,' he shouted, following her.

Amara shut the bedroom door. Her heart pounded against her chest. She couldn't take in another of Prashant's words. Still, no tears.

'Amara, listen to me. I know you don't want to hear it, but it has to be said!'

'Please, Prashant. Don't say it. Don't say anything right now.'

'I have to,' he said. She heard his voice through the door.

'Please don't say anything, Prashant.'

She heard him pause.

'I want a divorce.'

'No!' her voice rose like a sharp whistle. 'Please. Please, stop talking.' She banged her head against the door and buckled under the weight of her own body. Her hands covered her ears.

'I know you married me for financial security. That's okay. Because I married you for my mother's security.'

'Stop talking,' she said.

He continued, relentless, 'We've been married for six years. Never happily. We owe ourselves a chance for happiness. Amara, you owe yourself a chance to be happy.'

'You are just angry, Prashant. You are still in mourning. You don't know what you're saying. You don't mean all this,' Amara shouted, hoping to make him stop.

She heard a clunk against the door as if Prashant had banged his head or fist against the door.

'This is the first time I'm being honest in this marriage, Amara. And believe me I am sorry. I know this is unfair to you. I hope one day you can forgive me. You are a good person and you will be fine. You'll move on and meet someone. But this has to be done.'

'Go away, Prashant. Please. Leave me alone.' Her voice skittered over the walls and ricocheted back to her.

He didn't reply. She heard his feet shuffle. He was turning around. He was heading towards the door. She opened the bedroom door and ran after him. Something told her to let go, but she couldn't. She screamed, hysterical now, 'I didn't mean that. I don't want you to go. Let's talk about this. Please. Please, don't leave me.'

She fell at his feet.

'Don't do this to me, Prashant. You will ruin my life.'

He picked her up gently and forced her to look at him directly. 'Amara, I am sorry. But I know I'll be sorrier if I have to keep up this façade forever. I am giving you six months. Come to terms with this and get your life in order.'

'No!'

But he left the house, vanishing into the deep gloom of the night.

~ ~

Someone was knocking at the door. Amara opened her eyes. She was stretched out supine on the marble floor next to the front door.

What am I doing her?

Her fingers went to her neck. She thought a noose was wound around it. There was nothing there. Then it all came back to her. She took a sharp intake of breath, but there was no air in the room. She felt faint.

There was another loud knock. She sat up, steadying herself against the wall. Maybe it was Prashant. Maybe he had come to apologise. No, he never apologised. But she didn't even want his apology. She just wanted him to tell her that their marriage was going to be all right.

But he had a key, why would he knock at the door?

There was dried blood on the floor. And a sharp pain on her left foot.

Many times Amara experienced an urgent itch on the lower side of her left foot, which ate away at her before she slept, vanished when sleep conquered it, and was ferocious when she woke up. But its violence had never manifested like this before.

No, it wasn't that, she realised, as if even her senses could process only what her eyes dared to believe. A shard of glass was stuck in her foot. She plucked it out without flinching. As if swooning in relief, her head dropped back onto the floor.

There was that persistent knock again. She continued ignoring it, when she heard a baritone voice say, 'Ammu, are you there?'

For a moment she couldn't place the voice or the endearment. Then she knew. It was Baba's voice. Was she dreaming?

There was more knocking. And then the bell rang in a grinding tune that never failed to annoy Amara. She remembered how her parents hated ringing the bell to anyone's house, saying they didn't want to be known as inconsiderate guests who wasted electricity.

It was definitely not her parents outside this house.

'*Beta*, it be us. Biji and Baba. Open door.' Biji's voice rang distinctly through the door, rattling Amara as much as the bell did. She froze.

Sometimes half-asleep, Amara saw herself walking naked in broad daylight, cellulite and modesty forgotten, shouting obscenities, laughing loudly, cursing and screaming, dancing in the rain and singing to the moonlight. These visions disappeared as soon as she woke up to the static state of everyday life. And then ashamed at her own recklessness, she jailed these phantasms till the next such dream released them.

She knew she walked a fine line, where a single tilt could change everything, so she clung on to the sane side, stoically, bravely, not pandering to her whims. She asked herself now – has that day come today? Have I breached the line? Have I gone crazy?

She heard voices consulting each other. In her blurry state, she couldn't make out who was saying what.

'Why not we call her?'

'Her phone is switched off.'

'Maybe she gone somewhere.'

'Where will she go at eight in the morning?'

'Maybe she still be sleeping.'

'Ammu, open the door,' Baba's sharp voice penetrated through her hazy mind. His words gathered around her, giving her a focal point to bring her thoughts to. She wasn't dreaming or going crazy. Her parents were really at the front door. She stood up, leaning on the walls for support, and said with a croaking voice, 'I'm coming.' Her throat was heavy, as if carrying a lead block.

There was another knock. They hadn't heard her. She cleared her throat, made a small crack in the block, and said more loudly, 'I'm coming.'

She treaded softly to the bathroom. She looked at herself in the mirror and saw another woman look back at her. A woman with red eyes, a turned-down mouth, and a face bereft of any hope. It made her want to dissolve into tears. Instead she splashed cold water on herself and washed the dried blood from her feet.

'Are you okay, Ammu?' Baba's gentle voice cascaded in.

'Yes. I'm coming,' she said more loudly and assertively.

She walked to the front door and opened it. Her parents stood there with two plastic bags between them. They were the last people she wanted to see and the only people she wanted to see.

'What are you doing here?' she said, trying to force a smile.

'By God! What happens to you? Sick you are looking,' Biji said, placing a hand over Amara's forehead. Her mother's tender touch made Amara feel better.

'I'm fine. Just surprised to see both of you here.'

'Prashant call us last night. He say, you not well. He say, come here because he have to go to New Orlean for work for two week.'

Had Prashant done this to look out for Amara, for the first time in their marriage? Or had he called her parents so she could tell them what he had said?

'Yes, yes of course,' Amara said.

Her parents were holding a wet umbrella. Amara took it from their hands to place it on the ceramic stand. But there was no stand in the foyer. Why, Amara wondered, do we not have a stand for an umbrella? Everyone has one, why not us?

Baba hadn't spoken a word, but now he said, 'Ammu, are you okay? You're looking upset. Has something happened?'

Amara looked at her father to whom she never lied. She gazed into his old tired eyes that had worked so hard to see her happy. She forced her thoughts and voice to say, 'Nothing has happened, Baba.'

'Then why do you look like you've been crying? Did Prashant and you have a fight?'

Amara had put on her glasses so her parents couldn't see the state of her eyes, but clearly that wasn't enough to disguise her pain. She would have to use words. 'Everything is fine.

Nothing has happened, Baba.' She realised that she had just said these same words, so she quickly added, 'I haven't slept properly in the last few days. When you came I was taking a shower so it took me time to answer the door. I hope you didn't get too worried.'

'No, no. We happy to finally get call from Prashant. And see our daughter and great house she live in,' Biji said.

They came inside the house.

Biji touched her forehead to Gandhi's photo as if she was aching to worship something. While Amara showed them the kitchen and dining room, Biji cooed like a pigeon, touching everything as if she were in a free-for-all museum. When they entered the living room, Amara realised something, 'Watch your step!'

'Why?' Baba asked, not taking his eyes off his daughter.

Amara looked at the broken porcelain plate still lying on the ground; a poignant exhibition of everything she was feeling.

'I dropped a plate at breakfast this morning.'

'You have dal-chawal for breakfast?' Baba asked, looking at Prashant's unfinished dinner lying between the broken pieces.

Amara knew it was foolish to say something they all knew to be untrue. 'Yes.'

Fortunately for Amara, Biji yelled, 'Look!' She touched the flat-screen TV in slow motion as if it would give her an electric shock. For the next fifteen minutes, Biji was as excited as a child discovering the world. She took out her camera to click a photo of the Tuscan painting hanging over their mantel. She put the bedsheets in the guest bedroom on her cheeks and said it was like silk. It was. Amara was amazed at the simplicity of Biji's pleasure in things that Amara didn't even notice, from the Bunn coffee maker to the pearl-embossed champagne flutes.

She wished she could give Biji these things on her own terms.

'What good boy our Prashant is,' Biji said. 'Treating my daughter like princess. I wish I be so lucky. Sit at home and have everything at feet.'

Amara excused herself and went into the bathroom. She turned the tap on full while her tears fell softly against the gush of the water. She washed her face, pinched her cheeks so they would look as red as her eyes and went back out.

It didn't appear that Biji had noticed Amara's absence. 'You know, Ammu,' she was saying. 'After your marriage, we getting too much respect in community. Everyday we invited for dinner or to go to party. That stingy Patel has given to me a raise. My own brother has become too jealous. Your marriage is our full success here. Without it we be failure.'

'Without it no point to be here,' she added, and went into the guest bathroom.

Amara looked up at the ceiling fan that was revolving like a slow optical illusion. Why had Biji not warned her how tough marriage would be; that each moment was a minefield waiting to blow up; that a single wrong could negate all rights? Why had she only told Amara to be married at a prescribed age, have babies by a certain time and behave herself, whatever that meant now?

Baba put his hand on her shoulder. 'Ammu, you look unhappy. You are not meeting our eyes and you're far away somewhere. What's wrong? Tell me.'

Failure was not something Amara could discuss, not with society, not with Biji and not even with Baba. She knew she could speak to no one of her misgivings. It sprung from a sense of loyalty, not so much to Prashant as to the institution they were in. Talking about marriage in bad terms was considered sacrilege in the Indian community. Everyone around her was married, and claimed to be happily so, despite public fights and snide rumours. She often wondered if there was anyone else who had daily failures in marriage, like she did.

'Nothing is wrong, Baba,' she said. She grasped at the first change of topic she could think of. 'Tea?' she asked. 'I must at least serve you tea. Unless you want water.'

'Why don't you go to bed and lie down. You look ill. You should not be on your feet. I'll make the tea.'

Amara went into a deep undisturbed slumber and woke up in the evening to the aroma and sizzle of aloo paratha, her favourite dish. She walked into the kitchen to see Biji in Amara's silk robe using the one-touch appliances in the kitchen, while Baba looked relaxed smoking a cigar. This is how we'd imagined we would be on coming to America, Amara thought. This was Biji's American Dream – this house, this money, these gadgets and these comforts. For now it was a borrowed American Dream, for this was not their house and these were not their things, but that made each moment more special and momentous.

Amara missed having her parents around. In the last few years, she had visited them only three or four times and was amazed that they slipped back so easily into being a family. Even the house was different with them in it. Finally, there was something in it that she could call her own.

Yet, she had to get out.

'I'm feeling much better,' she said after dinner. 'I want to take you around Manhattan tomorrow. You will love it.'

～ ～

The next day, on the ferry to Staten Island, Amara tried to study Prashant's words, playing them over and over in her mind, wondering if he had said them in a fit of rage. During

*Lion King*, she waited for him to call, telling her that he hadn't meant a thing. On the top deck of the Empire State Building, she dialled his cell phone. She wanted to say, 'I love you,' so convincingly that he never questioned her again. He didn't answer.

Everyday, she pretended to talk to him and told her parents he said hello but was too busy to chat.

Exactly two weeks later Baba and Biji left. Biji presented Amara a pistachio-shell painting of a baby – an obvious hint.

After they left, there was nothing left to do except watch the days die.

# 12

It had taken her four months to say this: he wants to end our marriage.

Stacy spat the black coffee back into her mug, 'No way.' Realising that Amara was serious, she got up from her chair and wrapped her arms around her. 'I am so sorry to hear that, Am. Honestly, I'm completely shocked. I didn't know that you were having problems. I thought you Indians stayed married for like seven lives or something.'

Amara smiled despite herself, though her jaw hurt with the effort. Stacy looked Amara straight in the eyes and asked, 'Are you okay?'

'No,' Amara replied. She looked at the revenue graph on the desk, which Stacy had drawn in yellow and red. How typical it was of her friend to put life into the dullest things. 'Yes. I don't know. Today is better than yesterday. This week is more tolerable than last week. At least I'm finally able to talk about it.'

'I knew something was wrong when you said you wanted to come to office. But I never imagined it would be something like this.'

'I never imagined something like this either.'

'But what happened with Prashant? What changed?'

Amara thought about her reply, even though she knew the answer. There was no point in hiding things from Stacy.

'Nothing changed, Stace. It just took him this long to come out and say it. But his actions were clear from the beginning. He didn't want this marriage.'

'What about you? Are you okay with this?'

From the time she woke up till she fell into a fitful sleep, and sometimes even in her dreams, Amara's mind was clogged with questions. What would happen to her once she was divorced? How would her parents react? What would people say? What box would she tick in forms asking about her marital status? Who would want to marry her again? She was almost thirty; when would she have children? Amara couldn't even envision spending her life alone, leave alone actually do it.

'I don't know,' she replied, her voice faltering. 'I don't think I'm okay with this.'

'But you weren't happy with him. I saw the kind of person you had become. There was no life in you. I think this divorce will be good for you.'

A week ago, when Prashant was not in the house, as usual, Amara had stared at their wedding picture in the living room for over an hour. They were standing next to the sacred fire taking *satpadi*, their wedding vows. The fire was burning brightly, signifying the illumination of the mind, knowledge and happiness, casting a glow on Amara's face, filling her lips with a smile. Her head was bowed down, as Prashant filled the middle parting in her hair with vermillion, the red powder signifying loyalty and respect. She had looked at this photo for six years but never noticed that Prashant was not looking at her, his eyes unfocussed and faraway. Everything in the picture was a lie, except for Prashant's expression.

But all Amara knew in life was to be married, what was she supposed to do without it? She grabbed the photo frame from the mantel and went into the kitchen. She stood above the sink and broke the Swarovski glass frame – a wedding gift – with her hands. Her thumb got cut. As drops of blood fell into the sink, like mercury balls, she set the photo on fire. Ashes fell into the sink. Fire and vermilion. Ashes and blood. Her marriage from start to finish.

She began breaking and burning other things secretly. She started with small things he would not notice, like photos of them together; photos that she had printed and framed with care. Then she became bolder, and one day, not finding any outlet for her anger, she took a cigarette from the pack she was secretly smoking, and burnt a large hole in their mattress. The mattress was worth more than five thousand dollars. If Prashant noticed this, in the brief interludes that he came back home, he said nothing. None of this moderated her suffering.

'Stacy, I'd rather be married and unhappy, than divorced and happy.'

'Come, come. This is not India. You live in America where it's not a big deal to be divorced.'

Amara realised that Stacy may be her best friend and know more about Indian culture than many Americans, but she didn't understand its social complexities; knowing something was not the same as living it. 'Stace, as an Indian in America, divorce *is* a big deal. What is seen as liberating in America, is bondage for Indians.'

'Then go find a solution. Go for marriage counselling. Go right now to Prashant's office and tell him that you want this to work. That you love him. You do, right?'

'Do what?'

'Love him?'

'Of course. What kind of question is that?'

'Am, are you sure you want this marriage?'

'Yes. Yes, Stacy, I need this marriage.'

'Then go, now. Tell him all this.'

Amara thought she'd feel better talking to someone, but she felt worse. Stacy had understood neither her pain nor her dilemma. Amara had been pulled in so many directions recently, and Stacy's advice pulled her in yet another one. But Stacy was right about one thing – she had to tell Prashant what she was feeling. It was never certain when he'd be home, so she decided to go to his office.

Amara left McKarma's Lower East Village office and walked down Broadway to Pine Street. The last time she'd seen Prashant was three days ago, fast asleep in the guest bedroom. He was lying diagonally across the bed, covers thrown aside and his legs splayed, like a moth, wings outstretched, as if he'd already won his freedom and was relishing every moment of it.

After he'd come back from his two-week 'work trip to New Orleans' Amara had tried to act like nothing had changed between them. But he immediately moved to the guest bedroom and stopped talking to her. He'd leave early from the house and come late. He wouldn't stay in the house during the weekends. His absence or presence stopped bothering Amara, for she knew he wasn't there even when he was. His silence conveyed more than his words could have.

Maybe meeting him outside the house would open him up, Amara thought, as she took a right turn at the Fulton Street station. 'It's my fault,' she thought, 'I did so many things behind his back and I'm paying for my bad karma. I'm going to stop working, or eating cheesy curls, and I'll actually read the books he tells me to.'

She knew exactly what she would say to him: 'Prashant, I accept that you don't love me. From now on you can have your freedom and whatever else you crave. I will not ask you to talk to me, or listen, or even expect you to love me. Just don't divorce me.'

She was a building away from his office, when she saw *them*. Prashant was holding a door open as Riya walked into the café. Amara stood so still that she thought her heart had stopped beating. She waited till they were both inside, and then walked to where they'd just been; she barely knew what she was doing. She looked inside, through the umber glass door, and saw them taking a seat at a table for two. Prashant was looking intently at Riya. He set his hands down on hers. Amara couldn't look any more. She stumbled, her feet finding no ground, and fell on the sidewalk. She thought she'd hurl everything she had eaten this morning, last night, ever.

'Are you all right, young lady?' a man wearing a suit and a blue overcoat asked. He probably worked at the New York Stock Exchange down on Wall Street. 'Let me give you a hand.'

He lifted her to her feet though she didn't remember extending her hand for help. She thanked him, or maybe not, and ran into the door of the nearest establishment.

'What can I do for you, Madam?' she heard a voice ask. Amara looked up from the floor into very bright lights. She was in a hair salon.

'I need—' (a husband, a sister, a friend, help)

'A haircut?' the lady asked.

Amara looked at herself in one of the several mirrors. Her hair had always been long, the same style, covering her face, curly and unruly in the summer, wavy and dry in the winter.

She sat on the pink vinyl chair.

Chop-chop. Snip-snip.

She heard no other sounds, not even her mind's. She shut her eyes and opened them when the hairdresser nudged her. She looked in the mirror, and despite her numbness, gasped. Her hair was gone, leaving a crop afraid to venture below her ears. She looked at her cut hair that had been witness to all her suffering. It was good that it was gone.

All Amara could do was slap a hundred dollar bill on the counter and stagger out of the place. She thought she couldn't take another step, but somehow she walked to the nearest station, went on the nearest platform and got into the first train that came along. She didn't care where she was going. Inside the train, she remained standing, though there were several empty seats, it being early afternoon. The train was a fast one, not a local, and clattered noisily past blurry stations and slower trains. Amara's body became fluid and empty. Why was this happening to her? Was Prashant leaving her because of Riya? Were Prashant and Riya having an affair all these years? Was Riya exacting revenge on Amara for marrying Prashant?

'Make this stop! Make this train stop!' Amara yelled.

No one turned to look at her; it was as though she had said nothing. Amara noticed a man who was looking directly at her. He wore nothing save an orange skirt. The left side of his body, including his shaved head, was painted blue, while his right half was bare. On his forehead was a V-shaped line drawn in white and filled with red powder. His right ear had a *kundan* earring and on his left feet were small metallic bells strung together in two layers. He wore a huge silver pendant inserted into which was a five-inch long mirror. He continued staring at Amara when the train screeched to a sudden halt. The lights flickered and went out, plunging everything into darkness for a moment. There was complete silence. Even the tracks became quiet. When the lights came on, Amara was staring at herself, her eyes locked in the mirror on the blue man's breasts.

~ ~

Time clocked in, clocked out, till three months passed.

A big party was underway for Prashant's birthday, which

Amara had planned as a surprise on many levels. Instead of cooking the Indian way, preparing twenty dishes for days in advance, she ordered pre-made canapés, cheese and crackers. She kept the guest list to a selective twenty and had Chopin and Beethoven on the play list. Instead of wearing a sari, she chose a sequined black Versace dress. And this time she drank, already down four glasses of wine. Her head was light.

When she saw Prashant's surprised face as he backslapped his friends, she was glad she'd organised this party. She understood another part of him: that despite the loss of his mother and now his marriage, he considered it a greater loss to bore people. In the distance that had grown between them, Amara understood him better than when she had been living with him for years.

Though he looked at ease, he didn't notice her or thank her for the surprise. Every time someone complimented her, she looked to see if he had overheard, but he was never around her. Amara had already thought of a way he couldn't ignore her completely. She brought out his favourite sweet-toffee-date cake, especially ordered from Locanda Verde. Everyone gathered around, amidst hoots and claps, and Prashant had no choice but to stand next to Amara, blow out the thirty-five candles, and accept the piece of cake she put in his mouth. Amara took a mental snapshot of that moment, as a wave of excitement revved through her; everyone at this party thought of Prashant and her as a normal couple. She grasped at comments like, 'What a lovely pair you two make,' and tucked them away in her memory to keep her heart warm on particularly cold nights.

She drank two glasses of champagne to savour this feeling.

But Prashant continued to ignore her. Amara stood in front of him and lit a cigarette, convinced that nothing would catch his attention more than his wife smoking. He looked the other way. Her smoking caught the interest of another guest, who blew a smoke ring at her, and asked very seriously, 'How's everything with Prashant?'

Amara stared at the woman, perturbed even in her hazy state that someone had sensed their marital problems. 'Why? What have you heard?' she asked, as if they were gossiping about someone else.

The lady inhaled deeply before replying, 'I heard he was still in mourning. People see him alone at bars and restaurants, so naturally they talk. But who'd know better than you?'

Amara couldn't believe how easily she had almost slipped.

'He is better,' she said emphatically, as if she knew.

After the party was over and the last guest left, Prashant walked past the half-empty glasses, the unopened bottles of Sauvignon Blanc, and the unfinished platters of food, towards the guest room.

'Happy birthday, Prashant!' Amara said loudly, stepping up behind him. 'I've got you season tickets to a Yankees game. A small gift.'

Prashant turned around so slowly that Amara realised it was taking him the last of his effort. He said, 'Amara, don't do this to yourself. I don't think you are moving on.'

'I love you, Prashant,' she said, her voice sounding like a plea, instead of assertive, as she'd hoped. She realised it was the first time in years she had said these words to him.

He smiled at her sadly. 'You don't love me. You love the concept of me.'

Amara had come too far to give up now, so she replied, 'I'll do anything to make it work. Please, tell me what I'm doing wrong and I'll make it right.'

Prashant grabbed a glass on the table, which was almost full with red wine, and took a swig. He replied, 'You are not doing anything wrong. But if you spend your whole life doing something right, this marriage will still not work. My mother sacrificed her entire life for her marriage and it got her nowhere. For your own sake, Amara, move on.'

A strap from Amara's dress slipped off her shoulders. She had bought this dress ten days ago, and since then had lost more weight. She put the strap back in its place before replying, 'Please, Prashant. Give this marriage another chance. Don't ruin my life.'

'I will ruin your life more if we stay married.'

'Prashant, I am begging you.'

'Amara,' he said, and lifted his forefinger to emphasise his point. 'Don't you have any self-respect? Stop begging me. Give your love to those who deserve it. All I want from you is a divorce.'

'But I've changed. I've become American, like you wanted.'

'You're not in any way American. You came here later in life and have been cocooned from everything American. You have built India in America and nothing about this country has changed who you are or what you've become.'

'What do you want, Prashant? Do you want me to be her? Do you want me to be Riya?'

Prashant gave her a long and steady stare, but didn't say anything.

'I asked you something. Do you want me to become like Riya? Is that what it will take for you to stay married to me?'

'You can never be her.'

Something snapped in the warm place Amara was trying to build in her heart, 'Is that what it is? You've been in love with Riya all this time?'

Prashant's shoulders suddenly stooped and he leaned in, as if someone had punched him in the stomach. 'No.'

'Don't lie to me. Not now when you have nothing to lose,' Amara said, her teeth grinding against each other.

'How can I love someone who never belonged to me?'

'So you ended it?'

'No, she did, when she heard that we were getting married.'

'Don't lie to me. I know the truth.'

Prashant raised his hand as if shielding himself from a blow and walked out of the house. Amara was left alone. Her chest heaved up and down, and the nerves in her body beat up hard against her skin. It was as if her body had turned inside out, leaving her hollowed out. She grabbed a baseball bat from the storage room, and began to beat the chaise lounge with all her strength. When the boiling blood in her turned to a simmer, she fell down against the lounge, cried till she could no more, and got up to beat the patches made by her tears.

The next morning, Amara woke up feeling like her head was a mass of ice.

She went to the kitchen to fix herself a coffee when she saw a yellow post-it note tacked on the refrigerator. It said, in Prashant's handwriting: 'You have to move out.'

# 13

Amara knocked on the front door. A bold vermillion line had been recently drawn on it. Shoes were lying outside on the porch.

Baba opened the door.

'Ammu? What are you doing here?' he asked, removing his spectacles.

Amara didn't say anything.

'Your hair!'

She touched her hair, but, for the first time since childhood, she wasn't apologetic about her untameable mane. Instead, she picked up one of her two suitcases.

'Bags? Why do you have bags, Ammu?'

Amara entered through the front door. Baba picked up her other suitcase and followed her. She walked up the stairs and went into her room, which her parents had kept unchanged for the rare times she came visiting.

'I am getting worried, beta. What is wrong? You look so pale. Where is Prashant?'

Amara had to say something. She blurted out the first thing that came to her mind, 'Prashant is travelling on work for three weeks, so I thought I'd come here.' Baba looked rather sceptical, so she added, 'I need to sleep. Please don't disturb me.'

Amara shut the door and lay down on the cold, hard, unforgiving bed.

There was a knock on her door. Amara got up, startled, though she wasn't asleep. She couldn't remember where she was, though everything around her served as a clue. She needed desperately to see the time, as if that would put everything in place, but there was no watch in the room or on her wrist.

Baba and Biji entered the room.

Biji said, 'Ammu, we be very worried. We try to call Prashant but he not picking up phone. What is matter?'

There was no escaping it, Amara realised. It had to be said. Yet it was impossible, like trying to turn on a switch during a dream.

'I've already told Baba that Prashant is travelling out of the country, so you can't get through his phone,' she snapped.

Baba and Biji looked at each other. Amara had never flared up like this.

'Why you didn't say earlier? We could come to your home,' Biji said.

Amara looked away, feeling cornered by these questions, though she had practised answering them before coming here. 'I was a little unwell.'

'You been unwell lot lately. Good news?' Biji asked.

'Nothing like that.' She had to change the topic. 'You know what, I'm feeling much better after my nap. Let me help you around the house.'

The doorbell rang.

'That's my client. I better go,' Baba said, and ran down the stairway.

Biji and Amara went downstairs to the kitchen.

Amara asked Biji, 'What does Baba still have clients for?'

Biji looked away and bit her nail, as if she were hiding a secret as well. 'Baba consulting Indians here about their civic right in India. He love being lawyer again.'

'Biji, you told me you had paid off my wedding loan?'
Amara said, looking straight into her mother's eyes. She saw
a truth there that she couldn't find in her own eyes.

Biji hesitatingly added, 'Well, your wedding be bit expensive,
so it took long to pay loan back. Now house loan be pending.
So Baba be making little extra money on side.'

'Oh,' Amara responded.

'Don't think we poor,' Biji said, running her hand across
the steel pressure cooker in her hand. 'Or we mind doing
work.'

Amara gulped on hearing this. Her parents were punishing
themselves to continue building her life and she was throwing
that very life, crumpled up, back in their faces.

For two weeks Biji and Baba didn't talk about Amara's
sudden appearance. Amara stayed inside the house the entire
time, moving only from her room to the kitchen and back.
She often put her phone on silent and pretended to be on call
with Prashant when Baba and Biji came home from work.

One evening, as her parents were getting dressed for yet
another party at one of their Indian American friend's house,
Amara asked Biji, 'Don't you meet Dua Mama any more?'

Biji slipped gold earrings into her earlobes, which she had
surgically stitched back together, and replied, 'Tch. I not go
there now. They also not call. How it matter? Everyday I get
invite to party. I be saying no to people. Can you believe?'

Baba walked into the living room, dressed in a suit,
whistling. Amara smiled and said, 'Baba, you seem to be
enjoying this hard-partying life.'

Baba nodded his head in agreement. 'After living here, for
what, almost sixteen years, this—,' he swept his hands across
the room, '—is what makes me happy.'

'You've changed,' Amara said, remembering the night on
Tina's birthday when Baba had said that an immigrant's

happiness was like waving a picture of water before a burning man.

'Haven't we all?' Baba said and his eyes turned soft. 'Look at how serious you've become after marriage. And in the last year you've been falling ill, breaking things, snapping and looking misty-eyed all the time.' His eyes hardened as he added, 'If I didn't trust you so completely, I would say you're hiding something.'

~ ~

One Friday evening, Amara was standing by her room's large wooden window, watching the sunset shamelessly steal away the colours of the day, when Baba and Biji barged in without knocking. They stopped short when she turned to look at them, and stood close to each other, as if needing one another's support.

Baba cleared his throat and asked, in his lawyer voice, 'Ammu, a letter has come for you from a divorce law office. What is going on?'

Amara started. She had told Prashant to call her when the papers were ready, not mail them to her parents' house. It was too soon; she couldn't tell them the truth.

'Nothing, Baba. It must have been sent here by mistake.'

Baba held the unopened envelope in his hand as he emphasised his words, 'Ammu, we know that something is wrong. It's been almost a month since you've been here. You lie in bed all day. You are absent-minded and withdrawn. We haven't heard from Prashant. You're not talking about going back to your husband's house. Don't be scared to talk to us. We are your parents. What is happening?'

Amara looked at her parents. Baba was wearing wire-rimmed eyeglasses, which had slipped to the lower bridge of his nose, revealing roving watery eyes. His hair had thinned, from a bush to a tail. Around Biji's torso was tied a back-brace for the lower back pains she had recently started suffering from. She smelled of Tiger Balm and chemicals from the capsules she took for her knee and back. How similar they had started looking, Amara realised, with their wrinkling skin and greying hair, and the same weathered look that strugglers, like 'the earlys', carried.

When had they become old?

'We are – he is—,' she said.

'What?'

How long could she hide the truth? She had to tell them. Amara felt like a doctor groping for the right words to tell a mother that she had lost her only child.

She lowered her eyes and said, 'I – he – said – he – he doesn't love me. I thought about it. It's true. I – I don't love him either.'

As she voiced her feelings aloud for the first time, the truth painfully set in.

'What?' Biji asked and turned towards Baba as if he should decipher, as usual, what his darling daughter was trying to say.

Amara took a deep breath. It had to be said clearly, 'Prashant doesn't love me and I don't love him.' She didn't dare meet her parents' eyes, so she looked at the wooden floor under her bed and noticed with surprise that a large hole had formed in its cracks.

'What are you talking about? What love?' Baba asked.

'Love, Baba. Like marriage, love,' Amara said, impatiently, suddenly wanting this to be over as soon as possible, so she could face the consequences and be done with the anger and hurt.

'Cha! Love? What love? Marriage is not love. It be duty. Love is meaning you pick one person and no one after him,' Biji replied acidly.

Baba put his hand on Biji's shoulder. When had they started doing that? He said, 'There is no love. Fine. But what does that have to do with anything?'

'I – know this is shocking,' Amara said. She took another deep breath. 'Prashant has filed for divorce.'

Baba and Biji looked at each other.

'*Die-force?*' Biji said, repeating the word with disbelief.

'I am sorry, Biji. I tried hard to stop it. But it was beyond my control.'

Biji turned desperately towards Baba and said, 'What nonsense she is talking? What is this *die-force* talk nonsense? Our daughter have gone mad.'

Baba said in an even voice, 'Ammu, did Prashant and you have a fight?'

Amara grasped the table stand for support, 'It is not a fight, Baba. The marriage is over.' Her voice sounded as alien to her as her announcement. She had never thought that she'd be the kind of girl to say these words to her parents.

Biji plopped on the bed. 'Hai Ram! What she is talking? She have gone mad.'

'Ammu, we can't really follow what you're saying,' Baba said.

'Baba, I know this is unexpected. Believe me. I tried to save the marriage. I really tried,' Amara answered, looking from Biji's face to Baba's. They looked like crumpled paper that had been tossed in the garbage.

'Did he hit you?' Baba asked, his voice harsh in his throat.

'No.'

'Did he take another woman?'

Amara thought of Riya, but without proof how could she be sure? 'No.'

'Has his family treated you badly? It's the mother-in-law, isn't it? It's always the mother-in-law with women. Did you not like her? Was she not nice to you?'

'But she be dead. How it matter now?' Biji interrupted.

'Mummyji was very nice to me,' Amara said, tears welling in her eyes at how different things would have been if Mrs Roy were alive.

'Is he some sort of alcoholic or unemployed good-for-nothing? Ammu, give us some reason for this — this divorce thing.'

Prashant and Amara's marriage hadn't died dramatically. There were no adulterous dalliances or freakish discoveries. Their marriage had died of errors and neglect. It had died under a long protracted illness for which there was a diagnosis but no remedy. The disease had no name. So how could she explain it to Baba and Biji?

'I'm sorry, Baba. I don't know why he doesn't love me. But believe me, I tried.'

Baba let out a low curse, something Amara had never seen him do. 'What try? If you were really trying, you would have spoken to us and asked for help. You wouldn't have lied to us and pretended that all was well.'

Amara had no excuse for this. She looked down at the floor wishing it would open and pull her in.

'You think peoples will care if you try or not?' Biji quipped in, drying her tears against the end of her T-shirt sleeve.

'I knew we should not have come to this country. It corrupts our children with all these silly notions of divorce,' Baba said, his voice becoming a thin hissing buzz.

'Why blame country? It is our daughter. She have let us down. Woman must adjust in marriage. *Arre*, I sacrifice also so much for my marriage.'

'I am sure there has been some sort of misunderstanding. I will call Prashant right now and sort out this matter,' Baba said, the words bouncing off his lips. Baba dialled Prashant's number from his phone and went outside the room. Amara heard his muffled voice through the corridor but couldn't distinguish the words. She couldn't bear to look at Biji and sat down on the desk chair. Biji sat at the edge of the bed, silent with shock.

Baba came back a minute later and went straight to his wife. His voice was thick with grief and disbelief. 'Radha, he says he wants to divorce our daughter and that his decision is final.'

'No, no, don't say like that! He must have say something else.'

'He wished us all the best, as if he'd taken our interview for a job, and we had failed.'

'What have our daughter done? We be ruined. What be happen to us? How we will explain to people why they not married anymore?' Biji's voice was so fierce and choked that she could hardly get the words out. She got up from the bed and fell on the floor. Amara and Baba ran towards her. Amara reached to pick her up at the same time as Baba. Biji slapped Amara's hand.

'Don't touch me. You have shamed us. Peoples will spit at us because of you.'

'Biji,' Amara said, as if Biji had kicked her in the stomach.

'Don't call me mother. I ashamed to call you daughter. I wish I had boy instead of you.' Biji's voice was cold – raw and cold – and Amara tightened the shawl around her.

'Radha, come. I'll take you to your room,' Baba said, without looking at Amara.

'Baba,' Amara shouted. 'At least you have to understand me. You have to believe that I did the best I could to save my marriage.'

'I can't understand anything, least of all who you have become. You have hurt me more than anyone else,' Baba replied.

Amara watched her parents walk out of the door and into the darkness where she didn't dare venture. At that moment she finally understood what grief was.

~ ~

Amara was back on the train staring at the mirror on the blue man's chest. The train was going as fast as an airplane. Suddenly, it came to a screeching halt. Amara's body went flying towards the blue man and they were transported to Ridge Road in Shimla. The blue man jumped on Amara's favourite horse — Shera — and began riding it. Amara told him to get off but he ignored her. Then, right before her eyes, he rose to the air and split into two. She ran after his split blue body till it landed next to the yellow swing in her backyard. The man stood above the spot where Amara had buried her pendant, and started dancing on top of it. His feet made the mud fly off, and went deeper and deeper into the hole, till all the mud was gone. 'Where's my pendant?' Amara screamed. The blue man didn't reply but began to turn in circles, and turned and turned till he became a dizzying blur. Amara looked away so she wouldn't faint and when she glanced back, the blue man was gone. A giant green ringneck parrot stood in his place, with Baba and Biji sitting on top of its wings. It flapped and flew into the air. Amara ran after it shouting, 'Put them down! Bring my parents back to me!'

Darkness surrounded Amara's room when she opened her eyes. She sat up quickly, ignored the way her head spun, and swung her feet over the side of the bed. Her legs touched the icy wooden floor sending shivers through her already cold body. She threw off her quilt, put her feet into slippers, wrapped a shawl around her shoulders, and walked past the front door into the backyard. A blast of early morning air swooshed across her face like a heavy slap. She walked to the spot of the buried pendant. The wind rose and fell, shrilly like a gull's cry in the far sea.

Her hands dug a hole in the mud and pulled out the stone. Amara turned it in her hand feeling its smooth texture. Without giving it another thought, she broke the mangalsutra on her neck – the symbol of her married status – and threw it into the hole.

She sat on the yellow swing and remembered the day, sixteen years ago, when the parrot astrologer had predicted that she'd be a one-and-a-half wife. She had never understood what he meant, but after the dream its meaning had become clear. By virtue of not being born in America, Amara was neither a first-generation immigrant, nor a second-generation immigrant, but belonged to the group that reached this country's shore at a later age, the one-and-a-half generation immigrants. The parrot had seen that by virtue of this identity she would belong to neither Shimla, nor America, and this would affect her immigrant life, especially her marriage, thus making her a one-and-a-half wife.

Amara sat on the swing until the first glimmer of sunrise, a soft lavender glow dispersing like watercolour through the dark night sky.

~ ~

'Who allow you out of house? The neighbour see you in backyard and now everyone know you be here, living with us in shame,' Biji said. For six days, Biji had been ill at home, not allowing Amara near her. Finally, when her boss, Shambu Patel, threatened to sack her, Biji went to work. Amara volunteered to fill in, but Biji refused, saying she didn't want anyone to know that Amara was living with them.

Now she was fuming. 'I tell them that Prashant is gone on business, that is why you here. Don't step out of house again. I think peoples know about your di— situation.'

'Sorry,' is all Amara could say.

'What you are wearing on your neck? Where is your mangalsutra?'

Amara looked down.

'Hai Ram, this girl have gone mad. First your hair, now this.'

Biji removed her mangalsutra and gave it to Amara. 'I have my husband here so peoples know I be married. You have nothing – no husband, no marriage. You need proof, so wear this all the times.'

Amara removed her pendant and wore her mother's mangalsutra.

~ ~

When Baba came home from work, Amara watched him from the kitchen, not coming out for she couldn't meet his eyes. He plonked down on a chair, as if the weight of the world was too much for him. Biji sat next to him and started off dolefully, 'Shambu move me today from front desk to back. He say I better off keeping inventory. He have never made me do this type of work before, hiding me in back of restaurant as if I do something wrong.'

Baba removed his glasses and sighed, 'I think people know, Radha. I didn't want to tell you, but I went to Lakshmi Cash and Carry for grocery shopping last week. Remember, how they always give us a free sample, like basmati rice? That day they over-charged me and, for the first time, not one of them greeted me.'

There was rising panic in Biji's voice as she said, 'You right. Diwali is coming up and we not been invited to even one party. Why this happen to us? How it is our mistake?'

Amara realised that her family was living in the dregs of Indian American society – a situation that had so far been averted thanks to their association with Dua Mama and then the Roys.

'This die-force have ruin everything we try to build in America,' Biji said.

Baba shut his eyes tightly together, as if squeezing the pain out of them. 'I called Mr Roy today to see if he could talk to Prashant and help this couple save their marriage. He told me he didn't want to interfere because Prashant didn't listen to him. I tried calling Prashant again; he didn't answer his phone. I don't know what else to do.' Amara too had called, texted and e-mailed Prashant several times, but there was silence on his end. She knew her father-in-law was as helpless as they were.

'Yes, I call Prashant too, from different number so he not know it be me. But he not pick up phone. I think we go to his house and beg him to take our daughter back,' Biji said.

Amara almost screamed out, 'No, don't humiliate yourself any further,' when Baba said, 'No, I think there is nothing else we can do without losing our dignity.'

'Who care about pride when daughter life in danger?'

'Radha, what I mean is that there is nothing we can do even if we lose our pride.'

The bell rang furiously startling them all. Simultaneously someone knocked against the door, as if he were in a real rush to enter their house.

Amara came out of the kitchen just as Baba opened the door. Dua Mama barged in. He hadn't come to their house since they had moved into it. He walked straight up to Biji and roared, 'What is going on? What is this I'm hearing? People are laughing at us.'

With fear in her eyes that were as large as saucers, Biji feigned innocence. 'I not know.'

Dua Mama cut her off, 'I have worked all my life to build

a solid reputation in society. Now these same people who were scared of me, are laughing at me, saying that my niece is divorced. I have fallen in their eyes. How will I face society?'

No one replied.

He looked at Amara and said, 'We are Indians, my dear. We don't go around getting divorced. Especially when there is no reason to. And not from families like the Roys. You should have had more patience with a good boy like Prashant after all that he has gone through. I think you have got influenced by American people and their lifestyle.' He banged his fist against a wall. 'Do you know people are saying that Amara drove Mrs Roy out of the house when she came to visit them? And that's why she got a heart-attack and died.'

'No, that's not true!' Amara butted in.

'You think people are going to believe what comes out of her mouth,' Dua Mama added, without looking at Amara, addressing her in third person, as if she didn't exist. He turned to Biji. 'Have you not taught your daughter any manners? Or does she think she has become so modern that she can backchat? Remind her that a family is the most fundamental unit in our society. If families break down it weakens the fabric of society. When a society weakens, it shows in the national character. The rise and fall of nations depend on families. And this woman wants to destroy her family, her society and her nation, with her un-Indian behaviour.'

He added in all his fury, 'The worst thing about all this is that I have to hear from outsiders that someone in *my* family is getting divorced! I forgave you for a lot of things, but this time you have really stabbed me in the back, Didi.' Saying that, he turned around and left the house, slamming the door shut.

After he left, Biji went over to Amara. 'You stupid, stupid

girl. A daughter is reflection of her mother. Your shame mean my shame. Now I will have to carry your die-force shame on my head.'

'Radha,' Baba said, pulling Biji away. He turned to Amara and said, 'I have never been ashamed of you, Amara.' He had never called her Amara before. 'And I never thought I would be. But today I am. You have really let us down.'

~ ~

Early next morning, Amara woke to a noise in her room. She sat up in bed to see Biji packing her bags.

'What are you doing?' Amara asked.

'You not welcome in our home,' Biji said in an eerily quiet voice. 'Go back to your husband and save marriage before you show us face again. Leave before Baba wake up so he doesn't have to see your evil jinn. And take these die-force paper with you.'

Amara learned what happened to people who broke the rules and didn't adhere to life's brief. The door slammed shut to her old life.

# 14

Amara dropped off the timeline of her life, with its predetermined and prescribed milestones, set deep and dark with the blood of tradition. She had chosen her dreams and ambitions accordingly, so now, finding herself in unchartered territory, she didn't know what her next milestone could be, or how she could find her way back to the timeline.

She stood on the porch with her suitcases and divorce papers in hand. It was raining. Where could she go? What could she do?

A few people passed by, bent over umbrellas, not noticing her. Amara stared at the front door, hoping that Baba would open it and let her in. Surely he understood her. But there was no sound from the house, as if like their American Dream, her parents too had ceased to exist.

Amara turned back to the road. She didn't have money or a place to go to. She would just have to stand there till Baba or Biji forgave her. But they didn't want her in their house. First her husband had thrown her out, and now her parents.

Amara held back a sob rising from the deep pit of her stomach.

'I will not feel sorry for myself,' she said. She took her phone out and dialled Stacy's number. Stacy didn't answer but sent a text message: 'In Bahamas with Pete ;) Gonna scuba dive :) Wattup?' Amara gasped in exasperation; now she really didn't have anywhere to go. Still, she typed back, 'Njoy!' not feeling the joy her words were meant to convey.

A yellow taxi drove past her house. It stopped and reversed back to her porch. A window rolled down from the passenger's seat. A face peeped out. It was Riya.

Amara shut her eyes in disbelief.

Riya's thin voice asked, 'Why are you standing outside the house?'

Amara knew that her voice would turn to water, like the rain, if she replied. Riya was scrutinising her suitcases and the locked door behind her. She braced herself to hear a mock laugh, a harsh word, and then clenched her fists together: she would not let her fury get the better of her.

That's why it startled her to hear Riya say, 'Are you heading to the city? I'm on my way there with the kids. I can give you a ride if you want.'

Amara turned away and kept her eyes focussed on the grass. If she met Riya's eyes everything she feared to feel would surface.

'I think you'll need this,' a voice said, and Amara turned to find Riya standing next to her, holding out a black umbrella. With the other hand, Riya lifted one of Amara's suitcases and started walking towards the taxi. Amara had no strength to protest. Either way, she had no other option right now. She followed Riya and sat in the taxi.

Riya's daughters – Mallika and Shezan – were also inside. They've grown so much, Amara thought, as she returned Mallika's smile. The younger one, Shezan, sat on Riya's lap and pointing to Amara asked, 'Who that?'

Riya looked at Amara and after a long pause said, 'That is my sister, Amara Masi.'

Shezan stared at Amara, while Amara stared at Riya. She noticed what she hadn't seen in Riya before. Riya's eyes had lost the gritty leer of their youth and now held a muted softness. Her long slender arms were slightly dimpled, weight lending her an aura of vulnerability. Her typically coiffed hair was tied in a loose bun, moccasins replaced her stilettos, and she wore a hooded T-shirt instead of a glamorous dress. The biggest change was in her manner, which was poised and deliberate, yet possessed a hesitancy she'd never had in her younger days.

Before Amara could say anything, Shezan said, 'Tum-tum is hurting.'

Riya put her hand on her daughter's belly and asked, 'Where is it hurting? Here?'

Shezan put her thumb in her mouth and replied, 'Yes.'

Amara watched with envy as the mother held her daughter in a long embrace, to make the pain go away.

~ ~

When they entered Manhattan, Riya instructed the taxi-driver to drive to Amara's house. Amara didn't say a word, maintaining her silence through the hour-long trip. She wondered how Riya knew where she lived. She wanted to gag. When the taxi stopped in front of her building, Amara didn't get out.

'Amara, we're at your house,' Riya said.

Amara didn't move.

Riya looked at her for a long time, before turning to the taxi-driver to say, 'Continue to forty-third and fifth, please.' She asked Amara. 'Are you okay?' Amara turned her face to look outside the window at the passing streets. Riya sighed and added, 'You can stay with me for now.' Knowing she had no other option Amara didn't protest.

When they walked into Riya's apartment, Amara didn't say a word, ignoring her niece's play and the sweeping view of Times Square.

'It's not as big as your house, but it's nice, isn't it?' Riya asked, as if Amara's opinion mattered.

Heaviness overcame Amara such that she could barely walk. She turned to Riya and addressed her for the first time, 'I need to lie down.'

Riya's eyes widened in surprise before softening again, 'You can share Shezan's room while you are here. Shezu, show Masi your room.'

Shezan led Amara to a small pink room. Amara patted the little girl on her head and after drawing the shades, called Prashant. He didn't respond.

Alone, in the quiet, Amara's worst fears came to life, haunting her: how was she going to live as a divorcee; how was she going to talk to people who saw her as a failure; what was she going to do?

She stirred a few hours later, or maybe more, when darkness had already descended. Her pillow was wet. Her body was awake but her mind was still in a dream-like state. A pair of small hands were on her chest, directly above her heart.

Shezan's soft voice reached her ears like a melody, 'Where is it hurting? Here?'

~ ~

The next morning, Amara awoke to squeals and laughter. She smiled and stretched, before realising where she was. The happiness became jarring now and she put a white pillow above her head. She heard a man laughing. She sat up. Was Prashant here? She couldn't place the sound of his laugh, so rarely had she heard it, but it had to be him in such a good mood around Riya. Amara tossed aside the blanket that someone had placed on her during the night, and ran outside. She stopped short when she entered the living room. A man turned around. Her brain fogged as Prashant morphed into someone else.

Gaurav, Riya's husband, she heard him say.

Of course, how could she be so foolish? She ran her fingers through her hair, hoping to grant her appearance some order, and extended her hands in acceptance of his greeting. Gaurav's presence explained why there was such happiness in the house. He had a gentle face with a dovish nose, a noble chin and round eyes hidden behind spectacles.

'Welcome home, Amara. Let me know if there's anything you need.'

Amara blinked her eyes, surprised at his kindness.

'Thank you,' she managed to mumble.

Riya came into the room, putting apples into a tiny haversack. 'You're awake! Good. You must be starving. I wasn't sure when you'd wake up so I kept aside some spaghetti for you.'

Riya bent down to Mallika, wrapped around Gaurav's legs, as the girl asked, 'Masi, we are going to the zoo. You want to come?'

Amara barely had energy to walk across the room. Riya gave her a look over and turned to Mallika, 'No, my love.' She gave her a long cuddle and added, 'Masi wants to rest. Now let's get my princess ready.'

Amara excused herself to freshen up and when she came out twenty minutes later, the house was empty, save for Riya.

'Didn't you go?' Amara asked.

'No. I thought I'd spend time with you. Let me heat up food for you. Maybe I'll dig in as well,' Riya said.

'I thought you didn't eat carbs,' Amara said, following Riya into the kitchen.

Riya's eyes flashed for a second; Amara saw the coolness creep back in them. Then they became soft again. 'Time changes people, doesn't it? Look at you. Never thought I'd see a pixie cut on you.'

This was the first time that Amara didn't care how her hair looked around Riya. Riya continued, 'Anyway, looks never help a marriage. Beauty fades away from the outer self to the inner self. All that matters is how you are with each other. At least that's what our spiritual teacher tells us.' She put the dish to heat in the microwave.

Amara stared at a set of knives; Prashant had the same set in his house too.

Riya placed a gloved hand on Amara's shoulder. 'But you're in luck. My "Art of Living" teacher has told me to perform a kind deed everyday. You are going to be my kind deed for a few days.'

Amara stopped to consider this. 'Why are you being nice to me?'

Riya walked over to a kitchen stool and sat down. 'I – we are sisters, you know. I—' Amara stared at her. Riya shrugged her shoulders and took a deep breath. 'Okay, I don't have the right words for it. I heard Prashant and you were getting divorced and thought, in some odd way, that it may have something to do with me. I want you to know that was never my intention.'

The pain of that particular day when Amara saw Prashant and Riya entering the café came back. Though overwhelmed, she found a way to ask, 'Is this about the café?'

'Café?' Riya asked, and once again Amara was amazed that significant things in her life were so meagre to others.

'Yes, I saw Prashant and you at a café a few months back.' Five months, six days to be exact.

Riya ran her fingers along the edge of a napkin, and said, 'Amara, you know that Prashant and I were attracted to each other when we first met. But after you guys got married, I cut all contact with him. Then he called me up, seven or eight months ago, saying he needed to talk. I kept pushing him away, but he said it was about you. We met at a café one afternoon and he told me that he had asked you to leave. I asked him why he was telling me this, he didn't say why. But I firmly told him to work it out with you.'

'You said that?' Amara asked.

Riya leaned over. 'I may be what I am, but I'm not the type to steal someone's husband. Yes, I was furious for months when I heard Mrs Roy selected you as Prashant's bride, and that you agreed. I was surprised too, because I knew that Prashant and you wanted different things in life. But I didn't meet him after your marriage was fixed, except that one time at the café.'

Amara stared at Riya, again struck by the earnestness in her eyes. 'I spent my entire wedding life trying to be you, and didn't know what I'd become. I wish I'd been myself, maybe things would be different.'

Riya got up from the stool, took the dish out of the oven and walked towards the dining table. 'Time only moves forward, Amara. Now is your chance to be who you are.'

'Dua Mama, won't he mind that I'm here?' Amara asked, following Riya.

'You know I grew up keeping secrets from my parents. Don't worry. I won't tell anyone you are here and you don't let anyone know that you are here with me. They'll kill me,' Riya said, placing the dish on the table.

Amara noticed a picture of Riya and Gaurav on the mantel next to the table. They were on a sunny beach, kissing each other. 'Gaurav must love you a lot. Are you happy?'

Riya smiled at her. 'Sometimes we love each other, some days we can kill each other. So I guess we are happily married. And yes, I am happy.'

Amara rolled the spaghetti on her fork and took a bite. The food went hungrily down her body flooding her with a warm sensation. Riya was mouthing down her plate as well. Just then, Amara noticed the three monkeys' picture with Tina, Riya and her. She picked it up and smiled, seeing their rosy cheeks that Biji had painted in.

'You've kept the three monkeys' picture?'

'Yes, I am getting nostalgic in my old age.'

Amara put the picture back and noticed that next to it was a similar picture with Riya and her two daughters.

Amara asked, 'What went wrong between us?'

Riya put her fork on the plate and dabbed her mouth with a napkin. 'It's silly, really.'

'Do tell,' Amara said.

'Okay, so do you remember the last time we came to Shimla?'

'Of course,' Amara replied.

'You and I went out to play in the rain, and later I came down with pneumonia.' Amara remembered the apparition of death that had haunted them for twenty days and twenty nights. 'I was really sick and on the first day all I wanted was you by my side. You promised me that you would be with me the whole time. But a minute later, Dad called you and without a thought you left me alone. You didn't come back for hours. My best friend had left me in my worst hour. Through all those feverish nights, all I could think of was how, in your effort to please everyone all the time, no one really mattered to you. I didn't matter to you. After that, I didn't feel the same way about you. When you came to America, I thought maybe you had changed, but you hadn't. I treated you so badly but you kept trying to be nice to me. So many people were not nice to you but you just took it. It irritated me so much. Then my parents kept comparing me to you, Mom saying how well-behaved you were, and Dad making me stop violin lessons so I could get good grades like you. And I hated you even more.'

So many truths stood in front of Amara that she didn't know which one to talk about. She remembered that day differently. She saw Riya lying on the jute mattress, burning with fever, when Dua Mama called Amara to give him company and directions to the medical store for Riya's medicines. This turned into a long afternoon as everyone at Mall Road stopped to chat with the Amreeka-returned Dua Mama. When Amara came back home, Biji told her to help with clearing out the kitchen shelves to find some curative herbs for Riya. In her effort to help Riya get better, Amara didn't get a chance to meet her, and when she did, Riya turned her eyes away. Baba had said it was her disease.

'I'm sorry I did that to you,' Amara said.

'I'm sorry too. I know this is all from a long time ago. But we carry the scars from our childhood through our adult lives, don't we? Some things heal, most don't. I had my revenge and for that I should apologise. I have daughters now and I can't believe I lost a sister because of my pettiness.'

Amara forgot her problems for a moment. She put her hand on Riya's. 'You never lost me. I'll always be your sister.' Riya pressed her hand in return. 'So I guess you don't hate me,' Amara added.

'Amara, you are so concerned with everyone hating you that sometimes you don't give people a chance to love you,' Riya said in a caring voice.

'Maybe I'm not worthy of being loved. My own husband didn't think I was.'

'If you don't love yourself, how will someone else?' Riya said, standing up. 'By the way, you dropped some papers in the hall yesterday. I've dried them out.' She held out Amara's divorce papers. 'Let me guess, he's not giving you a penny in settlement.'

'I don't want his money,' Amara replied, wishing she could burn the papers as she had their memories together.

'That's very noble, my dear, but don't forget that you gave up your career for this guy, and your family. You're on your own now. You are homeless. And I'm assuming, penniless. How are you going to live your life and pay your bills?'

'I haven't thought about that. I'm sure he'll give me something,' Amara replied, getting up from her seat, which had suddenly become hard.

'The man wore imported underwear from India to save money. You really think he is going to give you alimony out of the goodness of his heart?'

'How do you know about his—'

'Never mind that.'

Amara continued looking at Riya.

'Fine,' Riya said. 'The day after Tina's birthday. One time only. Don't tell anyone.'

'That's how you knew where his house was,' Amara said. 'I don't know whether to laugh or cry.' Then she was laughing. 'What's wrong with me? Why am I finding this funny?'

Riya started laughing too.

'Remember how much we used to laugh in our childhood, for absolutely no reason,' Riya said clutching her stomach. 'Those days seem so far away.'

Amara laughed, but felt outside of it, for it didn't consume her like sadness did. She agreed with Riya. As a child, happiness had been a state of remaining in the present. Then came loss, due to which happiness came with an acute sense of awareness; it was never whole or in the moment again.

After they sobered up, Riya looked at Amara seriously and

said, 'Amara, I will try to get you at least something that you deserve from this divorce.'

Amara shook her head. 'No, Riya. I really don't want anything from Prashant. The faster I break contact with him, the better it will be for me.'

~ ~

One afternoon, almost four months later, Amara was on the phone with Stacy, who was trying to convince her to move to her place.

'I'm happy here,' Amara told her. 'Riya is taking good care of me.'

'I am worried about you,' Stacy said tenderly. After her return from the Bahamas, she came over to Riya's house almost every other evening after work. 'Can I take you out tonight at least?' Making Amara go out and get drunk was part of Stacy's grand plan to help her cope with a divorce. Amara smiled.

There was a knock at the door.

Amara looked up to see Riya and sat up when she noticed her expression. 'I'll call you back,' she told Stacy.

'What's wrong?' she asked Riya.

'I'm afraid there's some bad news.'

'What?'

Riya sat on the bed next to her and held her hand. 'Well — your mother had to be taken into the hospital today.'

'Biji?'

'Yes, she fainted and fell down the stairs. Don't worry, it's not serious and there's been no injury. But the doctors have kept her in observation for the next twenty-four hours.'

'How do you know this?'

'Mom called me up and told me.'

'But how does she know about Biji?'

'Dad is listed as her emergency contact on the insurance papers.'

Amara rushed to the hospital with Riya, and found Baba sitting on a bench outside Biji's room. She slowed down as she walked towards him, and seeing his bent head and limp body, felt a strong urge to hug him, to keep him from falling.

He looked up with tear-rimmed eyes when he saw her. 'Go see your mother. She needs you.'

'What happened, Baba?' Amara asked, barely able to enunciate the words.

Baba spoke slowly, as if absorbing the information for the first time. 'Last week, she got fired from her job. Patel told her it was because of the economy, but she was convinced it was because of your divorce, which everyone is talking about. After that she stopped eating. All day she'd lie in bed, refusing to talk. She woke up this morning screaming your name, "Amara, Amara" and started running down the stairs towards the door. That's when she—'

Amara held Baba as his shoulders hunched over, and he let out a whisper, 'What is happening to our family?'

Riya brought him some water and prodded Amara to enter her mother's room. Amara had never seen her mother ill and couldn't imagine her on a hospital bed. She entered the room, her fingers touching the wall for support. She couldn't recognise Biji. There were tubes running through Biji's nose and arms, her mouth was covered by an oxygen mask, and her head was bandaged from the chin to her temple. Amara went over to her insensate body and touched her hand. There was no response.

She leaned over her mother's heart and said, 'I am sorry for doing this to you.'

Riya entered with Baba, and said, 'It's past visiting hours, Amara. We have to go.'

'I am not leaving my mother,' Amara said, not taking her eyes off Biji.

'I am here to take care of your mother,' Baba said, his voice as tired as his eyes.

'You can stay here if you want, but I'm not leaving.'

From the corner of her eyes, Amara saw Baba take a step forward. Riya placed her hand on his shoulder and whispered something into his ears. He cast a long glance towards Amara and Biji, before Riya led him out of the hospital room.

Amara sat in the hospital room, motionless like her mother, till shadows fell on her mother's bed, and vanished, only to emerge with the next sunrise. Biji woke up, looked at Amara and smiled, remembered something and turned her head the other way.

'Biji, I'm sorry. Please talk to me,' Amara said.

She wouldn't.

The doctor came in. He examined Biji and told Amara, 'She's recovered quite well from her concussion. We'll watch her for another day, after which, if all goes well, she'll be dismissed.'

Baba came into the room after the doctor left. Amara watched as he fed Biji barley soup, spoon by spoon.

'You have told your daughter our decision?' Biji asked, after finishing the soup.

Baba wiped her lips with a napkin, 'Let's not discuss this right now.'

'What is it?' Amara asked, curious and scared at the same time.

'Now is not the time,' Baba said.

'No, please do tell,' Biji said, unrelenting. 'Tell her that everyday we be treated like failure, like outcast. It have become too much for us.' Baba placed a hand on Biji's arm to calm her but she was inconsolable. 'In our community, we be first unsuccessful immigrants.'

Amara cried out, 'I'm sorry, Biji. You know I am sorry. I'm not doing any of this on purpose.' There was a long spell of silence in the room, as though everyone was absorbing what Amara had said. She wiped the corners of her eyes and said softly, 'What decision are you talking about?'

Baba put the soup cup and spoon slowly back into a brown bag. He turned to face Amara, opened his mouth as if to say something and didn't say a word.

'Baba, you have to tell me.'

'Fine. Your mother and I have decided to leave America. There is nothing left for us here.'

'But where will you go?' she asked.

There was a smile beneath Baba's sombre expression when he said, 'We are going back to Shimla.'

Amara turned towards Biji in shock. 'Biji agreed to this?'

'Since my destiny meant for sorrow, I might as well be sad in own home than foreign land,' Biji replied, still looking at Baba.

They were serious about moving.

And who could blame them? Amara recalled her house in Shimla leaning so humbly before God. She remembered the familiar faces left behind – Shikha Didi, Langda Mr Lula and even Bakshi Aunty. She thought of her favourite parts: standing beneath the pine trees in Boileauganj or playing a game of rummy at a picnic in Glen valley. How simple life had been then, how attainable their needs.

'I have been thinking about moving back too. I miss Shimla. Can I come with you?' Amara said.

'No! What will you do in Shimla? It will be worse for you there. People will judge you even more,' Baba said.

'Yes, what if peoples find out? Remember what happen to Shikha? With the milk and—,' Biji said, before lapsing into a silence.

'If I am already as ruined as everyone says I am, then what do I have to lose by going back?'

'Your daughter will become burden to us,' Biji said, looking at Baba.

'I will not be a burden. I will make you proud of me. Just give me another chance. Please don't leave me here alone.'

'No, Amara. You belong in America with your husband. Your presence in India will make it worse for you and for us,' Baba said.

'Baba, neither America nor my husband have worked out for me.'

'Still, how can you take such a decision without asking Prashant?'

Amara heard her voice rising. 'How can I ask someone who doesn't care to be asked, Baba?' 'It Is His Desire' had ceased to exist in her life. 'Like you, I have nothing left here. All I have is Biji and you. If you leave me, then there's nothing for me to do except—'

A nurse entered their door and said, 'Quiet, please.'

'Baba, Biji,' Amara said softly. 'Can you really leave me here alone? We have never lived more than a hundred miles apart. Can you imagine life without me? I know that I cannot be anywhere without the two of you.'

Baba stared at Amara for a long time. His eyes melted as she gazed back at him, pleading to take her along. He looked at Biji, and Amara saw that Biji was also crying.

Finally he said, 'Fine.' He raised his forefinger to his lips when Biji opened her mouth to protest. 'But you must promise us, for your mother's sake, that you will tell no one about what happened.' Baba was still unable to use the word, 'divorce'. 'You must pretend that you're still married.'

Amara didn't care about any conditions that Baba was placing. He was not abandoning her and that's all that mattered. She found words through her tears.

'I promise.'

'And this not mean we forgive you,' Biji said, still looking at Baba.

'I know,' Amara replied.

'Then get your things ready, Amara. The Malhotras are going back to India.'

# 15

Biji pointed to a Subway restaurant. 'I always want to try one of them sandwich.'

Baba, Biji and Amara were on the way to the airport to take a one-way flight to India. It had been a quiet ride, with Biji sniffling into her sari *palu*, Baba cracking his knuckles, and Amara staring soundlessly out of the window.

These were Biji's first words that day and Amara couldn't help but take them seriously.

'Stop the taxi, please,' she told the taxi-driver. She turned to Biji who looked at her surprised and added, 'I'll get you a veg sub – you really must have one.' They had ample time to spare for their flight, for in his caution, Baba had insisted on leaving for the airport five hours before departure time.

In the Subway line, Amara stood behind an Indian guy with a moustache, glasses and a large haversack on his back. He was wearing brown pants that reached above his ankles. Amara could see his socks though he was standing.

He was telling the server in an exasperated tone, 'I want that—,' he pointed, '—the green thing.'

The server looked at where he was pointing and asked, 'You want pickle?'

'I don't want pickle,' the guy replied. 'I want that.' He pointed to the pickle again.

'I don't understand, Sir,' the server replied, puzzled.

The Indian guy got flustered and said something in an Indian language that Amara didn't follow. But she understood his dilemma and tapped him on the shoulder. He turned towards her with an irritated look on his face, which vanished to be replaced by a wide smile.

'Sorry to interrupt you, but the green thing is actually cucumber and in America they call it pickle,' she said. 'It's not our Indian version of pickle.'

'Oh,' the guy said with an exaggerated sigh. He beamed at the Subway server and said, 'One pickle, please!' He took his Subway packet and turned to Amara. 'You see, I am one week old in this country, so I bungle up loads. But it is so very nice making your acquaintance, Madam.'

As he was leaving, Amara called out to him, 'You know, you could go to this place called McKarma in Manhattan. It will help make your move to America a little easier.' She gave him the address and number, knowing he would be in good hands.

'Okay, I am very much grateful for your kindness, Madam.' He smiled, as a thread of happiness flashed in the blanket of Amara's sadness.

~ ~

As compared to their flight to America, things were starkly different on the trip back to India. Instead of twelve steel trunks with which they had come, they carried back five Samsonite suitcases. Unlike their grand farewell from Shimla, no one came to see them off on their last night in America. Dua Mama had come a week prior to sign papers finalising the sale of their house, and said of the move, 'This is for the best.' Sheila Mami came three days after that, entering their house for the first time (at which point Biji didn't even care about the tarpaulin on the sofa), with a dish of lasagna. A few

Indian Americans, who Baba and Biji had become acquainted with over the last few years, trickled in and said bland goodbyes. As they wrapped up their immigrant life in a few suitcases, Baba and Biji behaved like beaten soldiers of an army in retreat; Biji was either caustic or weepy, while Baba sunk into deep silence, finding it a better companion.

Through it all Amara was experiencing a growing dread. It occurred to her that America, which she had kept at a distance, had finally caught up with her and she could never shake it off. It would remain entrenched in her, forever. As the train for their departure drew close, Amara began to brandish the word 'India' like a cudgel, for India grew in her mind not as a home, but a place of foreboding and mystery, which would mould the rest of her waking hours in whatever way it deemed suitable. Never before had America felt so much like home and India so foreign. When Amara repeated her fears to Riya and Stacy, whom she met almost everyday till she left, both of them — more alien to India than her — tried constructing both her future life and country with much gaiety. They assured her that things were going to be better, and since Amara knew that their words were meant just to soothe, for there was never a way to know the future, she was not assuaged.

As she took her window seat in the plane, settling for a twenty-hour journey, Amara didn't have the energy to accept either the food or water being offered to her by Mrs Airhostessji. Her thoughts filled her, as she wondered what lay ahead after this airplane delivered her to a new life.

She looked outside her window. The world was full of blemishes, a pockmarked paradox. Between two fluffs of clouds Amara would see divinity, a shimmering lake, which would vanish beneath the murky brown of a hard mountain, only to reappear as a glimmering sheet of golden land. The world so big and overwhelming up close, seemed small and harmless from a distance, rather ridiculous in its chaos. And her life was just a speck in this universe of bloated dust.

At 5:09 a.m. IST, on 4 April 2008, the New York-Paris-New Delhi Jet flight landed at Indira Gandhi Airport, New Delhi. India.

They were in India after more than sixteen years.

Baba puffed up like a dandelion. 'We are home.'

'It is so hot. And smelly,' Biji said.

Baba didn't remind Biji that they were still taxing at the tarmac. He led the way, past the air-conditioned vestibule, past the billboards announcing Delhi's swanky new bars, past the luggage carousel area where Biji let the suitcases lie carelessly on the floor as if to say, 'Rob me, I don't care.'

They took a taxi from New Delhi to Shimla. It was nearing spring-time and leaves were still tightly blanketed in their seeds; but it wasn't the weather they noticed. Six pairs of eyes, for all three of them wore glasses now, noticed how much India had changed, the surprise of which was expressed by Baba and Biji. Neon-lit billboards dotted the roads seductively, for they were either of bikini-clad models inducing people to buy Armani or of brawny men in white vests challenging Indian men to don Lux underwear. Cranes in the sky, looming large like birds of steel, dotted the city's airspace. A frenzied pace of construction was underway, sending up abundant dust like prayers to heaven, embalming everything with the smell of black tar. The country announced its ambition with enough noise to shatter the very glass buildings that it was creating.

The taxi clambered up flyovers to touch the tall buildings and speeded down to where the slums lay prostrate at the city's feet. People were everywhere, jostling for space with the roads, buildings and sky, spitting out paan from their Mercedes.

Those brave enough to walk on the road wore stylish western clothing that clashed with the dust and clamour. It's as if I'm back in America, Amara thought, with the only giveaway being the potholes this taxi keeps dipping into.

In Shimla, they were going to live in their old house, or rather what used to be their old house. Seven years back, the Shimla Housing Board had informed them that their building was being broken down and built into a fourteen-floor highrise, of which they were entitled to a three-bedroom apartment. At that point it hadn't mattered to them, for the house had become a place they'd visit only in memory. So they'd left its supervision to their old friend, Mrs Bakshi, who informed them two years ago that the building and their apartment were ready.

After nine hours, when the driver announced that they'd reached their destination – the Shimla bus station – Baba, Biji and Amara looked at each other in confusion. The bus station was the hub of all activity in Shimla, a place where travellers stopped since cars were not allowed to go further, and then hired one of the hundred coolies to lumber their bags. But now the bus station was devoid of coolies and cars zipped past them into the town.

The driver sensed their dilemma. He said in impeccable English, 'I can drive you to your house in Lower Bazaar. Cars are allowed inside Shimla now.'

As they sped through roads not seen before, Amara had a growing awareness that they were foreigners in their own land. America had become as familiar to them as Shimla had become distant. She peered out of her window, not recognising her own town or her own people.

Biji seemed to be provoked by the same thought as she misdirected her anger at the taxi driver. 'He be cheating us, taking us in circle to make extra money.'

'Shh,' Baba said, knowing the driver could hear them. Within a minute they were in front of a McDonald's selling 'pure vegetarian burgers'.

'This our house?' Biji asked, looking at Ronald McDonald with animosity, an American symbol in the least expected place. The driver stopped a man passing on the road, said something in Pahadi, the local language they hadn't heard in almost two decades. He pointed to a building on the opposite side of the road, 'That's your building.'

Where earlier there used to be a run-down 'Snowhite' and 'Pinecone' marking the entrance to the building, now there was a palm-dotted driveway. The building looked fresh and crisp, as if painted recently, bearing none of the grime that Amara had anticipated. A glinting gravel road had replaced the previous part-gravel, part-mud lane outside the building. Boys roamed around with Pringles packets and the girls passing them wore bright red lipstick. None of the girls ate anardanagoli-churan-aampachan-lalimli-rasmola and the boys didn't smoke Phantom cigarettes. It was as if America was following them home. Baba and Biji probably felt the same way, for they turned uneasily to each other like victims who had become aware of a stalker.

They walked skittishly to the security guard manning the compound by way of a CCTV. When Baba asked him for their house keys, as instructed by the building's Managing Committee, he gave it only after checking Baba's ID. The building's walk-up was replaced with an elevator, which they took to the fourth floor. They walked gingerly towards Apartment 4D and stepped in, as if breaking into a stranger's house. The house was no longer a simple structure, but had changed like their lives. The cheap pinewood floors were replaced with mosaic ceramic tiles. The front door opened into a large living room with French windows overlooking the valley. A black leather sofa set with a matching coffee table had been placed at the centre of the living room. Their old belongings, the ones they hadn't sold or taken to America, lay among the new things – the Japanese doll next to the stain-glass lamp, the three-legged wicker chair next to the leather armchair; a blend of the old and new, nothing matching the other, reflecting their state of mind.

They touched each old thing, turn-by-turn, as if paying obeisance. Despite all the changes, it was good to be home.

There were three bedrooms, all of equal size, furnished with a bed, an in-built cupboard and a dressing table with a mirror. Amara walked into a room as if drawn by it and decided it would stay hers.

Biji, Baba and Amara hadn't told anyone they were coming back but within minutes of their arrival there was a knock on the front door.

'It is I,' said a familiar hectorly voice, but with a quaver, as though it no longer got its way. It was Bakshi Aunty, her frog eyes bulging with excitement and her skin stretched under a wide grin. Since her constant companion – Arjun – who they'd heard was married and had moved to Delhi – was not in tow, she'd gathered ample weight to compensate for his physical absence. Biji and she hugged each other tightly, with tears in their eyes, before Bakshi Aunty found the words to say, 'Hello-ji, Amreekan return. I cannot believe you didn't tell me you are coming. I had to hear it from the building watchman.'

She turned to greet Baba and Amara before asking, as per the protocol of a civilised visit, after Amara's husband. There was a collective intake of breath, which Amara was surprised Bakshi Aunty didn't hear.

Biji muttered, 'He on business in America. He come here shortly.'

They closely watched Bakshi Aunty's reaction to see if Amara's 'catch-de-horse-y' situation had been Shimla-whispered. But Bakshi Aunty didn't say anything. Amara saw Baba smile at Biji; the first part of their test was over. But there was more to come.

'No children?' Bakshi Aunty asked Amara.

'Soon, very soon,' Biji said softly, suggesting an impending pregnancy.

'But what brought you back from the great Amreeka to our humble town?'

'I be getting osteoporosis because of extreme cold there. We come back for health reason,' Biji said monotonously, as if reading off a cue card.

No shadow of doubt passed across Bakshi Aunty's face. To add to their growing comfort, Bakshi Aunty brought them tea and dinner, which they gratefully consumed. After dinner, the women stayed up to chat and Amara saw that Bakshi Aunty's penchant for gossip had survived the march of time.

Bakshi Aunty started off, 'In exchange for their shop and house, the Aroras were offered two houses in this building. And guess who moved into the second house? Shikha and her evil jinn.'

Amara should have jumped with joy on hearing about Shikha – whom she had lost touch with over the years – but she was still too overcome by grief to relish the news. Bakshi Aunty went on to corroborate her jinn theory in a three-by-three matrix, as if playing a winning game of Sudoku:

Shikha Got Remarried
To A Widower
With A Son

'What big deal is?' Biji said, allowing her biscuit – no longer apple-jam but Oreo's – to crumble inside her cup.

'Nowadays everyone says, "What is big deal?" But it is too much when people's jinn spreads. You should see what kind of people live in this building due to Shikha's bad karma.' Bakshi Aunty lowered her voice, 'There is a boy and girl living together − in same house − without marriage.'

'You mean they be living in?' Biji asked, barely able to hide her glee that there were more scandalous people around.

'Yes, nowadays they don't marry before staying in the same house.'

They stopped their gossip when Baba entered the living room. Suddenly Bakshi Aunty − since some things would never change − said she had to leave. They saw her off at the elevator. Biji couldn't let her go without asking, 'That young couple, what their parent be saying?' Right then the elevator door opened. A young man and woman were inside, kissing. 'Speak of the devil,' Bakshi Aunty murmured. Biji did a double take, her eyes widening, conveying, 'Is this them?'

Bakshi Aunty stepped into the elevator and greeted the young couple, as they slowly unwrapped themselves from each other. 'Did you see what the girl be wearing?' Biji said, as soon as the elevator doors shut. Baba smiled and muttered, 'Women were wearing skirts in the US too. That time you weren't as surprised.'

'Indian legs be different from American legs,' came Biji's pat reply.

~ ~

The Mikasa silver bowl was placed next to the Bastar statue. A Calvin Klein basso gold dinner set − Biji's most prized collection from America (which she had surprised even herself by buying) − was put next to their old steel plates. Although American culture had arrived at their doorstep, it was jarring to blend the old with the new, especially since the old felt new and the new felt familiar.

Everyday the Malhotra family made new discoveries, sometimes to their horror and sometimes joy. The horrors came when it took a month to set up the internet connection — as their application went from one department to another — or when the water supply went off in the middle of the day. The joys came in terms of Baba's job. He was hired as a partner by a national law firm and put on a salary twenty times what he'd made before leaving India and double that of America. 'This country is bursting with jobs, it's incredible,' he said, smiling enough to absent-mindedly include Amara — to whom Biji and he were still not talking.

For the first time, Biji was proud of her husband; he was finally a success in her eyes. This went wonderfully for her along with the fact that American shows were no longer restricted to *The Bold and the Beautiful* or *Baywatch* or *The Wonder Years*. 'No need to leave India to see Amreeka anymore,' she said. Biji happily relegated matters of the house to a retinue of hired help — a full-time maid, cook, cleaner, as well as a gardener for the four potted money plants — and flung back to her old life in India, watching American and Indian shows, gossiping with Bakshi Aunty and socialising on Mall Road. All she added to her life was visiting the parlour every third day, shopping every second day and watching a movie every week at the Gaiety Theatre. The 'it that shall not be named' of her past life was forgotten, like a slate wiped clean. She didn't acknowledge that she had worked at a restaurant in America or of her 'untouchable day', speaking only of the grandeur of her Green Card or ice-skating at Rockefeller Center.

Baba was hardly home, spending long hours at work, golfing on weekends and playing bridge and Housie every evening at The Shimla Club. Amara's parents were living the bourgeoisie life Biji had imagined for them, but Amara had been cast away, as if she didn't belong in their happiness anymore.

For Amara, neither the neglect, nor the joys or horrors made a difference. Having seen loss and failure, she lived in perpetual fear of disaster. Foreboding lingered by every corner, every telephone ring, and every incoming e-mail. She found herself incapable of feeling anything beyond terror.

There was no definition to any of her days. Amara woke in the morning or noon, whenever sunlight streamed in through the French windows in her room. She knew it was nightfall when dusk stole the light from the thick novels she was reading. She didn't remember what she ate though the cook came into her room with plates at regular intervals. Time remained remote, as did her feelings.

After a while, when she'd finished the Dostoevskys and Tolstoys, she clocked the passage of time by looking out of her bedroom window. Scattered in the valley below were some traditional houses, inclined at too steep an angle for even an ambitious builder to consider them. Spread out on their tin roofs were rows of red carrots, green lemons and white radishes, sunbathing on yellow cotton sheets. She watched women come to the roof in their nighties and oiled plaits and collect the dried vegetables to oil and spice for pickles. These were not women living away from their husband's home, signing divorce papers or mulling over their careers. Yet Amara didn't envy them, for she knew she could no longer be privy to the ordinary life.

In one of these houses, Amara discovered a schoolboy who stood at a red windowsill every evening and waved to her. He wore his white school uniform, and his face, crusted over with playground dust, was clean of judgment or expectation. It opened to her like a flower, demanding only a wave back. This boy gave a central point to her time, which would have otherwise remained undefined.

Her days would have continued like this, clocking in and out, blending into each other, had it not been for Biji who entered her room one afternoon and said, 'My husband's daughter, I decide to lock you inside your room.'

# 16

Since Biji hadn't spoken directly to Amara for many months, Amara couldn't immediately comprehend the nature of her statement. She put down the paperback copy of Kafka's *Metamorphosis* – in which she had found discomforting parallels between herself and Gregor Samsa – and made an effort to get up from the bed.

'I don't understand?' she said, once she was standing.

Biji paced up and down the room, as if she was going to be the one locked-up. 'Lot of gossip going around Shimla. Peoples notice you at home for three month and ask, "Why Amara not gone back to husband?"'

'But I haven't even stepped out of the house,' Amara stated, unable to meet her mother's eyes.

'Yes, but cook and cleaner come to your room everyday. They tell other peoples.'

Amara didn't know what to say to that.

'I lock your room and give you food after cook and cleaner leave. I say to peoples that you gone to Amreeka with your husband, and after two-three month you come out, and say you in Shimla for vacation.' Biji patted down Amara's life as perfectly as beads through a bracelet.

'And we're going to keep doing this till eternity?' Amara asked.

'Don't be sarcasm after what all I have do for you. I lie to

Bakshi Aunty, who be like my own sister, that you be fine and we be fine. I lie to peoples for you everyday,' Biji cried.

Amara saw the rest of her life boil down to cruel isolation and rejection. Her future fell into snapshots of dog-eared novels, lemon pickle spreads and solitary waves to schoolboys. For most people lived their lives as if it were a boat circling a lake, propelled forward by problems and fuelled by petty grievances. Rarely, if ever, did people head on to the sea just yonder, to the wide-open expanse, with sails as high as the laughter that moved it.

'It's time to put an end to this.'

'What?' Biji asked, halting in her tracks.

Amara looked into Biji's eyes and saw her own mistakes reflected in them. She found the strength in her voice to say, 'Maybe it is time for the lies to stop.'

'And who stop them?' Biji asked, her face in a knot.

Amara smiled as the answer hit her. 'It can only be me.'

Saying this, she walked past Biji, past the room and past the apartment. She heard Biji's yells as she waited for the elevator. 'Don't leave house! Peoples will find out!'

Biji was right. Amara almost stopped, but her legs dismissed the idea as she entered the elevator.

'It Is Biji's Desire' would have to be let down.

Amara stepped out into a drizzly day. A shopkeeper was haggling with a customer; a mother hurriedly pulled her child away from a toy store; friends were laughing at a joke; a beggar was singing for alms. The world had come alive again. But after the stillness of the past few months, Amara was overcome with uncertainty. What was she doing? In an act of defiance against Biji, she could end up humiliating her family. Worse, her promise to Baba in the hospital would come undone and he would never forgive her. She wasn't ready for this. She'd have to go back home.

'Aunty,' she heard a voice call out behind her. Before she could turn, a boy in gumboots came and stood next to her. She looked down into a face she recognised – the schoolboy from the window! Her astonishment came in the way of her ability to converse, but the boy seemed oblivious to her reaction. He said, 'I was waiting for my friends. But they are not coming out to play because of the rain. Then I saw you getting wet so I thought you can take my umbrella.'

Amara took the umbrella from his hand, happy that the distance between them had dissolved with this exchange. She said, 'That's very nice of you.'

He tilted his straw-like face towards her. 'You want me to get wet?'

'No. Of course not.'

'Then I'll go wherever the umbrella goes. I'll come with you.'

Amara laughed at his impetuousness.

He continued undeterred. 'Where are you going?'

She had no idea so she said, 'To Mall Road.'

'Good, you can buy me ice cream from Baljee's,' he said and put his hand in hers. Amara was about to admit that she was actually going home, but he tugged firmly at her hand. Feeling braver in his company, Amara began walking with him.

'What's your name?'

'Sanjay. Sanjay Guglani. You can call me Sanju.' Then he said, 'Aren't we going in your car?'

'Car? For Mall Road?' Amara asked. 'I've always walked to Mall Road.'

'Okay. No problem,' the boy said.

That was one of the many clues Amara was about to receive about how much Shimla had changed. As she began walking, Amara looked around at the new Shimla, which had eaten into the old Shimla and spit out an unrecognisable city. Roads were cluttered with traffic, dogs and ritzy shops. Dirt collected along sidewalks, as if the earth had turned inside out. Buildings crawled higher and higher, such that Amara had to crane her neck to see them. Human beings and concrete pressed down on the hills.

Holding Sanju tightly now, Amara shoved past scores of people. 'Is today a holiday? Why's everyone out on the road?'

Sanju shrugged his shoulders and said, 'It's always like this.'

They began climbing up the one-hundred-and-eight stairs to Mall Road from Lower Bazaar. Amara remembered the time when Shikha Didi's 'divorce' was Shimla-whispered in different tongues. Even now she could almost hear a squeak of disapproval from each stair: 'Die-force'. 'Dee-boss'. 'Die-wars'. 'De-horse'. She kept the umbrella low so her face could not be seen.

On reaching Mall Road, Amara got her biggest shock. Everywhere there were people and shops and cars. Wimpled nuns, turbaned gentlemen and over-dressed women in stilettos walked past angry cars with blaring horns. No one strolled nonchalantly, stopping to catch up with friends; people were rushing past each other with their ears pressed to their mobile phones. The singular factor defining Mall Road was its noise, which rushed towards her like an enemy she couldn't fight.

For so many months Amara had been dreading the moment she'd be on Mall Road – imagining the small community of people her parents knew gathering around her, shaking their heads in disapproval at her divorcee status. But she recognised no one here and no one recognised her.

With a long intake of mountain air – not as fresh as she remembered in her childhood – life throbbed back into her veins.

She walked up to Ridge Road hoping to see her old horse-friend Shera or the fritters stall owner who'd made the air thick with the smell of oil and spices. Not one of them was there.

'Where is the sweet-man?' Amara asked Sanju.

'Who?'

'You should know. He sells pink candy on Ridge Road and all the kids love him.'

'Never heard of him,' Sanju said. 'But you can get pink candy in any store here.'

Amara began to ache for a familiar sign of old Shimla. Then she saw the Weeping Willow. Once it had been a gem in the crown of the road, but now its long and slender branches stooped down, as if admitting defeat to such man-made devastation. Amara walked up to it, and spotted an old man, as decrepit as the tree, sitting under its shade. In his hand he held a lit beedi he wasn't smoking. One of his legs was wooden. This was Langda Mr Lula!

Amara was so happy to see at least one familiar person that she almost hugged him. But Langda Mr Lula tapped his metal stick on the tar road, making Sanju creep up behind Amara and say in a small voice, 'Let's go, Aunty.'

Through part faith and part fading recollection, Amara had hoped Shimla would retain what she'd build of it from her memory. But Shimla was now an entirely theoretical concept for her. Strangely enough, Amara's disappointments with her memories of Shimla were offset by Sanju's sheer loveliness. Around him, she became a happier and freer version of herself. She walked with him past some shops she could still identify (thankfully) till they reached Baljee's. The boy asked for a double-chocolate-chip ice cream cone as Amara laughed remembering how orange stick was the only ice cream she'd eaten there.

'You know, in our time we used to buy cream cones from

a man who ran a bakery on his bicycle. He used to ride up and down Mall Road and children would run after him all day long, sometimes their mothers too.' Her smile stopped short of extending into a laugh when she remembered that she hadn't carried any money.

'Gosh, I am so sorry,' she said to Sanju and put her hand on his lanky shoulders.

'It's okay,' Sanju said, digging a hand into his pocket. 'Mom says I should get used to paying for girls.'

'But you're only—'

'Eight,' he said, and thrust out his thin chest.

Amara ruffled his hair. 'I promise you a bigger and better treat next time.'

They walked back and Amara discovered that Sanju lived in her building on the sixth floor. 'But why did I always see you at that old building?'

'That's my Dadi's house. I go there everyday after school till Mom comes back from work.'

Amara reached home with specks of charcoal and sulphur, all pollutants, dotting her body; yet these were nothing compared to the dirt she had expected to be thrown at her. She didn't proffer an explanation or apology to Biji, but headed straight to her room to take a long hot shower. She came out half an hour later, feeling like some part of her old self had been stripped away and she'd slipped into a new skin, just like the city on which she stood.

~ ~

Biji didn't say a word to Amara or carry out her threat of locking her up. None of that mattered, for Amara was not in the mood to be compliant. Happiness was inching towards her like a wave, and knowing how fickle it was, she didn't want to scare it away with sudden bouts of despair.

She began walking around Shimla everyday, as the newness of it all started giving way to a fond familiarity. After a couple of weeks, Amara happened to pass by Baljee's and remembered her promise to Sanju. She bought him three flavoured ice creams and headed to his house. After ringing the bell, Amara was seized by a sudden childish desire to wolf down the ice cream, though she knew she wouldn't be able to take more than a bite, such was her appetite. Fortunately for her, just in time, a woman with short hair and a well-tailored khadi suit opened the door. Amara blinked. A jumble of memories lurched forward, and she looked away, unsure of her own ravaged mind. But when she looked back at the woman, peered closely at her dark eyes and bell-pepper figure, each memory stood up, distinct and articulate.

She said with surprise, 'Shikha Didi?'

'Yes?' the woman asked.

'It's me, Amara.' Amara smiled despite herself.

'Amara? Amara Malhotra! My God, you were a girl when I last saw you and look how beautiful you've grown up to be.' Shikha Didi leaned forward as if to embrace Amara, but with almost two decades between them, Amara became concerned that touching Didi would bring back memories she didn't want to recollect. She moved the bag of ice cream from her right hand to her left, and extended her hand to shake Didi's.

'Oh!' Didi said and shook her hand back. 'I didn't hear from you all this time. I used to wonder where you were.' Amara remembered the stacks of unsent letters she'd written to Didi. They were still with her. 'What brings you to Shimla after all these years?'

'I—' Amara paused. The passage of time and the chasm that had emerged between them compelled her to lie to Didi. 'I've come for a vacation, to help Baba and Biji move back.'

Didi looked bemused before catching Amara's hawkish gaze

and added soberly, 'I heard you got married. Congratulations! Is your husband also visiting?'

Amara cleared her throat before replying, 'He is away on business.'

Didi's eyes squinted but she said nothing. Amara changed the subject. 'I actually came to give Sanju some ice cream. Is he in?'

'No, he's at his grandmother's place. So you're the Aunty he keeps talking about. I was wondering who his new mysterious friend was. What a small world. Imagine that my son's new friend turns out to be you.'

Amara smiled at the coincidence of it all. She understood from where Sanju had got his wit and dry humour.

'Why don't you come in and we can catch up?' Didi opened her door wide, and Amara saw that Shikha Didi's house was laid out exactly like hers, as if lives could be so easily slotted and defined.

'I have to go,' Amara said, making an excuse that her husband was waiting for her on Skype. She turned to go and when the elevator doors opened, Didi called out, 'I can't tell you how happy I am that we met after so many years.'

'Me too,' Amara smiled, as the elevator doors shut Didi out of view.

~ ~

One evening, more than a week later, Amara heard the doorbell ring. Biji opened the door and a voice floated into Amara's room.

'Namaste, Aunty. Do you remember me? Shikha?'

Biji responded warmly with a 'how I forget you?' Normally, Biji would have shunned a 'de-horsey', but Amara guessed that having a divorced daughter at home had transformed Biji's loosely-shaped fixations; they possibly made her feel sorry for having acted out against Shikha.

Amara ran to the door and when she saw Didi and Sanju, a warm fist curled around her heart.

'You remember my daughter,' Biji said, pushing Amara forward.

'Yes, actually I came to meet her.'

'Hi, Didi,' Amara said. She bent down to ruffle Sanju's head. 'Hi, buddy.'

Sanju looked up at her and said shyly, 'Hi.' He looked at his mother and then added seriously, 'I came to say thank you for the ice cream.'

'Which is already over, might I add,' laughed Shikha.

'Please to come in,' Biji added in her warmest voice. Since they'd arrived in Shimla, she hadn't invited a single guest home, save for Bakshi Aunty, who actually invited herself.

Didi entered with Sanju. 'You have a lovely home.'

'Yes, yes. But you have son? Who is father?' Biji asked.

'Biji!' Amara said, putting her head in her hands.

'No, it's okay. I'm used to this.' Shikha Didi sat down on the sofa. 'I got remarried, Aunty. My husband's name is Karan and Sanju is his son from his previous marriage. We had our daughter, Gita, five years back.'

'Husband? Kids?' Biji said slowly, as if mesmerised, though she had already heard most of this from Bakshi Aunty. She paused as if doing a quick calculation and then blurted out, 'But you must be more than forty year then.'

Amara grimaced at Biji's gaucheness, but Didi threw her head back and laughed. 'I know. My life took a unique turn after thirty-seven when I met my soulmate, had a kid at thirty-nine and started my own clinic at forty.'

Amara looked at her in awe. Shikha Didi's shingle bob along with her suit gave the impression of power and strength, though her black eyes remained vulnerable and her frame small, like a woman in a girl's body. After all she'd gone through, how had she pieced herself back together with such perfection?

Sanju looked at Amara and asked, mimicking Biji's nasal twang, 'Husband? Kids?'

Didi asked him to apologise. But Amara bent down to eye level with Sanju and said, 'I want a kid, exactly like you. Maybe I'll steal you away one day.'

'I don't mind, but you have to buy me ice cream everyday,' came Sanju's pat reply.

Biji grew impatient with their banter and interrupted, 'So what bring you to our home?'

'We are going for a picnic tomorrow and wanted Amara Aunty to come,' Sanju said.

They all looked at Amara. 'I can't. I'm sorry. I have to meet someone,' she said.

Biji intercepted her, 'That can wait. Of course she come.'

'Well, let us know, Amara. We're leaving at nine. Please do come,' Didi said, getting up.

After they'd gone, Biji said, in a tone not unkind, 'My husband's daughter, I want you be friend with Shikha.'

'Biji, you wanted to keep me locked up a few weeks back. Now you're telling me to go out?'

'But for one month I see you go in public and nothing happen. Peoples knowing something not right in your marriage, but they not saying mean thing. That is why I also say nothing. And see that lady Shikha. She be die-force, but marry again and have children with no problems. Maybe we not have to hide you anymore.'

'Even if I go, Biji, I cannot spend an entire day with them, lying to them about my marriage and pretending to be happy.'

'We have to lie, that is not choice. You have made promise to Baba. But I still say go. Put foot which is best forward.'

～ ～

Amara went with Shikha Didi's family to Glen, a secluded and tranquil picnic spot, and this turned into more picnics and long walks. Their time together — at Viceregal Lodge, Tara Devi Temple and Summer Hill — was spent playing Rummy, eating sandwiches from silver-foil packets, singing songs, and laughing. The charm of old Shimla resurfaced through the innocence of Sanju and Gita, Didi's warm emotional embrace and the inclusivity of Karan — who with his hawkish nose and pointed jokes was the kind of person Amara had always imagined Didi with. They were personal without asking personal questions, and Amara welcomed their friendship like a life raft.

~ ~

One day Amara made Gita's favourite dish — khir. She went up to their house where she found Didi alone. 'Amara! What a nice surprise. Come on in.' Didi opened her door wide.

'No, it's okay. I came to give you this—,' she held out the khir, '—I made it for Gita.'

'Thanks,' Didi replied, taking the container. 'What are you doing? Want to hang out?'

'I — have to go — talk to — husband.' Didi and she only met around other people; Amara knew her armour would fall to dust if they were alone.

A fleck of suspicion passed through Shikha Didi's eyes as she went on to say, 'Well, I'm sure that can be postponed. There's a coffee place down the street that opened last week. Let's go there. No excuses.'

'Coffee?' Amara repeated dumbly.

'I'll take that as a yes.' Didi went inside the house before Amara could say another word and came back with a purse slung across her shoulders. 'Karan's taken the kids to his mother's. So there's no rush to be back early.'

They walked to the coffee-house, where once had stood an untamed garden and a rusty old pump with dirty water pouring out. After placing their orders, Didi said, 'I feel so bad that we lost touch. I kept waiting for you to call or write. I didn't know where to reach you.'

Amara hung her head, wondering why she'd forsaken a relationship to save a few dollars. 'I wrote, a lot, but never got around to posting the letters. Life got—'

'Overwhelming?'

'Nuh—'

'Look, I know we're meeting after ages. We can choose to spend the next hour filling time up with meaningless words or you can tell me what's wrong.'

Amara's eyes snapped wide open, like a wax doll with long lashes. 'What do you mean?'

Didi opened a sachet of brown sugar for her coffee and said, 'Your mother – who used to openly hate me – is being sweet to me; you're being evasive regarding questions about your husband; you aren't combing your hair or ironing your clothes; you've been here for four or five months and you're wearing what looks like your mother's old mangalsutra. I know the signs, Amara. I went through it for seven years.'

Tears collected in Amara's eyes as she realised that her family's best efforts had come to naught; nothing seemed planned and neat anymore. She tried to salvage the situation. 'I don't know what you are talking about.'

Didi touched her arm and said, 'Do you remember the roses?'

'What?'

'Do you remember leaving purple roses outside my house when I'd just got divorced? You probably don't know what a difference they made. Kindness in times of despair is more useful than kindness in times of happiness, Amara. I want to repay the favour.'

The gentleness in Didi's voice melted Amara's resolve. 'I don't know—'

'Know that you can trust me. Start by telling me how you're feeling?'

Tears flowed from Amara's eyes. In the last year, sadness had pressed down on her in all its fury. Everyone spoke of her divorce as if referring to a long and debilitating illness that common sense could cure; her parents with their focus on reconciliation, Stacy with her nonchalance and Riya with her practicality. In the order of the world, widows deserved sympathy, the dead respect and divorcees scorn. This was the first time that someone had acknowledged Amara's divorce as something that had hurt her beyond repair; a condition for which was needed, not a solution, but plain old compassion.

'No one has asked me how I'm feeling. They don't understand how it feels to hear your heart break. How it is to be lonely and scared, but have no one to talk to.'

'Talk to me.'

Amara hesitated, debating whether she should break her promise to Baba. Then she began to talk and became aware of how fast she was doing it, how eagerly, like winter buds reaching for the first ray of sun. She confessed that she held herself responsible for her failed marriage.

Didi said in an even voice, 'The first thing that you have to do is stop blaming yourself. It sounds like you did everything you could to save your marriage. Your primary fault lies in that you are observing life instead of participating in it. Take responsibility for yourself. Focus on the future, not the past. From now on, Amara, you will have to acknowledge that it will be more painful for you to remain in a cocoon than to fly. After that your life will be your prerogative and whatever happens will be your victory or loss.'

'But I am a failure. I have failed at the only thing I could succeed at.'

'Failure, like success, is a matter of opinion, Amara. Do you know how many things I've tried in life and failed in? Yet I consider my life a success.'

Amara looked down at her cappuccino that had gone cold. The server had made a heart-shape in the froth, which had dissipated, leaving a shapeless form. 'You and I may feel that way, Didi, but people judge me and my family. Indians in the US condemned me. They said I was an outcast. Overnight, my identity changed from Amara – the person, to Amara – the divorcee.'

'Amara, those are people who left India thirty or forty years ago. They're still holding on to the cultural norms of an India-that-was. India has moved ahead. We may not live in a big city like Mumbai where it's easier to declare a failed marriage, but we don't live in a small town either, where it's difficult. Seriously, is it really other people's opinion that is bothering you?'

Amara understood where Didi was trying to lead her, for society's sanction paled in front of her family's. There was a voice in her head that said out loud, 'I have hurt those who love me the most – my parents.'

Didi sighed audibly, 'That was the toughest part for me too. I could have gone through any form of criticism or humiliation alone, but to drag my parents in was unbearable. But I've come to recognise that we cannot always be our parents' calling card. Our parents hurt us, without ever wanting to, and we hurt them, in ways they deny even to themselves.'

'Didi, the most frustrating part is that everyone says have patience, everything will work out. As if it's the only solution that will yield something definite.'

'They are right in ways they don't know. Being patient through a divorce is rewarding.'

'You sound almost happy that you got divorced.'

'It's odd but divorce was the best thing that happened to me. It liberated me from societal norms. I tried to do the ordinary things that people do – getting married, having babies, going to work and running a household. No one said they enjoyed it but they did it out of this deep patronising sense of responsibility, as if living a lesser life in unhappiness was something to be admired. I followed them blindly and ignored my desires. So this energy I had inside me never took shape or became something extraordinary until after I got divorced. Once I was an outcast I no longer did things to please people. I was free to satisfy myself and once I began to love myself, people suddenly loved me.'

As Didi spoke, Amara had the strangest sensation wash over her, like she'd been caught on the brink of a raging storm only to have the sun break through the clouds and shine on her. The warmth sunk all the way to her bones. She could overcome things, be strong. She came clean with her lingering fears. 'But what will I do with myself?'

'Get in touch with what you desire. Think about what you enjoy doing, then go out and do that everyday.'

But Amara had no desires. Her desires were a culmination of what people told her to desire. 'I'm weak, Didi. I'm not strong like you.'

'You're only as weak as you allow yourself to be. Your mind can be as strong as it can be delicate. Just like your body. It can be both a flower and a rock. So learn to define yourself.'

'How?'

'Right now you're defining your world by your weaknesses. Remember when you watch TV, all the channels show you what is believable for them. The news channel makes you think that politicians and terrorists run the world. Pogo channel acts as though the world belongs to children. MTV makes you think the world is full of musicians. Similarly, you have to show people what to take away from you – that is, change the channel you show to others. Don't be scared of declaring the "Amara channel" to the world.'

Didi was right. When things got bad, she asked *Him* for strength not herself; when they were good, she thanked *Him* and not herself. But it was never 'Biji's Desire' or 'God's Desire' or 'His Desire' that had made things happen for her; she had made things happen for herself. She was a fighter from the time she struggled to come to this world, to the time she survived a fifty-foot drop, to the time she moved to a new country and as she coped with a bad marriage. It was always her.

Amara leaned back in her chair feeling lighter and happier. 'I'm so glad to hear all this. But tell me Didi, have things really changed here?'

'To an extent, yes. Take my profession for example. Fifteen years ago, people thought that going to a psychiatrist was for crazy people; now I've opened my own psychiatry practice and sometimes see fifteen patients in a day.' Didi looked around at the scones behind a glass case, the television channel playing Fashion TV and the hiss of steam from the coffee machine. 'But there is a flipside to this superficially modern approach. I won't bore you with that now.'

'Please do. I need to know whether my family will be all right if we come out in the open with my divorce.'

Didi cracked one of her fingers with an audible sound. 'It's not society that you have to worry about. They will gossip, yes, and sometimes you'll have to hear foolish comments. But otherwise they'll leave you alone. There's only one set of people you have to be worried about in Shimla and—'

Amara heard the steady drone of muffled voices in the café come to a hush. She looked away from Shikha Didi to see what the cause of this silence was. Her eyes fell on two young men standing at the entrance of the café. Both wore white cotton shirts, open down to two buttons, with a red stole flung loosely around their necks. They looked surly, as if they had a sour plum in their mouths. Rather disconcertingly, they were looking straight towards their table, pointedly at Didi. For a moment it was as though nothing moved, not even the models walking the ramp on the television screen. The two men turned towards each other and one of them whispered something in the other's ear.

'What are they planning to do?' Amara thought, a hot iron pressing down on her stomach.

The men walked up to a pale-looking cashier, said something to him and turned to leave. Before their feet were out of the door, the cashier announced that the café was closing.

Amara noticed that Didi had become completely still, her white hands holding on to her ceramic cup. Without a word, Didi pushed back her chair, jumped up from her table and walked out of the café. Amara ran behind her. When she stepped out, the warm and sunny day had been replaced by an evening wind. With a few long strides she caught up with Didi.

'What's wrong?' she asked, but Didi didn't reply. Amara followed her, barely able to keep pace.

On reaching the building lobby Didi pressed the elevator button and spoke. 'You must have heard the saying that there's no modernism without barbarism. That's what Shimla is going through. Strip away the young man's face and you'll find an old man's mind.'

'Who were those two men?'

'They are part of a local gang – Pranna – that protects what they refer to as "Indian culture". They're the ones who hurl stones at Hallmark stores on Valentine's Day and shut down discos at ten in the night.'

'Why were they looking at you?'

'They stalk anyone who they think does not fit into our culture. Their sole purpose in life is to make others miserable. The café was shut down because I was sitting there.'

Amara followed Didi into the elevator. 'Don't the police do anything about this?'

'Pranna doesn't directly attack individuals. They exercise their muscle in indirect ways, like at the café. And their chief, Anirudh Sharma, is aligned with an important party, so Pranna has political backing.'

'Have they made your life tough?'

'Yes, but what's cinder in a bed of coals?'

They reached Amara's floor. Didi placed her hand between the elevator doors to keep them open and said, 'Amara, don't worry about what you just saw. You should focus on yourself, not anyone else, especially not Pranna. Find something you love doing, which makes staying here worthwhile.'

'Thanks, Didi,' Amara said, knowing that it was too small a word. Didi would never comprehend what she had done for her.

~ ~

Amara spend another few sleepless nights. This time she was not furrowed under the blanket of her sadness but soaring in a magic carpet to her happiness. And how she flew. She mulled over her ways and errors. Over the last year the three desires she'd grown up learning – 'It Is His Desire', 'It Is Biji's Desire' and 'It Is God's Desire' had ceased to matter. There was a call for a new desire and she could only think of 'It Is My Desire'.

Her life so far lived in fear of others, whizzed before her eyes in the darkness of the night.

Then one day, dawn broke and the clouds parted. The

world reappeared, still there, like a bride, terribly shy, as if awaiting something new, unexplored. Amara opened the window in her room and took a breath of the light-blue morning wind. By the time she walked back to bed, she had made a decision. She opened her laptop and drafted an e-mail.

'Stacy, I have a business proposal for you.'

# 17

On the December of her thirty-first year, Amara opened McKarma's first Indian office at Mall Road, one-hundred-and-eight stairs above her house. The idea had germinated when she'd stood by her bedroom window one night and remembered the Indian guy she had helped at Subway on the day she was leaving America. It struck her that helping others made her happy.

'Why wait till Indian expatriates get to the States?' was Amara's rationale to Stacy. 'Start them off as soon as possible so by the time they're in America they already have a good understanding of American culture.'

Stacy loved the idea. Amara got to work, as this time she had the resources to bring her aspirations to life. Stacy offered to pay Amara seventy-thousand dollars for her previous work with McKarma. 'You helped me start and sustain this business, Am, and I haven't paid you a dime.' Amara used the money to buy a small furnished office, draw up a business plan, hire a secretary and advertise McKarma India's services in local newspapers. After the first ad itself, queries began trickling in.

Amara didn't know how to tell Baba and Biji her plans. She never saw Baba at home, and though Biji was around, she may as well have not been, for she treated Amara as a wholly invisible being. When they first came to India, Amara thought she deserved this treatment because of the hurt she'd caused them, but her patience was wearing thin. She began to feed off their coldness, mirroring it back.

When she found them home together one Saturday, three weeks before McKarma India's inauguration day, she told them. Biji was disapproving. 'Daughter of my husband, if you set up company, peoples will know that you not going back to Amreeka.'

'Biji, people already know that. Didn't you say so yourself?'

'I say peoples *think* something wrong, but they say nothing. But if they *know* something wrong, that you be divorced – full and final, then peoples will say something.'

Amara turned to Baba. 'I had promised you, Baba, that I would make Biji and you proud of me after we came back to Shimla. This is my chance and I need your support for this.'

Baba looked at Amara, for the first time since they had come back to India. Then he turned to Biji. 'Amara is right. People will find out whether we like it or not, Radha. She can't sit at home for the rest of her life.' Amara gazed at him gratefully but he wouldn't meet her eyes again; evidently he hadn't forgotten his pain and humiliation after Amara's divorce. Still, for Ammu's sake he said, 'Amara, go ahead with your plans. We wish you luck.'

This was the first time in her life that Amara's focus was on a career instead of marriage, and she didn't want to be distracted by emotions. So she started her first day at McKarma with no ceremony – alone at nine o'clock with Mrs D'Souza, her new secretary. Amara entered the office through a glass door on which was stencilled 'McKarma' in black with a red dot on top of the 'c'. She passed Mrs D'Souza's desk and opened a door on which was written, CEO. Inside the room – *her* office – was a desk and three leather chairs. She walked towards the desk in a trance-like motion.

She remembered visiting the McKarma office in New

York, after the first few weeks of her marriage, when doing what she loved had still been a possibility. It was a run-down place filled with endless paper and a tired-looking table, manned single-handedly by Stacy and two weary volunteers. For five years after that, she'd worked guiltily from home, against the whims of Prashant and Mummyji. Then the day after Mummyji left their house and Amara was alone and miserable, she'd gone back to the office to find it completely transformed.

As soon as she opened the door she saw a flurry of activity. Thirty to forty Indians were waiting in a lounge area. Several staff workers were walking in and out of the office doors. There was a young receptionist with a stern expression. Amara walked up to her, but before she could ask for Stacy, a voice called out, 'Will you quit wasting time being formal? We have work to do.' It was Stacy, spectacles at the bridge of her nose and stilettos on her feet, looking very much like a New York executive. After giving her a tight hug with one hand, Stacy dumped a few folders in Amara's hands and said, 'Follow me.'

'My, you're bossy at work,' Amara joked, remembering the Sheila Accounting days when she had to wake Stacy from her desk. She followed Stacy through the maze of an office, which now had two conference rooms and four office spaces. Every area was occupied.

'Before you get to work, I have to warn you that things have changed a lot around here. We have become more sophisticated,' Stacy said.

'Sophisticated in what way?'

Stacy kept quiet for a second before adding, 'Actually, we've not become more sophisticated but our clientele has. So we've been forced to adapt.'

'How has our clientele changed?'

'Let's just say, Am, that Indians are not what they used to be.'

'I have no idea what you're talking about.'

'Remember how we used to have a lot of "weeds" and very few "whales"? Let's just say that the equation has flipped completely.' Stacy had created different levels for immigrants fresh off the boat: 'weeds', 'waves' and 'whales'. 'Weeds' were those who had no idea about America; 'whales' were from big cities and knew their way around; 'waves' were in between.

'I'm still not clear.'

'You'll understand in due time. Now let's get you to work. Those people in the lounge want their money's worth.'

Amara had spent a few happy hours face-to-face with clients, wishing that she could do this everyday. But she didn't get the opportunity to work there again.

Now was the opportunity to make up for lost time. She set herself down on her chair and rang the buzzer. 'First client, please.'

Although it had been long since she'd followed the practice, Amara easily slipped back into consultant mode. The clients who came were usually young students embarking on bachelor degree programmes across America. They came with their mothers and wanted advice on a range of topics: American culture, how to apply for scholarships, how to obtain a driving licence or how to get resident assistance. Amara was nervous the entire time, hoping she could steer the course of people's lives in the right direction. But at the end of the day, when all work was done, a sense of exhilaration swept over her.

Four months passed with Amara navigating through 'whales', 'weeds' and 'waves', and many more who even Stacy hadn't experienced. Each day of those months Amara walked back home slowly, hugging the feeling she'd ached for. She began to wear nice clothes again and care about how her hair and make-up looked. The white and black winter passed, opening doors to a yellow and pink spring. It was a period that Amara embraced by working during the day and spending every free minute with Didi or Sanju.

Then one day, Amara reached home from work and entered her room to find that her French windows had bullet marks in them.

# 18

'This is the work of Pranna, my dear. They've seen us together; they heard you were back without your husband, and that you had opened an office here. It's pretty clear that you're divorced. I'm only surprised that they didn't do something earlier,' Didi said.

'It must be an accident. Somebody must have shot an air pistol to scare away the monkeys,' Amara said.

'Maybe it's because there are far too many divorcees now. They probably can't keep pace.'

'Didi, focus. What should I do?'

'Sit tight on this one. They won't do much, except make your life a little uncomfortable here and there. Be alert, don't walk alone – especially at night – and avoid hovering by your window.'

Amara looked out of the French windows, which were her favourite part of the room. She understood then that modern thought in India was gurgling along like a river with two polarised banks. By one bank was an aberrant section of people, who had diverted from conventional norms, and by the other bank were the extremists who wanted to protect society by controlling the aberrant people. The two banks could never meet.

'Well, there's a silver lining to this,' Didi said. 'If you've caught the attention of Pranna, then it's official that you're divorced. In that case, I think it's time you joined our weekly support forum for divorcees.'

'Weekly forum?' Amara asked, picturing a group of bitter divorcees bad-mouthing their ex-spouses to each other.

'This guy – I don't know if you'll remember him – General Talwar's son, Lalit, started it a few months back.'

'Who?'

'I assumed you knew him since he's about your age, but I guess not. Well, he was at boarding school in London and then worked there for a long time. He returned to Shimla three or four years ago when his father passed away. He went through a painful divorce and set up this support group. But it's by invitation only, so you'll have to come as my guest. The meetings are held at Kiara Mansion.'

Suddenly it hit Amara why General Talwar sounded familiar. 'Didi, you want me to come to Kiara Mansion? The same house where I stole purple roses from?'

Shikha Didi joined in Amara's laugh, and said, 'I promise not to tell Lalit.'

'What good will this forum do?'

'I believe it's cathartic. It'll make you realise that you're not the only one.'

But the idea of publicly acknowledging that she was divorced was too much. Amara shook her head. 'I'm doing fine, Didi. I don't need this.'

'Come this once. We have a lunch meet-up this Saturday, so you'll even get free food.'

Didi was more persistent than Amara expected, for she came to Amara's house that Saturday morning and waited till Amara got dressed to take her along.

'I'm really not comfortable with this,' Amara said to Didi, as they walked past their building.

'If you don't like it, you never have to go again,' Didi

conceded, and went on to tell Amara about Sanju's latest antics.

By the time they reached the Kiara Mansion garage, where the meeting was being held, fourteen people were already there. Everyone seemed to know one another. Gathered around a steel table piled high with strawberries and cucumber sandwiches, they were all laughing and talking loudly. Amara noted that many of the faces in the garage looked familiar; she had passed them often on her way to work and had never imagined that they were in the same situation as her. On seeing their smiles and informal gestures, Amara felt relaxed. Divorced people were leading normal lives, she thought. Didi and she weren't the only ones making that valiant desperate attempt.

'Don't stand there staring at people,' Didi said and dragged Amara by the arms towards the group. 'Let me introduce you to everyone.'

Amara found herself face-to-chest with a man and looked up into soft black eyes. She heard Didi's voice in the background. 'Amara, meet our group's founder, Lalit Talwar.'

'Hi, Amara,' Lalit said, his voice deep and thick, like honey in a bottomless jar.

'Hello,' Amara said softly, searching desperately for a smart repartee.

'I can't believe I'm seeing you here.'

Amara turned to glare at Didi. Had she told Lalit about Amara's purple rose antics? Didi shook her head in denial. 'Umm. Why?' Amara asked.

'Well, I've noticed you around, usually on Mall Road, and wondered who you were.'

'She's difficult to miss, right?' Didi added, as Amara turned to glare at her for the second time. Yet secretly she was glad for a diversion from Lalit's pointed attention.

An old man came up to Lalit and told him that the members were waiting for him to start the meeting. Lalit turned to Amara and said, 'I hope to catch up with you later.'

Amara followed Didi to a circle of old wooden chairs and they took their seats with everyone else. Lalit stood at the head and addressed the gathering. Amara was in a state of heightened awareness as Lalit's clipped British accent enveloped her. She noted that his shoulders were gently shaped, slightly hunched, yet he stood tall and burly as if the world started with him. His long nose curled at its tip. He spoke slowly and deliberately, and despite the smallness of his hands, his gestures were firm. There was power in his reserve. Her heart tingled as a sweet thought occupied it – of how infallible Lalit seemed. So when he sat down and his brown corduroy pants lifted to reveal that he wasn't wearing socks underneath patent leather shoes, Amara grinned to herself: Lalit was human after all.

She was concentrating so hard on him that his words slipped off her till he took her name. 'Please welcome our newest member, Amara, who we are very happy to have with us.'

Everyone clapped. Since no one had ever clapped for Amara before, a surge of warmth seized her. All the lingering sour after-taste – of her marriage and divorce, Biji and Baba's aloofness, the dread following the attack on her house – dropped off. Amara's smile lengthened from one ear to the other.

The meeting started. Each member was given a turn to speak as others listened and added their insights after. One member – a shopkeeper, who Amara remembered buying Tylenol from – discussed how he was moving on by taking photography lessons. Another member – Ganga, who Amara had seen by the balcony below her house – said she'd finally consulted a therapist for her pain and isolation. The old man – who'd earlier interrupted Lalit and Amara – expressed how angry he was with his ex-wife for poisoning their children's mind against him. At his turn, Lalit said that things were the same with him; Amara made a mental note to ask him later what he meant. The voices careening towards her showed Amara that her problems were not her own. She was glad that no one had forced her to share her experiences and opinions.

After two hours, the meeting ended, and Lalit stood up to say, 'In an effort to make our group more organised, we are going to assign it a name. Please come with your recommendations next week. Newcomers—,' and now he looked directly at Amara, '—we welcome suggestions on how we can improve our group.'

Amara let out a guttural mumble, which she herself was unable to decipher.

As everyone dispersed, Didi, sitting on the adjacent seat, leaned over and said, 'You haven't stopped smiling since you came to this meeting. I guess you liked it.'

Amara looked gratefully at her. 'You always know what I need.'

~ ~

It was evening when Amara returned home. The joy that had surfaced since afternoon curdled at once. For, sitting in the living room with Baba and Biji, was Bakshi Aunty, along with two men and a woman Amara didn't recognise. In itself it was a funny scene – seeing that the three strangers sat squeezed together on the sofa – but when they all looked up together and smiled (save for Baba whose hand was covering his mouth), Amara was discomfited. She grew suspicious, for Biji was smiling at her with the pretentiousness she adopted on social occasions.

Bakshi Aunty got up from her chair and led Amara gently to an empty chair, which Amara guessed had been drawn out for her earlier. 'Come, come. We have been waiting for you,' she said very slowly, as if Amara was retarded. She pointed to an unrecognisable man. 'You remember my son, Arjun? He has come with his Missus from Delhi.' Without wasting another breath she added, 'And this is Arjun's *very* special friend, Kumar.'

'Arjun! What a pleasant surprise,' Amara said.

Arjun grinned widely when she said that and got up from the sofa to give her hand a vigorous shake. He glanced at his wife mid-way and dropped his hand, aborting Operation Handshake.

Amara tried to quash the awkwardness by saying, 'Your mother told me that you got married last year. Congratulations!'

His wife stood up between them, and said in a high voice, 'Thank you. I am his Missus. Name is Sanaya Bakshi.'

'Nice to meet you,' Amara said and stepped sideways so she faced Arjun again. 'Well, Arjun, what have you been up to?'

'He is working as a chef for Taj hotel,' said his wife.

'That's wonderful. Do you like your job?' Amara asked.

'It has good days and bad,' replied the Missus.

Bakshi Aunty interrupted, 'Amara, you must say hello to Kumar. He has PhD in Sociology, runs his father's air-conditioning business, and is nice open-minded boy looking for nice open-minded girl. He's come all the way from Delhi to meet you.'

'Don't embarrass children. Let them talk alone,' Biji said in a mock-happy voice.

'Oh God, this is a setup,' Amara thought, as she remembered how a few weeks ago Bakshi Aunty had cornered her in the kitchen. 'Your mother told me everything,' she'd said. 'Don't you worry; your Bakshi Aunty will not let you die alone.'

She'd locked Amara in a suffocating hug and Amara was only thankful for the fact that Bakshi Aunty loved Biji enough to forgive Amara for her divorce.

Kumar's mouth opened and these words came pouring out, 'You know, I heard so much about you. My first wife was too traditional, and my second wife was little less traditional but still no modernity in her. I said to myself, find wife who has progressed like our time, independent, own business, lived in great US of A. I said to Mrs. Bakshi, "I am looking for exact like this girl." And see my luck, that time only she mentioned about you.'

'You – you've been married twice?' Amara asked incredulously, for Kumar looked no older than thirty-five.

'Thrice, but third wife, God bless her, committed suicide. Depression. Hereditary depression, you see. It's God's will.'

'And from what I've understood you want to marry again?'

'Oh yes, God disposes, man proposes, eh?' Kumar said, and began a chuckle that lasted through Amara's full minute of silence. When his shoulders stopped shaking, Amara looked around the room. Everyone – save Baba whose head was now in his hand – was looking at Kumar and her expectantly, with their mouths slightly ajar.

Amara knew that her next set of words would determine the course of other such unwanted arrangements, so she spoke slowly, enunciating each word, in a language that would be understood by everyone in the room. 'Man proposes, woman rejects, right?'

Kumar chuckled, but after another full minute of silence, his shoulders drooped before coming to a complete stop. He turned to Bakshi Aunty for help.

'Kumar is very wanted boy in the marriage market, Amara,' Bakshi Aunty said, getting up. 'Don't come crying to me later when you hear that he has found another wife.' Saying this

Bakshi Aunty stormed out of their house, with Kumar, the Missus and Arjun in tow.

'I not believe—,' Biji started off, when suddenly the electricity went off. Taking advantage of the darkness shrouding the room, Amara sneaked into her bedroom and firmly locked the door behind her.

~ ~

A few days later Amara related the incident to Didi, as they walked along Ridge Road, eating chocolate donuts from a new bakery in town.

'Arjun is one guy who really married his mother,' Amara said.

'So you don't want to have a match arranged with anyone,' Didi asked, her eyes studying the donut.

'No. I'm not ready for love.'

'Not even if it's with someone more appropriate for you, like say, Lalit?' Didi asked looking up in mock-seriousness.

'Lalit?' Amara repeated. As his name left her tongue her body tingled. She ignored the sensation, and forced herself to say, 'He's not my type at all. He's far too gregarious and looks like he'd bloat up if he missed a few weeks at the gym. Plus, I can't understand his British accent.'

'Really? You seemed quite enraptured by him at the meeting last week.'

'I was focussing on him because I couldn't follow what he was saying.'

At that point, they heard their names being called out: 'Amara, Shikha'. Amara turned around to see Lalit walking over to them in long easy strides. She wiped away a piece of chocolate she was sure was stuck to the side of her lips.

'Lalit,' Didi said in an exaggerated high pitch. 'Fancy bumping into you here!'

Lalit withdrew ever so slightly before becoming his old, open self. He said, 'Yes, yes. Umm, hi, Amara. We didn't get a chance to catch up after our last meeting.'

'Yeah,' Amara said, her tongue caught in her throat.

Lalit kept looking at her, till Didi said in a falsetto voice, 'Lalit, I think we forgot to make Amara sign the membership form.'

'We did?'

'Yes, remember? Every member has to sign it?' Didi continued. 'We can do it now. Amara and I have no plans the rest of the evening. And this way, you can better acquaint Amara with our group and what we do. I'm afraid I haven't done a good job of that.'

There was a beat of silence than no one disturbed.

Amara leaned over to Didi and whispered fiercely, 'What are you doing?'

'Like you said, I know what you need,' Didi replied softly, her eyes crinkling under a wide smile.

'Sorry about that, Amara. It's not Shikha's fault for bringing up the form. Actually, it's—,' he looked at Didi, '—it's compulsory to fill that form before the next meeting. My place is a two-minute walk from here. We can go over and be done with it right away.'

'Okay,' Amara said, seeing no way out. 'You're coming with us, right, Didi?'

'Well, I just remembered, I have to meet the children.'

'No, you don't. I know Karan has taken them to painting class.'

Didi conceded defeat with a smile. 'Right. Let's go then.'

They walked towards Lalit's house and on entering the gate stepped from a stoned stairway into an oak-panelled living room. The room was spacious and adult. A fire was burning, lending depth to the paintings hanging in rich colours of maroon, hunter and marigold on the walls. Perched against a corner was a tall three-part gold-painted leaf on which was etched the calm face of a Buddha. On the periphery was a patio, separated from the room by a milky sliding door. It overlooked a garden full of flowers and vegetables, which ended when the slide to the Himalayan valley began.

'Growing up, I used to wonder what your house looked like from the inside. It's as beautiful as I imagined,' Amara said.

'You knew my house?' Lalit asked incredulously.

'Yes. The hedges on your front lawn used to grow the most beautiful purple roses.'

'That's strange, because Shikha told me the same thing when she came home the first time. Didn't you, Shikha?'

Amara exchanged a long smile with Didi.

Lalit chimed in, 'What's going on, girls? You look like you have a secret.'

Taking heart from Shikha Didi's smile, Amara said, 'Do you remember a few of your purple roses missing one summer in 1991?'

Lalit's eyes squinted. 'Hm, that does sound familiar.' He brought his hand to his chin in deep contemplation before adding, 'I remember those roses were my father's most prized possessions. I was visiting from school that summer and – oh yes! – he was convinced that I was taking the roses to woo some girl. He even forced my mother to spy on me, while I kept spying on the bushes to catch the thief. What a wasted summer!'

Amara kept looking at him when he asked her how she knew of the missing roses. 'Blimey! You could know this only if you were – you were the purple rose thief!'

Amara smiled in acknowledgement, mildly disconcerted at how open she was being with him. Fortunately Lalit let out a loud laugh. Amara knew she was not going to miss a Saturday meeting again.

~ ~

Voices were heating up as members discussed the action to take against Ganga's husband, who'd allegedly stopped her alimony and moved to court stating he had a character witness who'd seen Ganga cheat on him during the course of their marriage.

'I would never do that,' Ganga cried, and the members joined in, promising to go to the media and form a legal alliance to help her out.

The outcry continued into another hour, when Amara cleared her throat and said, 'May I say something?' The members turned to look at her. 'I – I know I'm not an expert in these matters, but it seems to me that the problem here is not what Ganga's ex-husband is doing but the hurt his action is causing her. I think getting into a long-winding legal wrangle will only deepen this hurt. Ganga, I think you should tell your ex-husband to keep his money. You said you have ample family money and don't need his. So – cut him loose, sever all ties, because alimony is a way to keep a connection with your past going, and if that connection is causing you distress, it's better to end it.'

'It's not that easy to cut loose,' Ganga replied between her sniffles.

'I know,' Amara said. 'But I've done it.' She looked at Didi and Lalit, who'd specifically told her that she didn't have to talk about her experience until she was comfortable. 'I left my husband's city, country, money, everything. I didn't even take alimony from him, though I had the option, because I wanted to end all ties with him, because all he reminded me of was sadness. I set myself free and I'm happier for it.'

'Maybe you weren't as emotionally damaged,' a member said.

Amara laughed, a low sad laugh. Lalit said, 'Amara, you don't have to say anything.'

'It's okay. I want to. Is it less emotionally damaging if your husband doesn't love you because he's in love with your sister?' Her entire marriage whittled down to a sentence. Amara looked at Ganga, and repeated, 'Cut him loose.'

Didi put her hand in Amara's, as Lalit said, 'Let's take a break everyone. We've had a long session. Let's move on to lighter things like the corn puffs Nitin has got. After that, we'll vote for our group's name.'

During the fifteen-minute break everyone gathered around Amara telling her that she was brave, but it wasn't until Lalit's words streamed pleasantly into her ears, 'You're one gutsy lady,' that Amara started believing it.

They began the second-half of the meeting by throwing around names for the group. Three or four suggestions came forward, after which Lalit said in his slow deliberate voice, 'How about "Purple Rose"?'

Amara's jaw dropped before her lips curled into a smile. Lalit looked at her. She blushed, all the way from her tingling legs to her face. The group unanimously voted for 'Purple Rose'.

Amara went back home with Didi in high spirits, a weight lifted off her. Her cheerfulness lasted through the end of spring as Shimla burst into colour with an extravagant display of orange, pink, red and yellow flowers. Everywhere Amara looked — the roads, valleys or sidewalks — there was a blanket of daisies, dancing fuchsia, uniformed dahlias and wisteria. She went for day-long picnics with Didi and her family, going to beautiful spots in Karan's car. She learnt how to drive, practising on Sanju's insistence that he wouldn't go to his favourite Baljee's till Amara Aunty drove him there.

Lalit joined them on a few excursions as Amara grew better acquainted with him. She noticed grey flecks in his eyes that she hadn't seen earlier, and found in his burliness a comfort she could sink into. He was bold and frank when comfortable, and though he had the broad face of a child, his chin ended in a pointed sharpness, lending him the lurking handsomeness, which, from his tales, Amara gathered, women found irresistible. He was a man who carried the rinds of childhood when he played 'mock dumb' with Sanju, but he was decorous and polite when discussing adult matters with Karan. His occasional risqué comments allowed Amara to let go of her shyness, if only momentarily. Lalit slipped under her skin, till in a month's time, she thought she'd known him forever.

One day, during a long hike, Amara and Lalit were walking with Sanju, playing:

*There was a girl*
*So tall and thin and fair*
*Her hair, her hair*
*Was just the colour of ginnnnnn-ger*

Lalit turned to Amara and said, 'When was the last time you had the wholesome American fare of pasta and salad?'

'Well, I think that's more Italian fare than American, but I'm afraid it's been too long to remember the difference.'

'In that case may I interest you with a reminder of the difference?'

Amara accepted Lalit's invitation to a home-cooked dinner the coming Wednesday. Too shy to mention this to Didi, she spent the rest of the week agonising over it all alone, scavenging her closet and reading every online portal on how women should behave on their first date.

When the time came, and her feet found the way to Lalit's porch, she still didn't feel adequately prepared. But when he opened the door, and she saw his beaming face, she forgot why she'd been nervous at all. Her mind was helium light and she left everything she'd learned about first dates outside the door.

They spoke about this and that, the words not mattering as much as the pleasure of looking at each other. After an hour, Lalit served a lovely dinner of mushroom pesto linguini and corn salad. 'I haven't had this kind of meal since I left America,' Amara said, by way of thanks. 'How did you get lettuce leaves in Shimla?'

Lalit winked in reply. 'We timber men are very resourceful. Did you know, the earliest timber men in Himachal used to throw logs into the river from Manali and Kangda and, of course, Shimla, to be transported downstream to Delhi?'

As the candle in the sconces burned through the night, the topic changed from life to food to work to divorce. Amara asked him what he'd meant in her first 'Purple Rose' meeting when he said that things were the same for him, and Lalit spoke about his marriage for the first time. 'I couldn't make her happy. If I spent time with her, she said I didn't make enough money. When I made money, she said I didn't give her attention. After four years, it occurred to me that some women weren't the loving kind and she was one of them.'

Amara thought he was mouthing her sentiments when he went on to say, 'Marriage is the only sacred institution left in our lives. Otherwise all we do is survive – eat, work, play. Nothing is pure anymore.' He paused, then continued, 'What surprises me is that despite what your ex-husband did, you don't speak badly of him. Most divorcees can't stop complaining about the ex.'

'How can you talk badly about someone you once shared your life with? It's as much a dishonour to them as it is to you. Plus, I feel sorry for him. Imagine loving someone else and being married to another person.'

The night stretched on. By the glow of firelight, the clink of silverware and the soft whisper of heavy words, a tingle of pleasure flushed through Amara. This warm intoxication stayed as Lalit walked her home. Amara realised that she hadn't thought of Prashant in almost three weeks, a welcome relief, for he'd been in her thoughts every moment, even in her happiness.

But a rude shock awaited Amara when she got back home. She was turning the key in the lock when Biji and Baba opened the front door. Baba was breathing quickly and Biji's face was contorted.

'Someone threw a rock through your window,' Baba said. They didn't say another word as Amara followed them to her bedroom. Baba pointed to the debris of broken glass on the floor. Her French window had shattered leaving shards of pointed glass at the frames.

'I saw some young men running away when I looked out of the window. Do you know who could have done this?' Baba asked Amara.

'No,' Amara replied. She saw fear and concern on her parents' faces, and the old haunting guilt at having brought trouble upon them came back, along with the thought that she deserved their frostiness.

'We will not let such vagrants terrorise us. I am going to call the police and install wooden shutters outside all our windows,' Baba added.

Amara spotted her tape recorder lying smashed on the ground. She let out a shriek and ran towards it. She opened the recorder and took out a tape, 'Thank God my tape is safe.'

'What be so important about tape?' Biji asked.

Amara looked down at the ground and said quietly, 'Baba is singing songs in this tape. I listen to it so I can hear his voice, since he's not talking to me.'

There was a pause in the room. A soft breeze blew in through the broken windows, followed by a warm gush of air. A hand touched Amara's shoulders. She didn't dare look up. Baba knelt down next to her, broken glass or not. Tears came to her eyes when he touched her head, their first touch in many months. When he hugged her it felt like their first embrace.

~ ~

Amara went with Baba to the police station. She knew as per Shikha Didi's advice that these visits would be fruitless, but she had to try. The first time, they waited two hours and left since they were running late for work. The second time, they went in the evening after work but the police constable refused to lodge a complaint saying the miscreants were probably a bunch of kids playing cricket. Baba insisted on meeting the police inspector, who saw them only the next day. On the pretext of writing a First Information Report, he asked probing questions about Baba's personal life – why he had returned from America, why his married daughter was living with him, and why she was allowed to stay out late at night. After that meeting, Amara was glad that she was heading straight from the police station to Lalit's house for a 'Purple Rose' meeting.

Lalit came up to her the minute she entered the gate. 'I spoke to my friend in the police department. He's going to try and speed up the hunt for those goons.'

'Thanks,' Amara said. Seeing Lalit melted the hardness of the last few days, like a baby's smile melts an iron fist.

'By the by, remember you had suggested that we make "Purple Rose" an open group instead of by invitation? I posted today's meet on my blog and we have new people!'

Amara scanned the garage and her eyes fell on two fresh faces. One of them, a middle-aged man in a blue shirt, seemed to know everyone and was loudly offering legal counsel to Ganga. The other one was a waif-like young girl, her arms crossed around her chest as if cradling a hurt. She was staring at the ground, as if beckoning it to swallow her. She didn't look a day older than twenty; it was difficult to imagine her married, leave alone divorced, and more difficult to believe that she was pregnant, despite evidence of two full trimesters on her.

'She is the saddest pregnant woman I've ever seen,' Amara thought, feeling drawn to her, like one would to an abandoned child. She walked to the girl and extended her hand, saying, 'Hi, welcome to "Purple Rose". My name is Amara.'

The girl looked up at Amara — and although the first thing Amara noticed were her striking green eyes, almost the exact colour of Amara's emerald pendant — she couldn't ignore how frightened the girl appeared.

The girl in turn made a small circle with her foot before whispering, 'I'm Ka – Kanika – um – Bajaj.'

Amara smiled. 'Your last name doesn't matter here. How long have you been divorced?'

'I'm – not divorced, just thinking about it.'

Amara led her to a wooden chair. 'You've come to the right place. We'll try to help you through any problem you have. Come, sit next to me.'

The meeting started with Lalit introducing the new members, after which every member updated the others about his or her life. When her turn came to speak, Amara described what had been done to her bedroom window. The other members were furious. They shouted, 'Those Pranna hooligans are getting bolder. They only do this to divorced women. Do you know that their slogan is "Our Fists, Your Fingers"?' Through all this Amara noticed that Kanika sat with her hands between her thighs, quivering ever so slightly.

After the meeting, when only Didi, Lalit and Kanika were left, Amara went to Kanika with a plate of sliced apples in her hand. 'You look pale. Perhaps you need to eat?'

This time a newfound courage had crept into Kanika's eyes, as she said, 'You were wrong about one thing, Amara Didi. Last names do matter. My maiden last name is Sharma.'

'So?'

'I'm Kanika Sharma, the daughter of Pranna's leader — Anirudh Sharma.'

The plate slipped from Amara's hand, as slices of apple fell to the ground. She looked at Kanika askance. 'So what were you doing at our meeting? Spying?'

'No. Please don't misunderstand me. I'm in a lot of trouble. And you people are the only ones who can help me.' Kanika grabbed her arms. Cold bony fingers touched Amara's skin.

Amara pulled away, saying, 'I'm sorry, Kanika. I cannot help you. No one here can. It will only create more trouble for us.' Amara turned to go.

'My husband hits me,' Kanika said, almost hysterically, and her words gushed out like a geyser bursting from the ground. Shikha Didi and Lalit stopped talking to look at them.

Amara whirled back to face Kanika. 'What?'

'I have to escape from him. I have to protect my child. You have to help me. I have nowhere else to go.'

'What's going on?' Didi asked, as Lalit and she came to Amara. She filled them in.

'Well, we have to give you credit for being honest,' Lalit told Kanika.

'Let's hear her out,' Didi said to Amara. 'And give her something warm. She's trembling in this summer heat. Shall we go inside, Lalit?' Saying that, and ignoring Amara's bewildered expression, Didi led Kanika to Lalit's living room and sat her on the couch. Lalit set a cup of tea in front of

Kanika, wrapped a blanket around her and said, 'Tell us everything.'

Kanika explained, slowly, as if each sentence was burning a hole through her stomach. She was married at nineteen to a stockbroker, Gyan Bajaj, who her father had selected. Gyan started hitting her from the first day of their marriage. After two years, Kanika decided to leave India so she could end her marriage and applied to study Entrepreneurship at Boston University, where she was accepted. To book her university seat and make the advance payment for the first year that started that Fall, she'd secretly sold off almost all her wedding jewellery and gold. She found out four weeks later, in February, that she was more than two months pregnant.

The smoke from the tea hovered around Kanika's hands. The beverage had not been touched.

'Why don't you just divorce your husband?' Lalit asked.

'Gyan is the primary funder of Papa's political campaign to become the Mayor of Shimla. Papa needs Gyan. He'll never let me leave him. It goes against his conservative political image.'

'Have you told your father that Gyan hits you?' Amara asked.

'No. Papa thinks everything is fine between us.'

'Maybe you should tell him.'

'He won't understand. He won't let me leave Gyan and he'll think that I am questioning his decision to marry me off to Gyan. Papa cannot tolerate failure in his own children.'

Amara knew how Kanika felt. 'You may think you can't tell your father, but isn't your husband scared that you will?'

'In politics, every big boss has a bigger boss. If I tell Papa or anyone else, Gyan has told me he will cut the funding and end Papa's political career,' Kanika said.

Amara imagined how overwhelmed Kanika must have been

to come here and risk being found by her father or husband. 'So, by going to the US, you are running away from your husband and father?' she clarified.

'That was the plan. That way at least they would blame me instead of each other. We'd all be happy. But then I found out I was pregnant.'

'So go to America now and have the baby there,' Amara said.

'I sound horrible saying this, but I don't want this baby. I'm afraid to raise a child alone when I can barely take care of myself. It will ruin my life and in this state of mind I will ruin its life. I'm twenty-one. I want to live a little.'

'Why didn't you have an abortion?' Didi asked.

'No doctor would touch me here. They're all scared of my father. By the time I plucked the courage to consider going to Delhi or a big city, it was too late. I was four months pregnant."

'Then leave the baby with your husband,' Amara recommended.

'No!' Kanika screamed. 'He is not a good man. If I'm not there, he will inflict his viciousness on the baby. I may not want the baby but I can't leave it to such a bad fate.'

'In that case, I think your best bet is to leave Shimla before birth, to a place where no one can find you, then give this baby to an adoption agency or orphanage, and head straight from there to university,' Didi said.

'That's a good idea. But I'm due in August so all this will have to happen before I leave for university in September. It will take a lot of planning, a lot of money and I've used up my last resources,' Kanika added.

'Then how will you get by in America?' Lalit asked.

'The first year, as I told you, has been taken care of, and the university will give me a full scholarship for the second year, if I keep a good GPA. Till then, I'll work on campus or at Burger King. It's a risk but I want to take it.' They all smiled at her idealistic bravado.

Amara needed to consolidate her thoughts. She lifted her mug to her lips. Her tea had turned cold. But before she could speak more, Kanika said. 'I have to go. I told Gyan I was with my cousin, Falguni, and he's going to get suspicious. Thank you for listening. You are very kind people. I'll try to come back when Gyan is out, maybe next Saturday. You are my last resort and I beg you to help me.' Saying this, she pulled herself from the couch and was out of the door.

After she left, the three of them looked at each other.

'I feel so bad for her. There must be some way to help her,' Amara said.

'I see girls like her everyday. She's a lost cause. She'll end up staying with her husband and make her life as miserable as her child's,' Didi said, folding the blanket Kanika had used.

'I think that her only way out is to find someone to adopt her baby. That way, the baby will be in safe hands, she'll get rid of her husband and be able to live her life. But who'll get involved in such a complicated case?' Lalit said.

'No one,' Didi said. 'Not with Anirudh Sharma's daughter.'

Amara would have liked to stay back to talk but Biji had asked her to come home early. She walked back with Didi, both of them lost in their own deliberations, especially Amara who thought about how sad it was that while she had always craved a baby, others were trying to get rid of them.

It was good that her mind was clear when she got back home, for Biji was sitting in the living room with an announcement: 'I decide – enough career and going out at all time. I get you married again. Since boy I bring home not good enough for you, we will go to see proper boys.'

# 19

It had started when Amara handed Biji's mangalsutra back to her – 'I don't need this anymore' – and put on her emerald pendant. She didn't realise that Biji saw this as a sign that Amara wanted her own mangalsutra.

So now when she told her mother that she wasn't ready to remarry, Biji – unaccustomed to Amara's defiance – said, 'Not ready? You was ready ten year back? Now when you so old you are not ready? It be too embarrassing that peoples know you are divorced.'

'Would you have felt this way if I was your son, Biji? I'm running my own company, earning well, and if I were a man you would be proud of me, not ashamed.'

'But you not my son, eh?'

Biji went on to say that Bakshi Aunty had recently arranged a *hori kirtan* and *daan-dakshina*, lighting a gold fire to swallow Amara's jinns, during which Biji had donated a gold coin, a goat and a silk shirt to the priest, so he could pray for her daughter's life to return to 'normal'.

Amara knew that Biji couldn't believe that the onslaught of modern thought had aligned itself so neatly with the biggest tragedy in her life, and encouraged by this, she wanted to repaint her family's presence in the social picture, like with her photos. Amara also knew that there was a more pressing reason behind Biji's interest in Amara's remarriage.

Biji was bored.

Baba worked. Amara worked. They both made enough money for Biji to finally lead the life she had yearned for. She spent her mornings bullying the cleaner into gossip, her evenings bullying the cook into gossip, and her afternoons gossiping with Bakshi Aunty. She fired the massage woman who she had been raving about earlier. ('Imagine she take only one *dallar* for one-hour massage.') She fired the driver who she claimed drove her mad instead of driving her around. She fired the *dhobiwallah*, convinced he'd stolen a handkerchief from the pile of clothes she gave him to iron everyday. Then she hired another retinue of sassy drivers and maids and dhobiwallahs, and devoted the same energy into firing them. She moaned about mysterious aches and pains that gripped her right leg, her upper ribcages, or her left toe, while the numerous doctors she consulted declared her 'fit as a pin'.

Biji slept on a mattress of wealth and behaved like a biddy. She wasn't at peace. It was time to interfere in her daughter's life again.

Amara wished she could hit the pause button on her life, or at least have a stop-and-start pattern, like with the Morse code, to study and understand her existence. But even without the luxury of time, she wasn't in a position to further embarrass or inconvenience her parents. So around a fortnight later, when Biji bellowed, 'I will arrange meeting with family soon. Be ready,' Amara stood at the door at nine in the morning, wrapped in a mauve sari (the colour of compromise, for it was neither hot purple nor cold white). Baba was coming too, for he was a loving father, who when faced with 'for Ammu's sake' could not reply in dissent.

The first sacrificial pit, or so Amara thought of it, was a suitor who lived in Jakhoo Hills, whose cosy inhabitants, less than two decades back, were deafened by echoes of

A frank question doesn't always get an answer.

The boy-man got up, muttering, 'My blackberry is ringing.'

On the way out, Biji held Amara's arm. Her nails dug into the underside of Amara's elbow, as she said, 'Our Prashant was too much better.' On finding no reaction from Amara, Biji let go of Amara's hand and said, 'For my sake, blame marriage failure on Prashant. He not here to defend himself.' She walked away in a huff to their car.

They drove to the house of the second suitor, which was stark after the opulence of the previous house. The second boy-man sat between his parents, on a sofa, with his feet and hands close to his side. He lifted his hands every few seconds to rub his sniffing nose. His eyes were red. There was a silence during which Amara braced herself to be asked anything. But the boy-man ran his hands below his nose and said, 'Please call me Chabi.' Amara looked up at him; no one she knew had ever requested to be called a 'key'.

'Why?' Biji asked, her curiosity getting the better of protocol.

'Because I dance like one. I really love dancing.' No one responded; no one knew how. They needn't have worried, for Chabi started off again, 'I will be completely open with you. My wife left me a year ago because she thought I had addiction problems. Four months later I was fired from my job. I haven't found a new job yet.' Amara noticed that he twitched every time he said 'I'.

'Aren't you doing your father laundry business?' Biji asked, trying to make up for her gaffe, like the builder of a falling building.

'He refuses to hire me. But no problem. Amara has Green Card, no? We will go to America and I will do laundry business there. I hear the richest laundry people are there.'

Amara almost sighed out a sense of relief. The scale had tipped back in her favour.

Baba, Biji and she left immediately and headed to the home of the third suitor, a widower who lived across town in Chota Shimla. The third boy-man was well-dressed, soft-spoken and mild-mannered. He lived alone, without any hired help, and offered them ginger tea and cucumber sandwiches he'd made himself. He asked polite questions about Biji's health and Baba's job, even throwing in some vignette about the weather. His conduct was impeccable, as if they were at a tea party. He pleased Biji immensely, for she drew him into a monologue of Amara's good traits and bad luck. He listened politely for a few minutes and then said, 'With your permission I would like to talk to Amara alone.'

'Yes, yes,' Biji said enthusiastically, and when the boy-man's back was turned she put her fingers on her lips, motioning Amara to keep her mouth shut. Amara followed him outside to his balcony. He turned to her and said, 'I loved my wife a lot. Losing her was the toughest thing I've had to deal with. You have a right to know that my wife's memory will always be my priority and I will not be able to love anyone that way again.'

Amara knew her answer before it left her mouth. 'I can't be in a loveless marriage again. I'm sorry but this will not work.'

Biji was furious when they left his house. During the car ride back home she rambled on for a few minutes, 'Three, okay, one of most eligible man I show to her and she say they not good enough.' When she was met with silence, she turned to her husband and said, 'Why you never say anything?'

'I think you speak enough for the both of us,' Baba said.

Biji glared at him. In response he said, 'Haven't you heard the new democratic diktat in our country? According to the decree passed from the young to the old, we have to keep our minds open.'

'We shouldn't open mind so much that our brain fall out.'

Baba laughed, then added seriously, 'Radha, our daughter is an adult. We have to let her decide what she wants.' He smiled at Amara as she smiled back appreciatively.

But Biji was not one to give up easily. She turned to Amara and asked in her mock-sweet voice, 'What you want, Miss Amara Malhotra?'

'I don't know what I want, Biji—,' except a child, a voice in the back of her head said, '—but I do know what I don't want.'

'Hai Ram! I am never going to see the face of my grandchildren.'

Amara saw Biji dab her handkerchief on her cheeks, as though wiping off tears where there were none. 'It's okay,' Biji said, as though consoling herself. 'Oprah say that some women not meant to get married.'

~ ~

Didi laughed when Amara recounted her experience. Amara was sitting on Didi's bed, as Didi came out of the bathroom with a wet towel wrapped around her head. 'Don't try the arranged marriage route as a divorcee,' the older lady said. 'You'll find men who are insecure because they think they've failed, or very angry because they feel victimised, or those at forty who ask their parents to make decisions for them. Most of them carry such emotional baggage that wading through that will be a lifelong chore. The best thing to do is find someone on your own terms. You'll be surprised at how many eligible men there are if you go out and look.' She smiled sweetly then and asked, 'Talking of eligible men, what do you think of Lalit?'

Amara twirled the end of an orange bedsheet in her fingers. 'I try not to think of him. It's all too soon.' She had told Didi of their dinner after it was over, much to Didi's ire.

Didi said wistfully, 'Why do people find it difficult to talk about the things dearest to them? If you don't think of Lalit then why are you at my house, making sure I'm ready on time, when there are still two hours to the meeting?'

Amara picked up a plastic *Lord of the Rings* hobbit from the floor, 'To help you clean up the kids' mess, so you're relaxed before the meeting.'

'In that case don't ever stop!'

Amara turned serious. 'Didi, the person I'm actually thinking about is Kanika. What are we going to do?'

'I don't know. I can't think of a way out for her. Why do you even care?'

Amara thought about it. 'There were people like you who came to my rescue when I needed it. And then there were strangers who performed small deeds of kindness that I couldn't have lived without. Like a man in New York who helped me get up from an alley, or even Sanju, long before I knew he was your son, whose smile I looked forward to everyday. But I've never helped anyone. So I took one look at Kanika and knew I had to help her.'

A little later, when they walked into Lalit's garage – slightly wet, for the first of the pre-monsoon showers had set in – Amara looked around for Kanika. She wasn't there. Amara's eyes remained focussed on the door throughout the meeting; she was barely able to concentrate on the meeting, and she saw that Lalit kept his opening speech to a sentence and Didi didn't contribute her opinions as she generally did with gusto. The meeting ended and Lalit, Didi and she stayed inside the garage hoping to see Kanika.

'I hope she didn't get caught,' Amara said, her fingers knotting the end of her scarf. 'She said she'd be here more than three Saturdays ago.' They stood next to each other, not talking, for another twenty minutes. When it became pointless to wait, Amara agreed with Didi that they should head home. It was only on stepping outside that they saw a tiny figure, soaked to the bone, standing behind the rose bushes next to Lalit's gate. It was Kanika. They ran up to her.

'Are you okay?' Amara asked, unable to see Kanika's face, for – oddly enough – big sunglasses covered it. 'We were so worried. Where were you?'

Through chattering teeth, Kanika said, 'Gyan got suspicious after that day, so I couldn't get away. But he's out of town today. I came to apologise for dragging you all into my problems.'

'Please don't. Why are you standing in the rain?' Didi asked.

'I didn't know whether to come in.'

Lalit grew concerned for the shivering girl and insisted on taking her inside. When they were seated in his living room, he went to the bathroom to get towels. Didi leaned over to Kanika and gently took off her sunglasses.

'I knew it,' she muttered angrily. Kanika's left eye had a large purple bruise. 'Why did he do this?'

Kanika didn't reply. Lalit placed a thick white towel over Kanika. Kanika didn't lift it to wipe herself. He said, 'Kanika, you're safe here. Talk to us. Why did he hit you?'

Kanika said in a voice that seemed to have been sliced open, 'I don't know why. I ask myself that everyday when I sleep with a knife under my mattress, just in case one day he takes it too far. I've tried to fix myself, and fix him. But you can't fix something that's meant to be broken.' She seemed to lose the strength in her body and gripped the edge of the sofa for support. When she spoke again her voice was low and rough. 'Now all that hurts is what's shattered inside me.' She started shaking so hard that her teeth rattled.

Warm tears stung Amara's cheeks. Her own pain, pushed to

the pit of her stomach with time, seemed shallow now. At Kanika's age, Amara had hopes and dreams, so she had enjoyed the innocence of youth. Over the last few months, she had been witness to stories of messy divorces – legal wrangles, gold-digging wives, wife-beating husbands, shattered children, stingy alimonies – and she realised that, comparatively, she'd had a quick divorce, a clean cut, which hurt when it happened, but healed quicker because it was firm and definite. She leaned over and hugged Kanika tightly, wanting to shield her against anything bad.

'Amara Didi, please don't feel sorry for me or I will give up on myself. Just tell me what I should do,' Kanika murmured, looking straight into Amara's eyes. Amara didn't know what to say.

Shikha Didi said, her voice quivering and thin, 'I don't want you to get your hopes up, Kanika, since – and I hate saying this – there is nothing we can do. We want to help, but how can we, given your circumstances?'

Amara watched Kanika and at the black end of her consciousness she saw herself – frail and broken, her fire diminished by the rage of one person. She put her hand into Kanika's cold ones. 'We will help you get to America.' She said this so instinctively that she surprised herself. But as the words hit the air, they gathered strength and conviction; she would make this happen.

Kanika looked up with wonder in her eyes, 'Really? How?'

'I have someone in America who may be able to help us,' Amara said, her words leading her plan of action. 'Before the due delivery date we will take you to a big city, say Delhi. You give birth there and then take off to America. No one can get hold of you then. When is the baby due?'

'Eight to nine weeks from now.'

'What we do with the baby is going to be the tricky part,

but we'll figure something out. This baby is no longer your concern, but our concern. We'll make sure it finds a good home.'

'Not it. She.' When Amara looked askance, Kanika clarified, 'Between my husband and father it's difficult to keep anything legal. They forced the doctor to tell them the gender.' Suddenly Kanika grabbed her stomach and seeing her grimace, they all asked, 'Are you okay?' Kanika smiled at them and in that full smile Amara saw what a happy child Kanika must have been. 'She just kicked. Every time she does this, it's like she's coming to life, but it hurts like hell. See—,' Kanika took Amara's hand and put it on her stomach. Amara felt the strong kick of feeble feet. The kick was as surprising as a tiny shoot growing in the cement crevices of a pathway. Crushed under the foot of the world it had no chance of survival, yet it managed to grow and sometimes even bloomed with little yellow flowers. Amara wondered if she could allow this baby to serve the punishment that awaited it on birth.

Another hand wrapped over her hand. It was Lalit's.

'You are not alone in this,' he said. Although Lalit was looking at Kanika, Amara knew that the words were also directed towards her.

The next day Amara placed a call to the one person in America she knew would help.

'Have you married Lalit yet?' Riya's voice, sharp and pointed across the phone line, asked. Despite not understanding her own feelings towards him, Amara had surprised herself by talking about Lalit to Riya and Stacy. She thought she was behaving like a schoolgirl with a crush, yet – again surprisingly – she relished this unfamiliar emotion.

'You do know that a dinner doesn't mean a marriage proposal?' Amara teased back.

'If I had taken you under my wing in high school, it would

have,' Riya said, and burst into laughter, warm and tender. Amara remembered the first few months on her return to India when this very laugh had helped her through some rough days. 'In fact, I met Stacy at Vermillion for dinner, before she left for another beach vacation with one of her new boyfriends, and we wagered a bet. I stand to win fifty bucks, so make something happen with Lalit before the year ends.'

'I should stop telling you girls anything,' Amara said with an exaggerated sigh.

'Lalit! Lalit!' Amara heard girly voices chant in the background. Shezan and Mallika, she thought, before saying, 'I see the whole world knows.'

'Hi, Ammu Masi,' the girls chanted together, and once again a warm fist curled around her heart on hearing the children's voices. She exchanged some kiddie talk with them before telling Riya, 'I need to talk seriously. Do you have a minute?'

'Of course, give me a second,' Riya said, and Amara heard her telling the girls to continue playing, and the bedroom door shut.

'I guess you heard,' Riya said.

'Heard what?'

'You haven't heard? Well, I thought I'd call you about it, but kept finding excuses to avoid it. Okay, don't shoot the messenger, but I heard that Prashant got married.'

Amara felt a jolt. As the aftershock of the news set in, she realised that it wasn't Prashant's remarriage — which in itself was to be expected — that struck her, but him being brought back into her memory after so long. She remembered how Lalit always found something to laugh about in sombre moments. 'I hope his new wife gifts him some nice underwear.'

Riya grunted. 'I'm impressed that you can joke about this. Sounds like Lalit is doing you good. So, what's your serious business?'

Amara related Kanika's story and situation to Riya. 'I promised to help her, and if I send her to New York to settle in before she leaves for school in Boston, can you look after her, like your own sister?'

Riya sounded serious when she said, 'What I didn't do for you when you came, I'll do for her. She can come live with us anytime. I'll show her around, make her meet Stacy, help her with paperwork, and show her your favourite place – the Central Park Zoo. Whatever it takes.'

'Deal!' Amara said, and then, 'I really don't know how to than—'

'Don't even say the word, what are sisters for?'

Knowing she had Riya's promise made Amara more confident about helping Kanika. She placed another call, this time to a travel agent, and bought Kanika a one-way open ticket to New York.

She paused to reflect over whether she was doing the right thing by sending a young woman to America; the same place that had almost destroyed her. But she realised that Kanika's experience would be better, for the American Dream meant different things to different people.

On doing some research Amara came to the conclusion that Delhi was the right place for Kanika to deliver a baby. The city had scores of private maternity clinics and adoption agencies. Her research got more interesting when Lalit volunteered to help. They spent every evening of the next few weeks together. After she'd wrap up the day's work, Amara would go to Lalit's house, a ten-minute walk from her office, and stay with him until after dinner. During this time, she discovered another happy fact – that they were the perfect working team; for she was organised at filing and recording, while Lalit was good at research and talking to people.

They narrowed in on a clinic, 'Little People', which

seemed clean, professional and discreet. Having been around for a couple of decades had given the clinic foresight to tie up with a reputable adoption agency.

'This is not going to work,' Lalit said, getting off the phone with 'Little People'. 'They assign each patient a doctor and staff, and have regular check-ups. They are insisting on meeting Kanika. But how will we take Kanika out of Shimla? It's much too risky.'

'But this place is perfect,' Amara replied, looking at the photo gallery on their website.

When they consulted Kanika, however, she came up with a solution. She ran a small business making novelty items like lampshades and photo frames from mermaid tears. Her supplies were delivered or personally bought by her from Delhi every month. Kanika could pretend to run out of supplies for a big order, and tell Gyan that she had to leave for Delhi immediately. Gyan was too preoccupied with the plummeting stock market to question the details of her trip or volunteer to come with her. He would however insist on a chaperon, so Kanika said she'd ask her sympathetic cousin Falguni to come along.

Lalit scheduled Kanika's appointment and they decided to meet ten days later at the Shimla taxi stand.

~ ~

It was a soft mist-hung morning. Amara watched the vast hillsides and the snowcapped mountains. Low-bellied clouds scudded in front of her, their white skin gliding across the earth.

Amara stood in a gazebo, surrounded by the bounties of nature. The garden was flush with violet milkweeds dripping from baskets, a red rose-covered arbour, white clematis by the banks and yellow daisies playing with pink tulips in merry-go-round pots. Birds plump with songs in their chests hopped around, from creeper to branch, lending music to the beauty. The sparrows chirped, the koyal sang and the mynah mimicked them all to a crescendo.

Amara inhaled the fertile smell rising from the green of the earth. Behind her, standing by the cedar trellises, Lalit cleared his throat. 'You look spellbound.' His voice bounced around with the chatter of the birds and the soughing of the breeze in the branches overhead. It's a lovely voice, thought Amara, like dewdrops on lilac.

It took her a minute to come fully to herself, after which she replied, 'I am.'

'So am I.'

Amara blushed. She found that she was unable to form a coherent thought. All she was aware of was a tingling happiness at the edge of her hands, her feet and her lips. Everything else was mush.

The rain began. Raindrops fell, big and dreamy and scattered, making the shingles tap-dance to their beat. Without another word, they walked into the house, past the rustic stone path with the curving yew hedge. Amara was surprised her legs were working; she couldn't feel them.

A warm fire sparkled in the living room and they sat opposite it. Amara had come here to discuss Kanika, but the weather, misty and nostalgic, distracted both Lalit and her, drawing them to each other like moths to the eternal flame.

Amara found herself at the centre of her life, her hand on its pulse. This is it, she realised with a warm shock, this, this Sunday in July, as her mind turned to liquid and her only worry was keeping herself from falling completely.

'Shouldn't we be—,' she said, just to hear herself, to know that she could still talk.

Lalit smiled, guessing her thoughts, the evidence of which was everywhere. As his lips came down on hers, she allowed herself to float, like driftwood on a lake, embraced by the depth of water and the expanse of the sky.

She faded away, and emerged again, wondering if this moment was what they called perfect. This was no time to dwell though, as she returned Lalit's embrace.

～ ～

The clouds had stopped sweating the day they left for Delhi, and despite the serious purpose of their trip, they were all in a festive mode. Two taxis were hired, a separate one for Kanika and Falguni so they wouldn't be seen leaving Shimla with Amara and company. Shikha Didi – who came only as Amara's alibi with Baba and Biji – took motion sickness tablets and passed out, while Lalit and Amara spent the journey talking and singing their favourite songs. They left behind the mountains, which seemed to crumble to dust as they got to the plains, and that dust rose to become buildings once they entered the city premises.

They reached late into the night, and met at the nondescript hotel they were going to stay at. The next morning they went to the 'Little People' clinic, which was all they'd imagined. Most importantly, it had a doctor who Kanika warmed up to. When the doctor took Kanika's sonogram, Amara stared at the white and black image of the baby curled up like a cashewnut, holding in her four-pound body all the dreams Amara had about rearing a child. A tear rolled down her eyes. Lalit's hand drifted down on her gently. She didn't want to be seen right now and she appreciated that he allowed the moment to pass with the dignity it deserved.

'Are you okay?' he asked her later, when they came out of the clinic. She said she was fine, and realised that she was not just fine, she was feeling great, really feeling great.

With the day stretching ahead of them, they went to India

Gate, stood right below it and gave it a sharp salute, for it had existed long before they were born and would stand long after their life was over. Then they went to the Bengali market and ordered mounds of street food, sizzling potato-pakodas and spicy chaat, and Amara bought Kanika milk and bananas to eat for the baby. With full bellies they walked around the markets of Connaught Place, where Kanika picked up jars of mermaid tears to show to her husband, and gifted Shikha Didi, Lalit and Amara a jar each of colourful mermaid tears.

Then she called Amara over and said, 'Didi, I want you to listen to something.' She put Amara's face against her stomach. Amara heard a low rustling rumble. 'It's her heartbeat.' Amara put her arm around Kanika's stomach and listened more closely, smiling wistfully to herself.

As a present to the baby fighting so hard to stay alive, she dragged Lalit to a baby clothes shop, and was enthralled by the tiny bodysuits, onesies, hats and bibs.

'This is not very wise, you know. Gifting baby clothes to a girl about to give up her baby,' Lalit said.

'I don't want Kanika to be ashamed of this baby, Lalit. I may be wrong, but the least this baby deserves on birth is clothes on her back.'

Lalit agreed with her by picking up a pink winter jacket for four-month-old babies. 'She'll need it this winter,' he said.

After a few hours of milling around, Kanika grew tired and retired to the hotel with Falguni, while Shikha Didi split to meet a relative. Lalit and Amara continued their tour of Delhi by going to the heart of the city – Qutub Minar. They walked on the laterite ground and stared in awe at the red sandstone minaret beset with beautiful and striking carvings. Seized by a sudden boisterousness they started running around the tiny pillars, and Amara went back to her childhood, chasing someone for no reason, hearing the wind blow in her ears, watching her shadow run ahead of her.

She began to laugh, Lalit fed off that laugh, and they reached a crescendo of laughter that caused them to double over and sit on one of the stone steps facing the fluted minaret. Lalit removed his jar of mermaid tears, filled with colours of brown, amber, jade, lime green, and a rare red one that Kanika had mentioned. He handed Amara a piece, picked one for himself, and held it up against the sun. Amara also let the white light shine through and saw the world taking on hues she had never imagined, a psychedelic paradise.

Lalit turned to her, his face happy and flush. 'The label on this jar says that if you want to make a wish come true, you have to bury one of these in mud.' He dug a little hole in the ground and handed her the rare red mermaid tear. 'Make a wish.'

'Aren't you going to make one?' she asked.

'I already got my wish.'

'And what's that?'

'You were the wish I made when I was a little boy,' he said, his face wiped off the laugh-lines it had just a moment ago.

Amara turned her eyes away, convinced she had turned as red as the mermaid tear in her hand. She closed her eyes, made a wish and buried the glass in the mud.

~ ~

There was heavy rain on their return to Shimla, so they took a taxi to Kalka and then, to avoid mudslides, took the toy train from Kalka to Shimla. During the entire five-hour trip Amara kept her hands out of the window, touching the mist, the ferns and petals unfurling coquettishly at her fingertips.

One stop before Shimla, Lalit, Didi and Amara moved to another compartment, so they weren't seen coming into Shimla with Kanika. A half-hour later they got off at Shimla station, laughing and joking, while Kanika and Falguni walked ahead of them, as if they were strangers.

But peace was never enough. Therefore, it never lasted.

Kanika froze, as if they were in a battlefield and she was the first soldier to be shot. Amara saw a man standing a few feet in front of Kanika, staring straight at Didi, Lalit and her. Five doppelgangers surrounded him, like extensions of his head, but by virtue of the power and strength he exuded, he loomed over them, appearing like modern-day Ravana. His white shirt was open to his chest, he had a red stole around his neck, and a large tika on his forehead, as if he had come blessed for battle. His eyes were the same shade as Kanika's but they did not carry flecks of vulnerability; instead they were sharp and calculating, like the green of cacti. His body was stiff but he turned his neck to the right and then swung it to his left, like a bell ringing in a hurricane.

As realisation dawned on who this man was, a sense of horror consumed Amara.

It was the beginning of a waking nightmare.

# 20

The evening wind swept across, threatening to buckle Amara's knees. A nip in the air chilled her spine. Her blood quickened. She followed Lalit and Shikha Didi's cue, managing to somehow walk up to Kanika.

Kanika started to say something in a high querulous voice. The voice choked on itself when Anirudh Sharma raised the palm of his hand upright, urging her to keep quiet.

His cronies came slowly towards them. Their breaths — levitating like dialogue balloons in a comic strip — were on Amara's neck. They surrounded them. Amara looked at Lalit, rising to his full height, swivelling around as if to scan possible escape routes. Amara was trembling like a leaf, as was Kanika. Then it hit her — the baby, surely they wouldn't touch her. For the baby's sake she had to say something, talk in a reasonable way to Anirudh Sharma, ensure that no harm came to Kanika. When she opened her mouth, her voice lurched to the pit of her stomach, and by the time it reached her throat, Anirudh Sharma had already nodded his head in Kanika's direction. His cronies lifted Kanika and dragged her to a car.

'Papa, please don't hurt them. They're good people,' the girl shouted, before the car zipped away.

Anirudh Sharma didn't acknowledge Kanika's comment, as if she was a bit part, like a tree in a play. Instead he stood rooted to his spot, towering over them. He didn't blink. Or say a word. He shot them contemptuous looks, such that if his eyes were swords they would be hacked into a million pieces. Without warning he turned around and walked to another car. His men trailed behind him, like spilled blood.

For a moment nothing moved. Not the wind. Not the standers-by. Not the cop holding a banana. Unlike life, Amara thought, that has big things and small things, big fry and small fry, big mistakes and little mistakes – violence is never little or big. Administered even in small doses, violence achieves its full effect.

So in the setting darkness, without being a victim of shoves or blows, Amara walked back silently with Didi and Lalit, feeling as if she had picked herself up from the gutter after being lynched.

But there was more, for troubled waters neither reflect the clarity above them, nor reveal the depths below.

Amara returned home to find that her family's shoes, which were usually put outside the door, were slashed, as if they'd been put through a paper shredder. She rushed inside and seeing Baba and Biji eating obliviously in front of the television, sighed in relief. Seconds later a familiar number flashed on her mobile and Didi's frantic voice directed Amara to come to her place. She darted to the sixth floor and saw that someone had made a long deep red slash across Shikha Didi's door.

Then Lalit called Amara to say that all the flowers in his front lawn – including the purple roses – had been crushed.

Amara and Shikha Didi questioned the building watchman who swore he'd seen nothing suspicious. Baba called the police, who said that without incriminating evidence they could do nothing. Amara watched concern crease Baba and Biji's face as it dawned upon them that the attacks on Amara were becoming more frequent and daring.

Amara lay awake that night, wrought with guilt. First, she'd brought violence upon her family by being a divorcee, running her own business and letting her parents house her. Now, by protecting the daughter of a local goon, she was being deliberately disobedient, more so because all this remained invisible to her parents' eyes. What would happen once Pandora's box opened and revealed what she didn't disclose to Baba and Biji? What about Kanika and her baby? What was the local gang going to do with her? How much did they know?

Overwhelmed by agitated thoughts, Amara lay awake till the first rays of sun emerged.

~ ~

Two days later – as Amara was deliberating on whether to go to Anirudh Sharma's house and explain Kanika's side of the story – Lalit called and asked her to come to his place immediately. 'Don't come alone or walk, it's not safe yet. Bring Shikha with you in your car.'

At his house, Lalit showed them an unstamped letter that had arrived in his letterbox that morning. The letter was from Falguni – Kanika's ever-loyal cousin – who assured them that Kanika's situation was not as abysmal as they may have thought. Someone had informed Anirudh Sharma that Kanika was talking to divorcees on the toy train to Shimla and he had assumed that they'd actually only met on the train. The local council elections were round the corner so Anirudh Sharma did not want his daughter to act contrary to his political agenda. Kanika was placed under house arrest in her home and her father had posted a guard to ensure that no one could enter or leave that house without permission. Her e-mails and calls were being monitored, which is why Kanika was unable to get in touch with them. Falguni continued in her curlicue handwriting that though no one suspected their plan, Kanika thought it was 'as futile as trying to win the lottery and as dangerous as climbing the Everest', and hence best abandoned. The letter ended with Falguni saying she'd pass by Lalit's house every three or four days, and check his letterbox, in case they wanted to send Kanika a message.

Multiple reflections caught Amara's attention and dissipated. One clear thought emerged – the baby was okay.

'Let's write back to her,' Amara said.

Didi touched her arm and whispered, 'Ammu, I have to tell you something. I can't help you anymore with Kanika. I've been dealing with Pranna for many years now, but they've never come near my house. I have children to worry about and Karan is insisting I stay low-key. I think Lalit and you should drop this idea too. It's not worth it.'

Amara and Lalit looked at each other. Amara leaned over to Didi. 'I respect your decision, Didi, but I can't stop myself. I've told you already, this is my one chance to help someone. I don't care about the consequences.'

'Me too,' Lalit said. 'I feel sorry for her. I can't turn away.'

'Don't make excuses, Lalit. We all know why you're doing this,' Didi said, winking at him.

Lalit laughed loudly, taking the joke in his stride. Then he said in a sober tone, 'We need you, Shikha.'

Didi paced up and down Lalit's living room for a few minutes before saying, 'Maybe I can help with things that don't require me to be directly involved. Like, if you need ideas for a plan or want me to keep my eyes open.'

Lalit and Amara agreed. Then they wrote to Kanika telling her that the plan would not be abandoned; in fact they were more determined to help her, and would write soon telling her the next step. Lalit urged Kanika to go to her father or come to him if Gyan hit her again. Amara told Kanika to eat right and stay cheerful and positive so the baby would be all right.

After they put the letter in Lalit's letterbox, Amara said, 'Kanika's baby is due in three to four weeks. What should we do?'

'Let's give ourselves a few days so we can think about this objectively,' Lalit said, and they all agreed to do that.

~ ~

The next day, while Baba and Amara helped themselves to a breakfast of semolina cutlets, Biji strode into the kitchen and asked Amara, 'What be your relationship status?'

Amara knew that just weeks earlier Biji and Bakshi Aunty had joined Facebook, a godsend that allowed them to spy on people from the comfort of their living room. They maniacally checked people's photos, commented on their status updates and spent long hours discussing everyone's profile. They tittered about their friends' daughter wearing a bikini in Goa, or Mr Mehra cavorting with a young trainee at his office party, or Mrs Shroff being caught with a cigarette in her hand.

'Biji, what are you talking about?'

Pat came the reply, 'I am being open mind.'

'Open-minded? Why?' Baba asked slowly, suspiciously.

'You only said that be our country's new policy.'

'Great. America didn't succeed in modernising her, but India has,' Baba said. He got up with a jerk and headed towards the front door. 'I am going to play golf.'

'There is storm outside,' Biji pointed out.

'That's okay. I've already been hit by thunder today.'

After Baba was gone, Amara turned to Biji, 'Biji, what's going on?'

Though Biji tried to look interested in her cutlet, her voice was thick and her tone quiet. 'I ask your relationship status.' This was important for her.

Amara knew that she was better off answering her, so she said, 'It's complicated.'

'What complicated? He is too good boy. Timber business, nice looking, only son, all alone in big house. Our families go long way back. Baba's grandmother used to be cook in Talwar house. But don't tell anyone that.'

Though she could hazard a guess, Amara asked, 'How do you know about Lalit?'

'Nowadays we hear about children from Facebook. I saw your both photo in Shikha page, some picnic or something; then Bakshi confirm to me.'

Amara made a mental note to kill Shikha Didi for tagging her photo with Lalit.

Biji continued, 'I send to him friend request this morning and invite him for dinner tomorrow night.'

'You did what? Biji, we're not ready for families meeting and all that yet.'

'What nonsense. You will not get boy like this. Don't let him go.'

Amara looked at her mother, and her guilt caught up with her once again. After what she was doing behind Biji's back, she knew she couldn't deny Biji a simple thing like a meeting. 'Fine, call him.'

'Good girl,' Biji said, getting up. 'I call your Baba and tell him to pick chicken for Lalit. He will be too surprise. When I should tell Baba that you and Lalit are getting married?'

Amara didn't reply, the question fazing her. She opened the kitchen window and took in a breath of fresh air. 'Not before dinner, Biji. Not before.'

~ ~

The word 'dinner' that Biji had mentioned so casually became a full-blown affair, acquiring epic significance. The chicken

Biji asked Baba to get from the market got clubbed with lamb and fish. The cleaner was told to dust and sweep everything thrice. The gardener was cursed for being unable to produce a single flower in their ten pots. The cook, accustomed to making four dishes a meal, was told to whip up fourteen, to impress the future son-in-law. 'He's not our son-in-law, Radha,' Baba implored, when she asked him to bring out the scotch he'd been saving for five years. 'He's seen me before, you know,' Amara implored, when Biji insisted she buy a new silk sari to wear for the occasion. But there was no stopping Biji.

The effort was worth it when Amara saw Lalit at her front door, holding a bouquet of purple roses for Biji and a Blue Label bottle for Baba. Seeing his tall frame loom in the hallway, as if he owned it, made Amara glad that these four walls would bear his mark in the future. And when Lalit smiled at Baba and Biji, giving them his entire smile, with enough left in his eyes, Amara knew he would never repeat Prashant's outright exclusion of her parents.

During dinner Biji fawned over Lalit, laying dish upon dish in front of him, pulling up their common family connection, while skirting around the exact nature of the relationship. She threw Amara long warm looks, to show that her own mother could not get enough of her. Lalit regaled her family with stories about his days in London and his timber business, adding how happy he'd been to meet Amara after seeing her at Mall Road. Baba and he discussed golf and scotch.

After dinner, they had a round of green tea, which Biji insisted on; she'd read it in *Cosmopolitan*. When Lalit accidentally spilled hot tea on himself, Biji asked him to open his mouth and put something in it. Lalit mumbled 'Thanks,' before his face turned sour.

'It is Hajmola, it will help,' Biji said.

Baba let out a soft chuckle and whispered to Amara, 'She is sacrificing her Hajmola for him. I think he is welcome in this family.'

The next day Biji declared that she was no longer looking for suitors for Amara because she was a modern Indian mother who didn't intrude in her child's life.

# 21

'The clinic is ready, the adoption agency is ready, the tickets are ready, her visa is in place, we just have to find a way to get Kanika out of that house,' Amara said that Saturday after a 'Purple Rose' meeting. 'There are only two weeks left for her delivery and we have nothing.'

She saw Lalit and Didi exchange a smile. Lalit said, 'You're talking like a lioness that'd do anything for her cub.'

'And, might I add, completely out of character. The Amara I knew would tremble at such a bold suggestion,' Didi said.

'I've learnt in the last year that life is like a standardised test, it's the smarter person who gets tougher questions because he can deal with difficult things,' Amara said.

'In that case, Miss Smart, how will we make Kanika escape, considering she's being watched, as are we in all probability?' Didi said.

Lalit interrupted her. 'I haven't told both of you something. I've been watching Kanika's house for the last five days.'

'Lalit,' Amara said sharply, her voice thick with concern. 'Why did you do something so risky?'

Lalit looked at Amara. Following a sweet silence, he continued explaining, 'There are two or three men lurking around the house during the day but there is no one there in the night. I think they monitor Kanika's activities only by daylight.'

'That means we can sneak Kanika out in the night.' Amara said.

'And if the elections are round the corner, as Falguni's letter said, we have an advantage as they may not make her escape public for some time,' Didi said.

'But it will look suspicious if we all go missing together,' Lalit said.

Amara, pacing up and down Lalit's living room, suggested, 'One absent person should not arouse suspicion. I'll drive her to Delhi, say the Thursday after next. Lalit, you stay behind and ensure all is smooth here. Didi, you keep us updated if you hear anything.'

'We can't let you do this alone,' Lalit said. 'There has to be a better way. Maybe I can host a big party in my house the day after the escape, which is Friday, which Shikha can also attend, so we have proof that we were in Shimla. I can leave immediately after the party and join you in Delhi. That way, you'll have to manage things on your own for only a day or two, after which I'll be there to help till Kanika leaves for the US.'

They discussed the plan in greater detail and penned a letter to Kanika with the exact information. Amara added a last line to the letter: 'Take care of yourself and your precious child.' Kanika would know who wrote that. They put the letter in an unstamped unsigned envelope in Lalit's letterbox late Saturday and found it gone by Tuesday evening. Early Friday morning, Lalit had a reply. Kanika confirmed the plans.

Over the next five days, Amara checked her watch every few minutes to confirm the date and time. She forgot to eat lunch or dinner, much to the chagrin of Biji, who was making special health food for Amara before 'her wedding to Lalit'. Amara insisted on seeing Didi and Lalit everyday and went over the plan again and again, till Didi inserted cotton buds in her ears every time Amara spoke.

On the designated night, Amara and Lalit left for Kanika's home, dressed in black, in a black rented car, with a number plate covered with a black cloth. Amara's ears hammered as if her heart was in them. If caught, Amara knew it would be impossible for her to continue living in Shimla. She thought of Baba and Biji, fast asleep in their bed, unaware that their daughter, whom they'd forgiven several times over, was not going to Delhi for work, as she'd told them, but to help Shimla's most notorious gang leader's pregnant daughter escape.

They drove half a kilometre to Kanika's house without headlights. Lalit cut the engine and got out. Amara took the driver's seat. The previous night, Lalit had diffused ten or eleven streetlights around Kanika's house with a rock. Shards of broken light bulbs still lay on the ground, glistening. Lalit deftly approached the house.

Amara sat in the car waiting. The car windows were rolled up and her cell phone was on speed dial with Lalit and the police.

Time slipped by and Amara tapped her fingers against the wheel. The weather was cool but Amara, who didn't sweat (unlike her mother), had trickles of perspiration roll down her face, as if her car were parked on a furnace. 'Where are they? What's taking them so long?' she whispered fiercely to herself. She realised that she needed to calm down; anxiety was not an emotion she'd monitored like this before.

After ten minutes, or three hours, she couldn't tell, she saw Lalit and Kanika walking towards the car. Kanika was also wearing black and her head was covered. Lalit trailed behind her with a large suitcase. Amara was surprised at how gaunt Kanika looked, not like a healthy mother but a starving model. Her heart went out to her. She took a deep breath while Kanika got into the passenger seat and Lalit put her suitcase in the trunk.

Amara asked Kanika, 'Did someone see you?'

'I don't think so.'

'Is anyone following us?'

'No.'

The street lamp in front of them was still lit. Without prelude, they heard the sound of feet tapping against the road. Clickety-clock. A long shadow appeared in front of the car.

Lalit sprinted like a deer into the bushes. Kanika ducked her head low in the car seat. Amara thanked God she had some vellum on her face; no one could see her clearly.

Amara heard Lalit shout, 'Move!'

She hit the pedal and the car almost collided with a figure that lurched out of nowhere. She continued to drive and turned around to see if the person was okay. A man was waving a metal stick in the air. His hair was long and matted; his teeth were big and decayed. He was the very embodiment of terror. The reject. The boogeyman. He was Langda Mr Lula and he was smiling, Amara realised, with a warm shock. She saw him in her rear-view mirror, waving his stick in the air, a call for victory, a send-off to their mission.

Amara drove hypnotically in the dark. The only light came from the blinking red digital clock next to her dashboard, and when she looked at it, it was 3:06 a.m. She had driven for more than two hours. She saw the village of Barog loom ahead of them and realised that they were already around sixty kilometres out of Shimla. No one was following them.

She turned to Kanika, amazed that no word had come out of either of them, and asked, 'How are you feeling? Has everything been okay?'

Kanika's voice crackled from the long silence, 'I don't know, Didi. I am so scared. I haven't slept in days. And my stomach has been hurting a lot like something's pulling inside it. I can't feel her at all.'

Amara stopped the car by the mountainside though she knew this was dangerous. 'What happened? Is she okay?' She put her hand on Kanika's stomach, trying to feel a sign of life. There was nothing. 'We need to get you to the clinic fast.'

'We don't have a booking till day-after.'

'I don't care. Something is wrong. I've been feeling it for a week.'

Amara drove fast. Everything passed her by in a blur, as if there were no wrong or right turns. After a while she looked up at the mountain and scanned the treacherous turns she'd negotiated. She understood that the pull of the flatland and the push of the mountain kept her car from spinning out of control on the steep curves. Her entire body tingled. She kept driving – a black car in the black of the night.

Amara and Kanika reached Delhi late next morning, when the sun had spread its mellow orange arms across the plains. They headed straight to 'Little People' clinic, where the doctor took one look at Kanika and immediately admitted her.

Amara followed him to outside Kanika's room. 'What's happening? Is she okay?'

'We're going to do a proper examination once she has changed,' the doctor replied.

'I'm asking about the baby.'

The doctor looked at her for a long second. 'I can't make a decision before we examine Kanika.'

'Make a decision for what?'

The doctor touched Amara on the arm and said, 'Why don't you get some rest. I'll let you know when we have something more concrete.'

'I just want to—,' Amara said, as the doctor went into Kanika's room. She was about to follow him when her phone rang. It was Lalit saying that he hadn't heard anything in

Shimla so Anirudh Sharma was probably keeping his daughter's escape low-key.

'You don't sound happy about this, Amara. What's the matter?'

'It's Kanika and the baby. They aren't doing very well.'

'I'll leave right away.'

'What about the party? We can't let anyone get suspicious.'

'You're right. I'll leave immediately after the party and make sure it closes early,' Lalit said.

Amara sat on a white bench in the clinic and heard Kanika moaning as the doctor and nurse ran in and out of her room. She tried to distract herself by reading the instructional charts posted on the walls, but it didn't work. By afternoon, Amara had chewed off all ten fingernails. She couldn't take it anymore and stopped the doctor. 'You've got to tell me what's going on.'

Maybe it was the look on her face or the tears welling up in her eyes, but the doctor responded, 'There's some meconium in the amniotic fluid and irregular cardiotocography. We're—'

'English please, Doctor.'

'The baby's heart rate is abnormal. She's showing signs of foetal distress. We're doing the best we can to save her. Please just sit on that bench and cooperate with us.'

Amara sat down with a thud.

A few hours later, the doctor poked his head out of the plastic curtains and asked her to come in. 'Kanika wants you to sit with her.'

Amara went in. Kanika had changed into a hospital gown and her skin was the colour of the sterile drapes around her. Amara took the girl's small hand in hers. 'It's going to be okay. Be strong,' She turned Kanika's hand to kiss her palms, when she saw purple slashes on her wrist. Her head jerked towards Kanika. She opened her mouth to ask her for an explanation when she saw that Kanika's upper arm had bruises on them, as if someone had twisted it. The bruises had turned yellow; someone had done this to her a few days ago.

There was nothing to be said.

Amara slept on the clinic's bench that night, not even bothering to stop by the hotel she'd earlier reserved. Lalit woke her up early the next morning, saying he'd just reached. They sat on the bench and only when he forced her to take a bite of the croissants he had bought did Amara realise how hungry she was, not having eaten in over thirty hours.

Soon the doctor declared, 'Kanika's not been taking care of herself or the baby. This is going to be a close call.'

Amara got up. She grabbed Lalit's hand and said, 'Take me to the Qutub Minar.'

During the car ride, Lalit asked her if she was okay. She couldn't reply, knowing that if she opened her mouth, incoherent sounds would emerge, not words. They were there in fifteen minutes, the first of the tourists. Amara walked to the spot where she had buried her red mermaid's tear and dug a hole next to it. She yanked out her emerald pendant and put it in the hole.

'Amara, that's your talisman. You have to keep it with you,' Lalit said.

'The talisman is to make one wish come true for me. And I've made the wish.'

'What did you wish for?'

'It's a wish I'm making for a little girl, Lalit.' She looked one last time at the emerald sparkling in the sunlight and buried it in the hole.

They got back to the clinic, Amara feeling calmer, ready to face any news. The nurse told them that the doctor had begun performing a caesarean on Kanika and the initial abdomen incision was made. Kanika had left instructions with the nurse that she wanted Amara inside the room with her.

The nurse thrust surgical gloves, a face mask and a plastic gown at Amara, and said, 'Scrub your face and hands thoroughly, put these on and then come in.'

Amara washed and changed, and went into the delivery room. She walked up to Kanika and held her limp anaesthetised hand. She glanced at the features on Kanika's face, finally relaxed. How ironic it is, Amara thought, that it's at the operating table, while giving birth to her child, that Kanika is finally looking her age. She observed the rose red blood that Kanika seemed to be swimming in as they further sliced her stomach. Like hurt, rose red had so many variants, dark in the hollows, lighter at the edges and softly granulated under the light. Would Kanika and her baby survive both those things: the hurt and the blood?

Before she could recover from worrying about Kanika, she saw the baby's dusky blue head peep out of Kanika's abdomen. Right before Amara's open mouth – and the overpowering smell of medicines, the loud ticking of the machines, the studied movement of the medical team – the baby came out. The newborn girl was covered in slime and blood, but lay in the doctor's surgical gloves, quietly, as if nothing could faze her.

'She's beautiful,' Amara said, feeling as if something inside her had broken, or been born. There was a strangled quiet in the nursing room.

Amara asked, 'What's wrong, Doctor?'

'The baby has not cried.'

Amara remembered Biji's story of how she had not cried on birth until hot coal had forced her to declare herself to the world. Amara placed her hand on the baby's foot and held it there. 'Don't do that. You may infect the baby,' the doctor said.

'Chance is sometimes more effective than effort, Doctor,' Amara replied. The newborn let out a lone ear-splitting cry. There was a pause as everyone turned to look at her. Then the baby gave a full long wail, not holding back at all. Joy burst through Amara on hearing that declaration of life. 'It is Her Desire,' thought Amara. She wants to live.

'The mother?' she asked.

'We had some scary moments there but she's going to be fine,' the doctor said.

The nurse gave Amara something in her hand, a small glass jar containing a bluish-white two-inch stub. 'What is this?' Amara asked.

'It's the umbilical cord. The mother wanted you to have it.'

~ ~

'I'm going to name her Kiara, after your house, Lalit. Because that's where I met all of you,' Kanika said.

'It's a beautiful and suitable name,' Lalit said, looking at the baby.

Amara walked over to the incubator where Kiara lay sleeping. She rubbed the back of her forefinger on Kiara's long eyelashes, her soft cheeks and down her small arms. How long Amara had ached for such a moment with her own child! She cooed Kiara's name. The baby opened her eyes. Without a sound she held Amara's finger and went back to sleep. The moment froze into complete happiness. Amara knew that no emotion could ever equal what she was feeling now.

She looked over at Kanika, who was advised complete bedrest for three days. Gentle tears were spilling over her face. 'What's wrong?'

'I wish Papa was here to see his granddaughter. He was so excited.'

'Kanika,' Amara said, turning to face the frail mother. 'Are you sure you can let Kiara go?'

Kanika looked at the white sheet where her cut wrist lay. She thought for a long time before replying, 'Didi, my mind has not changed. Do you see me holding Kiara unless it's feeding time? I don't want to look at her the way you do or I will never let her go.'

'Why didn't I see this before?' Amara wondered. She understood Kanika's lanky look and the troubles during her delivery. Kanika didn't want the baby to be born. A stillborn baby would free her of the guilt of giving her up for adoption, of knowing she had abandoned her child, and of living with the knowledge that her daughter was out there somewhere.

Amara heard words – a little hysterical – come out of her. 'How will Kiara survive without a mother? I know you think Kiara will have a better life away from you, but we're all here to help. You don't have to go to America or back to Shimla. Stay here, in Delhi, Mumbai, wherever you want. I'll buy you a house where the two of you can live together.'

Kanika looked at Amara and held her gaze for a moment. 'We've already established that this isn't possible. My father and husband will hunt me down in India. Why don't you just say it, Didi? You want to say something more, don't you? You want to say that I'm selfish. That I'll live with this guilt for the rest of my life.'

'You stupid, stupid girl!' Amara said, walking towards her. 'I'm not judging you. Given your circumstances, you are doing the right thing. All I'm asking is for you to consider that there may be other options for Kiara.'

'I *have* been thinking about this, Didi, every second for the last seven months. You know that, you've been a part of the process. There are no options.'

'Maybe you need to think more,' Amara said, surprised at the anger in her voice.

Lalit came up to Amara and said, 'Let's not upset Kanika right now. She's just gone through surgery.'

He led her towards the door, but Amara turned on her feet and walked to Kanika's bed, 'I'm sorry, Kanika. I have no right to say these things to you when I can't even imagine what you've gone through. I'm just really concerned about Kiara.'

Kanika took Amara's hand and said, 'You're not wrong, Didi. But right now I don't have the will to fight for someone else. I'd rather be selfish and feel guilty.'

'I know. I don't know what's come over me.'

Kanika's laughed softly. 'Yes, you're behaving like an overprotective mother.' And as the words left her mouth, Kanika withdrew her laugh and looked sharply at Amara.

Amara turned her eyes away, and said, 'I'm sure you're tired. Get some rest. I'm going to be at the hotel if you need anything.'

'Kanika,' she heard Lalit say, 'I've called the adoption agency. They'll send someone after six days. That will give you time to recover and get organised before you fly out to America. Do you want me to confirm your ticket for the twenty-fifth?'

'Yes, please,' Kanika said sadly, or so Amara thought. She knew Kanika's mind was made up and it was wrong to ask her to change it when her life was taking off on the path she craved. But what about Kiara? Why did she have to suffer for decisions others had made for her? And wasn't Amara as much to blame, having suggested a plan to abandon Kiara? What could she do to make amends to Kiara?

A bold thought crept into Amara's mind, a thought haunting her since the preceding month, but she pushed it to the edge of her consciousness. Nothing had changed about the circumstances or intentions, but for Amara everything was different, nothing would be the same again.

~ ~

'I think Pranna is on to us,' Didi's thick voice, laden with concern, came through the phone line. 'Today, two men came to my house saying they were from the Shimla Population Consensus Bureau. They asked to see all my family members. I asked them for their ID, but they said they'd left it in office. I looked online and there's no such bureau.'

Amara called home and Biji confirmed the same men had visited her. 'Very polite, but they keep asking to see you. I tells them you in Delhi for work.'

'What do we do?' Amara asked Didi.

'This can only mean that Anirudh Sharma knows that we may have something to do with Kanika's escape, but – since there's no news of Kanika missing yet – he's not letting word out till the election is over in a week. We're safe till then, I hope.'

During this time, Amara watched Kiara constantly. Flaying her arms playfully, kicking her legs, opening her mouth, staring innocently upon the days ahead. She had no idea that she had been born into the world as scrap. A reject. Her fate drawn out for her. Sleeping on the bed, feeding on her mother's breast, bathing in the nurse's arms, resting on Amara's shoulders, gurgling in Lalit's lap; her long journey started with these little trips. Seven days old and it was time for her to take her life's longest excursion from the clinic to the adoption agency.

'Kiara,' Amara thought, 'you'll be told of this trip when you've lived five winters and five summers. You'll try to make peace with the horror of your rejection for another fifteen winters and fifteen summers. For the sixty winters and sixty summers after, you'll learn that no peace will come, for the stamp of rejection has an imprint that is much too deep. Forgive us for gifting you this life.'

'The adoption lady is waiting and she doesn't look happy,'

Lalit said, entering Kanika's room. Kanika was packing a new sweater Lalit had gifted her. Her flight to New York was booked for the next day and she was to stay with Riya for two weeks before her college semester started.

'Tell her to give us five more minutes,' Amara said, stroking Kiara's cheeks.

Lalit looked worriedly at Amara. 'Ammu, she's been waiting for forty minutes now. I can't hold her off any longer. I'll take Kiara from your hands now.'

Amara kept looking into Kiara's eyes, as the girl stared back at her. At that moment, Amara's consciousness had a purity equal to that of Kiara's, full of the abundant hope of a child and the wisdom of an old soul.

It dawned on Amara that she could not let go.

'Lalit, tell the agency lady that she will not have to take Kiara.'

'But that—'

'I'm going to adopt her.'

# 22

Kanika and Lalit turned to look at Amara. 'Absolutely not!' both of them said together.

'Why not?' Amara asked, leaning against the wall for support. She looked at Kanika. 'I've been in love with Kiara from the first time I felt her inside of you. She is the only thing I've ever desired. I will love her more than any adoptive parent, more than anyone else, more than you, if you could. I'll give her a good life. You know that, right?'

'Didi, I can never doubt your capacity for love; look at what you've given me,' Kanika said. 'It's Papa I worry about. He suspects you already. He has made your life uncomfortable, and when he sees you with a baby he'll make your life hell.'

'Ammu,' Lalit added, 'It's not just Pranna. What about your parents? What about Biji? Do you think they'll welcome you as a single mother into their house?'

'I don't care. Kiara needs a mother and I need a child. And we both need love. We'll be fine.' She turned to Kanika. 'If she's with me, you'll always have her in your life, and she'll have the love of two mothers.'

'I cannot imagine her happier with anyone else, Didi, but—,' Kanika said slowly.

Lalit walked towards Amara with small steps. 'No, Amara. Absolutely not. You cannot take such a risk. I will not let you.'

'I've taken risks before, Lalit, and because of them I found you. All of you.'

'Look Amara,' he said loudly. His fists were curled and his breath hard. 'I've been supporting you in everything you've done, even when it was dangerous. But now you're being irrational. You're getting carried away with emotion and I cannot support you blindly when you're doing the wrong thing.'

'I'm doing the right thing for once, Lalit. Can't you see that?'

'You're being so headstrong that my opinion doesn't even matter. All I've become to you is a knight in shining armour and nothing more.'

Anger rose in Amara but she looked at Lalit and saw hurt slapped across his face. She took Lalit's face in her hands and leaned her forehead against his, whispering, 'You know that my love for you will not decrease with this. Will yours?'

'Come on, Amara, that is not a fair argument. You need to be practical. Imagine your future with the kinds of choices you're making. You will not be able to carry this through.'

Resignation crept into Amara's voice. 'I'm tired of people telling me what to do and how to feel. Lalit, we've known each other for a few months. I love you and always will. But I've wanted a child for more than a decade now. Is it right to deny myself what I really want?'

She turned to look at Kanika. 'Kanika, I ask you one question. Do you think I will give this baby all the love it deserves?'

Kanika said, 'Guys, please don't fight over this.'

'Kanika, answer me. Will I not love Kiara as my own and give her a good life?'

Kanika looked at Lalit apologetically and said, 'Yes, I already said that; you'll be great.'

Amara continued, 'All this girl will want growing up is to have someone love her. I will be that love.'

'Excuse me,' a voice interrupted them. A stranger's head poked into the room. 'I've been waiting for almost an hour. I have to go back to the agency now. Shall I take the baby?'

Amara looked beseechingly at Kanika. Kanika did not meet her eyes. There was a spell of silence, before Kanika turned to the social worker and said, 'Absolutely not!'

~ ~

Amara had survived divorce, displacement, loneliness, unemployment and violence, but as she stood outside her parents' apartment door with a baby in her hands, she knew she couldn't take the next step. She couldn't invite into their lives the kind of societal scorn they had worked so hard to avoid.

She also felt awful dragging Lalit with her. He hadn't spoken to her since their argument. After dropping Kanika to the airport the previous evening, they'd stayed overnight in a hotel, and driven back to Shimla at noon in silence. When they reached her building later that night, Amara had gritted her teeth and said, 'I need another favour,' so he'd come up with her to hold Kiara while she spoke to her parents.

But now, outside the door, she said, 'You know, I'm exhausted. It's been a long car ride, dropping Kanika to the airport, getting no sleep the whole night, driving up the hills with a baby. I'll tell them later.' She looked at Lalit knowing she deserved to hear him say, 'I told you so.' Instead he took Kiara from her hands, rang the doorbell and said, 'You are doing this now.' He vanished in the darkness of the passageway and Amara knew she was alone.

Baba opened the door. 'You're back. How was the trip? Were the clients happy?'

'Who there?' Biji's voice came from their TV room.

'Ammu,' Baba replied.

'Then why you are missing this scene? Heroine about to be murdered.'

'Let's catch up in a bit. We're watching that silly show your mother's got me addicted to, and right now the blind daughter has got into a fight for her family,' Baba said, and ran into the TV room.

Amara followed Baba skittishly. At that moment they were devouring the very values − of fighting for the family − that she was going against. Maybe she would tell them after the show. But what would Lalit do with Kiara till then? She had to tell them now, she determined ruefully. After all, the worst news never came with a prelude.

She entered their room with the guilt of a devotee wearing shoes inside a temple. She walked over to the television and turned it off.

'What you are doing?' Biji snapped.

'Sorry. I'm sure there will be re-runs of this tomorrow. I have to talk to you about something important.'

'Good news?' asked Biji, the eternal marriage optimist.

'Depends.'

'Shall I call priest to fix date?'

'No. I'm not getting married.'

Amara knew if she looked into their eyes, especially Baba's, she would weaken. So she focussed on the carpet and said, 'I know it has been tough on all of us because of me, and I want you to know that I appreciate both of you taking me in against all odds. But now something new and unexpected has presented itself, and because of that, what I'm going to ask of you is more, and maybe too much.'

She watched Baba and Biji turn to look at each other. After living through a nightmare, her family lived in a perpetual expectation of bad news, anticipating being swamped in the tsunami of bad luck. What could she say to protect them from the shock of her disclosure? She gave the situation a last thought; she had been musing over the words she would choose for the last two days, and knew there was no way to explain this except directly. She found her voice again. 'You know I've always wanted a child – and you, a grandchild. I haven't been able to fulfil this in the traditional sense, but during my trip to Delhi I decided to adopt a baby.'

'What?' someone said, or both of them, she wasn't sure because of the intensity of that word, the fact that it swallowed all the noise in the room, even their breathing and the nervous tick of the clock.

Biji and Baba both looked so shocked, Amara could cry.

Biji broke the silence and Amara almost admired her at that moment. Her own voice had become a desert, dry and mute, and she could tell by Baba's turned-down lips that he too had retreated and was looking inward. 'By God! You have gone mad? We give you freedom and you betray us doing this type of thing? Have you not given to us enough headache? Have you not put us through enough?'

Amara let Biji's angry babble continue, till her mind gathered shells of thoughts back. Her parents had been placated under situations where it was more difficult to come to an understanding. She had to make them see her point of view.

'We not deserve this,' Biji said.

'I know you don't,' Amara finally said. 'But do you remember how much you craved for a child before I was born? I feel the same way. Both of you should understand my desire to have a child.'

'Your desire? What about God's desire or our desire?'

'This is the only thing I have ever wanted. Please understand where I come from.'

'And Lalit? He will not look you again if you say to him that you take someone else child. You want to lose him also?'

'Lalit knows everything and he supports me,' Amara lied.

Baba spoke and his tone was mild and genial, as if the shock hadn't set in as yet. 'Ammu, have you considered the consequences of this adoption? What are we going to tell people? What about those scoundrels who have been harassing you? They will make not only your life hell, but also ours and the baby's.'

'I am not concerned with people or those goons. I love this baby and I want to give her the life she deserves.'

'Whose baby it is?' Biji asked.

Amara had never faced a more ill-timed question in her life. She looked from Baba's face to Biji's, with the strongest urge to lie. But they didn't deserve it. Slowly, she explained the whole story to them. Amara watched with horror as curtains drew upon their faces and their expressions grew distant. There was a heavy silence in the room, as if they were watching a play and the heroine had walked off in the middle of a crescendo, leaving the audience aghast. Even Biji lost her usual hold over words.

'Have you thought about what Anirudh Sharma will do when he finds out that you've adopted his grandchild? Do you want to invite violence and louts into our house? I am sorry, Amara, but we cannot accept this baby,' Baba said, finally.

Amara hung her head, allowing the silence to enclose her. Baba was right. Then she thought of her beautiful baby and the strong protectiveness of a mother took control of her. She would mortgage her life for Kiara. 'If there is no place for my daughter and me in this house, then I'll leave.' Amara turned around and left the house.

Outside, she met Lalit's eyes and without having to pronounce it, he knew.

'You may go,' she said, tears filling her eyes like steam by the rim of a teacup. She didn't know where to take Kiara. She could go to Shikha Didi's house now, since Lalit was upset with her. But after that? She made mental calculations of rental prices of one-bedroom apartments around her office.

'No,' Lalit said, and before Amara could gather what he was doing, he strode into the house with Kiara in his arms. She ran behind him. Biji and Baba looked up from the sofa they were quietly sitting on. If they were surprised to see Lalit, they didn't show it; their faces were devoid of any emotion.

'Sir,' Lalit said to Baba. 'You have to learn to trust Amara. She is trying to do the best she can. She loves both of you and she will not be able to stand losing you again.'

'Son, we supported her through her first mistake, but we cannot watch our daughter destroy her life for the second time,' Baba said.

'She's not destroying her life, Sir. She's making it. We should all support her.'

'Lalit, it's easy to talk when it's not your family and you don't have to watch someone you love throw away the life you're giving them,' Baba said.

'Amara means more to me than family, Sir.'

'Words are easy, Son. It's the actions that are difficult.'

'In that case, if Amara wishes, I can put my words on paper by making her my wife.'

A cry of astonished jubilation rang through the room, before Amara even registered what Lalit had said. Biji ran towards him and twirled both her palms in blessing around his head. 'May God bless you with hundred children.'

'We will not need a hundred. This one is enough,' Lalit said.

Baba walked over to Lalit and hugged him, and then, shy about his display of emotion, he patted him on the back. Kiara woke up with all the excitement around her and let out a small cry.

'That be the baby?' Biji asked. She looked at Kiara bundled in a blanket. 'You wrap her too tight. Give her to me.' She took Kiara over to the sofa and re-tied her blanket. She smiled, muttering, 'She look just like Amara when she was baby.'

Lalit turned to Amara. Amara tried to smile but only partly succeeded. Without saying another word, they left Kiara with Baba and Biji and walked outside the front door.

'Lalit, thanks but there was no need to lie like that,' she said.

'Amara, I meant what I said in there. I know it's not very romantic to propose in front of the parents, and I know it's premature, but I love you. If I hadn't proposed today, I would have in a few months,' Lalit said. He rubbed his palms together in nervousness. 'Anyway, what do you say?'

Before she could say anything, Amara's phone rang. It was Kanika, calling to say that she had reached. 'I love it here. I feel so alive. And free.'

Amara remembered that during the drive to the airport the previous evening, Kanika had rolled down her window and stuck her fingers outside, aimed to the sky. The night wind whistled in Amara's ears. Kanika's voice, as high as the sky she was looking into, said, 'My fingertips are tingling. Is this what freedom feels like?'

'Yes, this is what freedom feels like,' Amara replied, taking Kanika's free hand in hers. Though America had not been a place of freedom for Amara, it would be for Kanika, Amara realised.

Kanika's voice turned serious on the phone line. 'What about Kiara and you — are you safe? Have you told your parents?' Amara assured her that all was well. 'And Papa? Any news of my escape?'

'There's a rumour that you've flown to Geneva, some say Sri Lanka, for your delivery. Shikha Didi was clever at planting that idea in people's head. But otherwise, nothing. The election is on its last leg, so I guess your father is waiting till after it's over.'

She heard Riya clucking in the background, a mother hen to three children now. She confirmed Kanika's state of joy when she took the phone from her. 'Kanika is as excited as a kid.'

'She is a kid. A wonderful kid,' Amara said.

She hung up to hear Lalit ask, 'So, what do you say about marrying me?'

Amara remembered her time in Manhattan — when she used to look out of her window every evening at the loving man who came home to a woman and their baby; the only thing Amara had ever been jealous of.

'But that was *their* life, and this is mine,' she thought now.

She couldn't meet Lalit's eyes. 'You are such a good boyfriend, Lalit. I don't know what I'd do without you.' She stood on her toes and hugged him, her arms around his shoulder, her face so he couldn't see it. After a moment, she looked into his eyes to find a pensive look flash across them.

Lalit scanned her face for something, and his expression changed, from confusion to consternation and, finally, to resignation.

~ ~

Early one morning, with the smile of the dawn behind her and the smile of her child in front of her, Amara sat by the window, phone cradled in her hand, working from home. When Baba had advised her to stay indoors for her own safety, she didn't protest, but took the chance to be wholly devoured by motherhood. The apartment became her sanctum for the second time, but this time she loved it.

She was e-mailing a client, 'No, Kismet. H1N1 is not a visa class,' when there was a call on her mobile phone from her secretary, Mrs D'Souza.

'Come to the office at once. I came in and – they're trying to ruin us.'

'What?'

'Come right away. I'm calling the police.'

Amara left Kiara with Biji, trying to look calm. She ran up the stairs to Mall Road. On reaching her office she stopped short, as if a door had been slammed on her face. Her office shutters were spray-painted in red with obscenities and nude portraits of women, along with an epithet, 'If it feeds, it bleeds.'

Mrs D'Souza was sobbing into a handkerchief. 'I came in early to send a fax to Stacy and saw these boys, two of them, doing this. They ran on seeing me. Praise the Lord, that I wasn't attacked.' Amara's suspicion was confirmed when Mrs D'Souza said that the boys were wearing white cotton shirts, open at the collar, and red stoles around their neck.

Twenty minutes later when there was no sign of the police, Amara got impatient and, though it was early in the morning and Lalit was still not talking to her, she called him. As she put the phone down, two policemen came straddling along. Their outfits ended in white socks outside their pants, and black shoes, making them look like zebras. They wore beret khaki hats adorned with red wool feathers, which lent them the bearing of peacocks.

'You are Mrs – *Miss* – Malhotra?' one of them asked, while the other one furiously moved his tobacco chewing mouth. 'We have received complaints of a baby wailing in the night. But you are not wed, eh? Die-wars? Then who is baby?'

'That's none of your business.'

'Then this is also not our business.'

'Yes, it is. A business property has been damaged. If appropriate action is not taken, the life of the proprietors could be in danger. We have a witness who can identify the two men who did this, so you have proof to register this case.'

The policeman snorted in disgust and folded his arms across his chest as if wanting to prove a point. 'You expect us to take proof from die-wars lady and old lady?'

Amara cursed her enemies for never showing their faces to her, so she could confront them the way they deserved.

At that point, Lalit came up behind the policemen. He shook hands with them and asked what the problem was. At once, the policemen were deferential, before the wealth of a man and the man of wealth; they took out their register, lodged a First Information Report, heard Mrs D'Souza's description of the culprits, clicked photos of the shutters, and left with the promise of solving the case, their voices wholly ambiguous. A potato plant may as well have claimed that it would grow mangoes.

After the policemen left, Amara entered her office with Lalit. The words 'if it feeds, it bleeds' were tattooed in Amara's mind. 'Lalit, Kiara needs to be protected from this violence.'

'And you as well,' Lalit said. 'But you are not even accepting the solution I offered. What can I do?' Lalit's words, thick around her, ensconced her. She lost herself in his deep soft eyes, full of love for her. He would make a wonderful husband. He would make her happy and protect Kiara. Yet—

She looked out of the office window at the autumn leaves. Each leaf was a distinctive shade, standing out in its own right, its individual beauty lending to the picturesque whole.

'I want love to be the foundation and cornerstone of my life, not a solution to my problems. You understand this, right?'

Lalit shook his head. 'I feel like no matter what I do, I will never be your number one priority. Is it me? Are you not able to love me?'

'Lalit,' Amara whispered softly, grazing her finger against his cheek. 'No man I've met has your sense of love and loyalty, courage or fairness. You've loved me so entirely that I couldn't ask for more. I could not be in love as much as I am with you. But marrying you will be an escape, a way of running away from my problems. It will be unfair to you.'

'What is unfair is that I thought you were a rational, courageous, strong woman, who was doing amazing things with her life. What I loved most about you is how you completed me with your level-headed behaviour. I thought you would be my touchstone, my balance, something my ex-wife couldn't be.' He looked away as if the pain of his words was too much to bear. 'But I feel like your behaviour is becoming irrational. You want to do everything in as rebellious a way as possible, from adopting Kiara – when we can have our own children, to not marrying me – when this will make life better for Kiara, you and me.'

'Lalit, look at me,' Amara turned his face towards her. 'If I marry you under the given circumstances, you'll always look back and think I did it for a lack of options. You'll never know how much I love you. And I'll never know if you married me out of pity or love.' She wiped his tears falling onto her fingers. 'Do you understand?'

Lalit held her hand in his and looked at her for a long time. 'I understand but I also worry about you. How will you be free without a husband?'

'I will be free only when I'm in a state of unknowing.'

He smiled gently and said, 'Look, frankly, it doesn't matter to me if we're married or not, as long as we're together. Your love is enough for me. But what about your parents?'

'There's a risk that they'll throw me out of the house once I tell them that we're not getting married.'

'And Kiara?'

'I hope she'll respect me more if she knows that I fought for her and didn't act like a coward. And if things get worse then I'll move to a city where women like me are not singled out.'

'There's another way, you know,' Lalit said. And he told her. When she agreed, he took her in his arms and said, 'So are *you* going to tell your parents or am I?'

~ ~

There were no clouds that day, but by late morning an unseasonal rain came pouring down. Biji and Baba had gone to the market for shopping while Amara was home alone with Kiara. She finished patting down her daughter's body with talcum powder, enjoying the baby smell that reminded her of all things soft and gentle, like the underbelly of a fluffy cloud.

The doorbell rang.

Amara picked up Kiara and mumbled to her, as she walked to the door. 'Now who could that be? We aren't expecting guests.' She opened the door without looking through the peephole and her blood froze. Immediately she shut the door hard but a large foot stopped it from closing. Her hands were not free, as she was holding Kiara with one and protecting Kiara's head with the other, so she put the entire weight of her body on the door. Still, the door pushed open and the uninvited guest entered her home, carrying a hat in his hand, behind which could be— 'a gun, a knife, oh God he's come to kill us.'

'Help! Help!' Amara hollered, but the man put his hand on her mouth, clamping it shut, and pushed her against the wall. Amara knew she could do nothing unless she dropped Kiara, which was not an option. As her body slumped against the strength of his big hands, she knew she was powerless.

Amara didn't feel any more horror, just pure sadness that she hadn't been able to protect her baby.

She looked straight into her murderer's eyes. His green eyes seemed to be melting, as if they couldn't bear the glint of their own sharpness. He looked shrunken, wet and slouching, doubled over as if he had vertically folded in half. She realised that Anirudh Sharma wasn't here to kill her, at least not right away. She stopped struggling. Immediately he took his hand off her mouth. He stared at Kiara.

'What do you want?' Amara asked, edging towards the kitchen, hoping she could grab a knife. He probably wanted answers from her and would then proceed to kill her. He shifted his hat from one hand to the other, and she noticed he had nothing behind it.

He reached out and touched Kiara. 'Can I hold her? My lovely granddaughter?'

Amara stopped moving backwards. He took Kiara from Amara's hands and gave her a long hug. His tears streamed down her blanket. He hung his head. 'My daughter is a fool. But I am a bigger one.'

'How did you find out?'

'How could I not find out? Gyan was so caught up with the elections that he didn't even notice that Kanika was gone for a full day. When Kanika didn't return my calls, I got suspicious and asked him to check. Turns out that she was missing. I was convinced she'd been kidnapped. I've made a lot of enemies and I thought this was a political coup before the elections. I had the whole of Shimla searched, worried to death since she was due to give birth. You people figured on my list of enemies. So I sent two of my men to determine whether the three of you were at home. Turns out, Lalit and you weren't, and it was clear that both of you had something to do with Kanika's absence. I didn't know what your intentions were. Lalit has no family, but you had parents, so I made a plan to have them abducted to negotiate with you – when Falguni interjected.'

'Thanks for saving my parents,' Amara thought gratefully about Falguni.

'Falguni told me about Gyan and Kanika's unhappiness, that Lalit and you were trying to help Kanika. I asked her where in Delhi you'd taken Kanika, but she didn't know.'

'Good girl,' Amara thought. If Falguni had told him about 'Little People', for she knew the location, their lives would be very different right now.

'I left for Delhi immediately and my men and I went to over a hundred maternity clinics and hospitals in two days. I couldn't find her. Then my spies called up to say they'd seen Lalit and you near your building with a baby. It was not difficult to guess that it was Kanika's child.'

Anirudh Sharma paused to look down. A lock of hair fell on his forehead and Amara realised from the dirty cloud of hair on his head that he hadn't combed it for days.

'But I had to hear this story from Kanika to believe it. I wanted to scare you so you would tell Kanika to come back and take care of her own daughter. Why do you think I staged the attack on your office and not home, where it could have injured my granddaughter? You didn't get scared. I admire that. So I made Falguni tell Kanika about the attack. Kanika, as I'd expected, felt guilty. She called me up and told me everything.'

'Did she tell you about Gyan?'

'If only she'd told me earlier. I would've broken his neck. But I've taken care of him.'

'What did you do?'

'I lost the elections, didn't I? What better way to free myself from him? The day the results came, I sent the police with a chargesheet of domestic violence. He's in jail now, signing the divorce papers we've sent him.'

'He had it coming. But Mr Sharma, how did you lose the election?'

'Power can create and destroy, Miss Malhotra. I have men who control more than just our society. The very people who my men had bribed or bullied to vote for me, were told, at the last minute, to do the opposite. I think most of them complied happily.'

'Losing the elections in that manner must have been difficult.'

'This month I lost my daughter, granddaughter, son-in-law, my funding and the elections. And the truth is that the only thing that's hurting is losing my daughter. Why did my own daughter think I'd give her second priority over work? Why did she run away from me?'

'How could she come to you when you hate anyone even slightly unconventional?'

'But she knows why I am the way I am. Yet she didn't trust me. People like me aren't born; our beliefs are shaped by what we see. She knew that.'

'What do you mean?'

'I'm afraid it's a long story.'

'I have time.'

Amara pointed him to the kitchen. She put Kiara in her pram and set the tea to boil, as Anirudh Sharma started talking. 'My favourite aunt, Sani Tai, was the kindest person I'd met. She took me in when I was eleven and orphaned, and raised me as her own son, though she had two other children. Then, her husband left her. I remember no one used the word divorce in those days; it was considered much too shameful. But she became a single woman, all alone, a helpless mother with three kids to look after. I watched her, my favourite Sani Tai, slowly descend into madness. Like her divorce, we didn't label her schizophrenia because it would become true to us. She talked to herself in different voices, most of it gibberish; she grew scared of her real voice, cried when she saw herself in the mirror, or otherwise laughed hysterically. This continued for twelve years, till her death. You know, she never signed her divorce papers, they lay on her desk, and now I keep it in mine, to remind myself of what a single woman goes through. I cannot tolerate the sight of a divorced woman. Or even a divorced man, because that means he's abandoned a woman somewhere.'

'I'm sorry to hear that. But does your sadness have to translate into violence?'

He smiled sadly. 'I thought I was doing a great favour to society. But then I heard Kanika tell me your side of the story. You didn't think or act like a victim, even though you did not become single by choice. I admired your strength. Then I heard my daughter on the phone, single by choice, and sounding happier than she has in a long time. I'm a traditional thinker, but I realised that making mistakes, admitting failure, living on despite tragedy, are not signs of defiance, but signs of courage. Being an exception to the rule does not mean you're wrong. I became conscious of how outdated my notions were, how presumptuous my behaviour. Forgive me. You've been a sister to my daughter and a mother to my grandchild. Yet I've made your life difficult.'

'It's okay.'

'No, it's not okay. I will not allow Kanika or myself to pass on our responsibility to you. It is very kind of you to adopt Kiara and I will always be grateful for that. But from now on, Kiara is my responsibility. I will take care of my grandchild.'

'No!' Amara said, her voice high. 'How can you ask a mother to give up her child? Kiara *is* my daughter and no one, not even her biological grandfather, can take her away. I will not let anyone take Kiara from me.' Amara looked at Kiara, who nodded as if in approval.

Anirudh Sharma looked hard at Amara and an old fear crept back in her. Would he take Kiara by force? But he began laughing, soft and warm. He held his palms upright in the air and said, 'You are really something else. I am sorry for even making this suggestion. Kanika told me you'd react this way but I wasn't sure about your feelings. I must add that Kiara is one lucky girl.'

'I'm the lucky one,' Amara replied, blushing at how wary she was of him.

'I would really like to give my granddaughter's mother something. Ask for anything.'

'Please, help me find a good nanny. I really need to get a good night's sleep.'

~ ~

Baba and Biji were at the doorway, two hours later, a smile stretching from Baba's ears to Biji's.

Biji started off, 'Today be luckiest day of our life. We go to electronic store and owner give us free flat-screen TV. Then Baba get call from his company saying he be promoted. We come home and outside door the cable company chap be adding wire, saying they upgrading us so we get all American channel without paying extra cost. Imagine.'

Amara's imagination did not have to go far. She knew why these sudden favours were being bestowed upon them. Power can destroy. It can create.

'I think Kiara is bringing us luck,' Baba said.

'She is indeed,' Amara agreed.

Baba gave Amara a tight long hug for no reason and said, 'I'm so proud of you, beta.' He looked at Amara, some heaviness taken off the lines around his eyes. 'You know our Big American dream didn't come true, but our Great Indian Dream is turning real. And how!'

Maybe this is a good time to tell them that I'm moving in with Lalit, Amara thought.

Biji interrupted her intentions and said, 'We have surprise for you. Look who we find in Mall Road and bring home.'

A tall lanky frame entered the hallway wearing a Himachali cap. He carried an iron-corrugated cage with a green Indian ringneck parrot inside it.

He stroked his long beard and said, 'I have come to see Babyji's future.'

Amara looked at Kiara, who was staring intently at her mother's face as if they shared a secret, and said, 'Her future will be what she chooses, Punditji, not you.'

The astrologer didn't let out a 'karr'. Instead he released a long sigh and said, 'I give you this. It is meant only for Babyji. You will see its value when time is right.'

In his hand he held an emerald pendant.

~ ~